I0761177

Isle of Misfortune

a novel by

Geoffrey Leavenworth

TCU Press
Fort Worth

Library of Congress Cataloging-in-Publication Data

Leavenworth, Geoffrey.
Isle of misfortune : a novel / by Geoffrey Leavenworth.
p. cm.
ISBN 0-87565-269-7 (alk. paper)
1. Galveston (Tex.)--Fiction. 2. Stalking victims--Fiction. 3. Relocation (Housing)--Fiction. 4. Police--Texas--Galveston--Fiction. I. Title.
PS3612.E24 I85 2003
813'.6--dc21

2002009351

This book is a work of fiction. Names, places, and events either are products of the author's imagination or are used fictitiously.

Book Design and Illustrations by
Barbara M. Whitehead

This book
is dedicated to
Simone.

Acknowledgments

I will always be grateful to the people who helped us, sometimes putting themselves at risk, during the dark days that inspired this book. They include Richard Ferguson, Judge Susan Baker, Earl Myhre, Dennis and Mylene Dressler, former Galveston County District Attorney Michael Guarino, and our families.

Many thanks to those who offered advice and encouragement during the writing, including Mary Gardner, Rob Lallier, Larry Brill, Janet Christian, Barbara Burnett Smith, Marsha Moyer, Cecilia Derkits, Claire Holman Thompson, and to editors Judy Alter and James Ward Lee of the TCU Press. I consulted several of the many translations of the journal of Cabeza de Vaca, and I leaned most heavily on *The Account: Alvar Núñez Cabeza de Vaca's Relación*, translated by Martin A. Favata and José B. Fernández. Special thanks to Tom Zigal, friend, colleague, and man of letters. And to Simone, Mark, and James, my constellation.

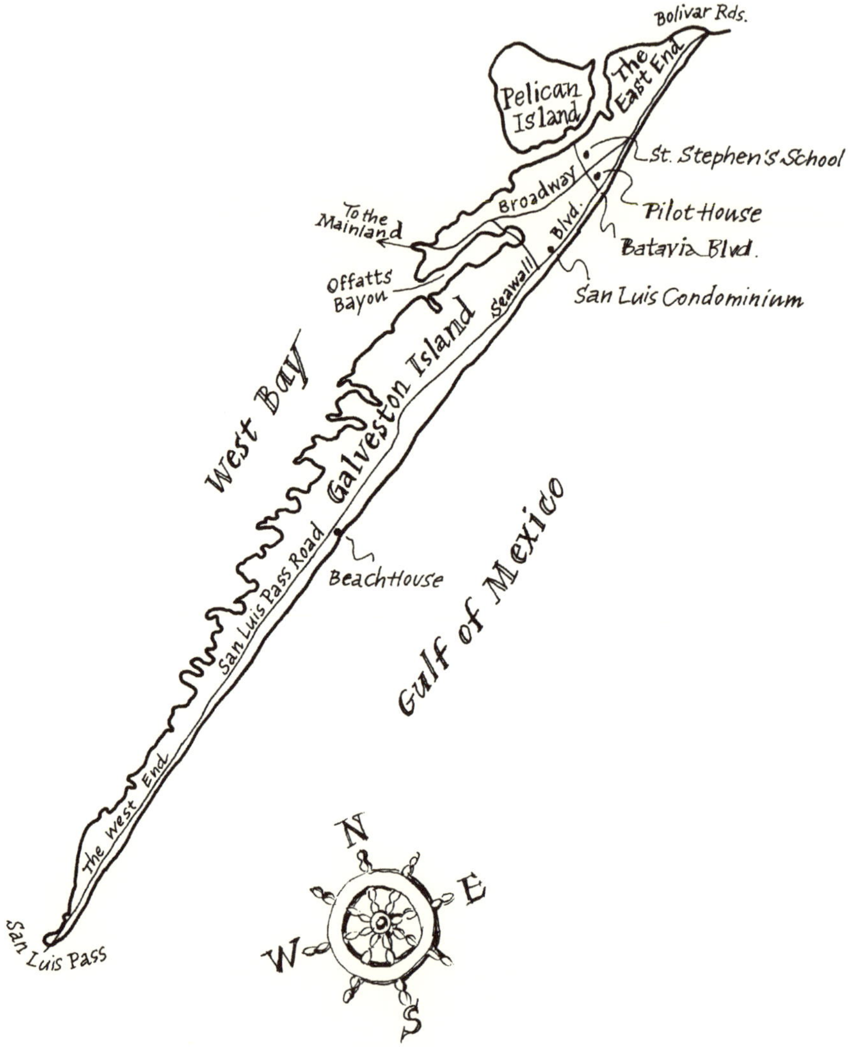

Bolivar Rds.
Pelican Island
The East End
St. Stephen's School
Broadway
Pilot House
To the Mainland
Blvd.
Batavia Blvd.
Offatts Bayou
Seawall
San Luis Condominium
Galveston Island
West Bay
San Luis Pass Road
BeachHouse
Gulf of Mexico
the West End
San Luis Pass
N
E
W
S

When they came to kill us,
the Indian who kept me interceded.
He said: If we had so much power of sorcery
we would not have let all but a few of our own perish;
the few left did no hurt or wrong; it would be best to
leave us alone. God our Lord be praised,
they listened and relented.

We named this place Malhado—
the Isle of Misfortune.

Alvar Núñez Cabeza de Vaca
1542
La Relación
Account of Cabeza de Vaca's
Odyssey in North America

One

The night Gordo's life spun out of control he made pasta. An unwitting last supper in the big old house on Batavia Boulevard. He'd been unable to resist the overpriced sweet peppers at the grocery, so he sliced them, along with purple onion, garlic, and a few stalks of broccoli discovered on the bottom shelf of the fridge. As the olive oil heated in a skillet, he stepped outside to pick sage and rosemary from Ana's clay pots on the back porch. Then he threw everything into the oil and inhaled deeply.

Such a wonderful smell from such simple food. About the time he was reaching for capers and feta cheese, the front door creaked sharply.

Got to oil those hinges, he thought.

Click, click, click. Heels on the longleaf pine floors. Ana.

"It smells like we'll be eating well tonight," Ana said. Three long strides put her at his side. "Mmm."

Gordo pushed his face into the straw colored hair that fell to her shoulders. He had discouraged her from cutting it after Jake was born.

"I'm glad you didn't cut it too short," he said, placing his hand on her stomach. Gordo remembered a small sense of loss on that postpartum day when her long straight hair was shorn to her shoulders. But it could have been worse. "The first thing these new mothers do is cut their hair. 'Sorry, hubby, got to dowderize myself, and quick!'"

"Dowderize?"

"Verb form of dowdy."

"Oh really?"

"It's a well-known word. Describes a well-known phenomenon."

"And why does this happen?"

"Puts Dad in his place," he explained. "Lets everyone know that maternal duties take priority. No time to fuss. Got to dowderize. Quick!"

"Maybe new moms do it because it means the difference between mere sleep deprivation and life-threatening sleep deprivation."

"There are all kinds of deprivation . . ."

"I know what you mean. Fathers are deprived of morning sickness. Indigestion. Labor pains. Then there's the snickering as you walk through the office to put expressed breast milk in the freezer."

"The bastards! Who snickered?"

"Who didn't? I've been thinking of cutting my hair."

"Please don't."

"You don't have to blow-dry it in a hot steamy bathroom and then climb into a dress and pantyhose. It's such a hassle. And it is my hair."

"Some natural resources can't be owned. They are too lovely to be regarded as property."

"You're really full of it tonight."

Gordo liked the smell of her hair. From the morning's squeaky clean just-shampooed scent—was it tea tree oil these days?—to the more complex smells of evening. A curled shaving of spruce falling from a carpenter's plane mixed with a stray waft from one of Bertie's cigarettes laced with a faint reminder of the day's intensity—the perspiration of an elegant woman.

"I am a dog following his nose," he said without explanation.

Ana was used to such naked pronouncements. "You are a dog, all right. Where are the puppies?"

"The puppies are rotting their canine minds in front of the television."

"If you have everything under control here in the kitchen, I'll just go upstairs and give them a pat."

Click, click, click.

Batavia Boulevard. It was named for the Dutch-established port of Batavia in Indonesia. Galvestonians pronounced it with a long second *a*, so that it rhymed with Moravia. In the nineteenth century, major streets running from the port of Galveston to the Gulf were named for distant seaports. Thus, Veracruz Street, Marseille Boulevard, and Port Royal Avenue. But Batavia was the broadest boulevard running north and south. Today, it was anchored by the old Santa Fe Railroad Station and the Strand district near the harbor, and, at the opposite end, by the Flagship Hotel, built on a pier over the Gulf. A double row of palm trees and magnolias, interspersed with pink and white oleanders, extended from Broadway to the beach. When the city's tourism bureau bought magazine advertising, it often included a photo of a row of Victorian houses on Batavia Boulevard. Right in the center, partially obscured by a camphor tree, was Gordo's house.

• • •

Had he known this would be the last supper, Gordo would have savored the light slanting through the green louvered shutters, casting a warm glow on Sam's white blond locks.

"What are these little *wownd* things?" asked Sam, who at six, was still struggling to pronounce his *r's*.

"Capers soaked in balsamic vinegar," he replied. "They add a little salty flavor."

"It looks like it adds a little *wat* poop."

"Spoken like a true food critic," Ana said.

Professional eating, as Gordo called it, was one of the patchwork of writing jobs that he stitched together to make a living. Sam and Jake had been dragged along to restaurants for years, having unfamiliar plates of food set before them so their father could sample the right mix of appetizers and entrees for the benefit of magazine readers. On a number of occasions, Jake's pronouncements had found their way into the reviews. "The seven-year-old in our party reported that the Belgian mousse was 'a whole new chocolate adventure!'"

In his role as cook, Gordo was used to complaints from the customers—the boys were picky eaters. "I don't think I can use your view of the capers in my next review."

"Why not?" said Jake, who, now at nine, was beginning to enjoy arguing about anything. "You think people want to eat food that looks like rat poop?"

Gordo might have also savored the mere presence of the family together at the dinner table. Ana, Jake, Sam. His constellation.

The boys had been born on the island. They knew no home other than this tall airy Victorian. The broad porch with its gingerbread skirt and crown of turned spindles and lacy brackets. Balconies on the south and west sides that seemed to embrace the street. The south balcony was washed with sunlight and the comforting music of palm fronds rattling in the wind. And the west balcony, projecting toward the street and shaded by the camphor tree, resembled the pilothouse of a riverboat. When the boys were little, he and Ana had rocked their way through countless bedtime stories, night terrors, and sleepy fall afternoons on their porch swing in the trees.

For mosquito bites, you could just reach out and grab a few of the leaves, as green and glossy as if they'd been lacquered. Crushing them, the smell of Gordo's childhood summers burst forth. Aromatic Campho-Phenique in its green glass bottle, hot musty canvas tents, and the red eruptions from chiggers burrowed into flesh.

The boys called it Pilot House. They all called it that. Their home on Batavia Boulevard seemed to make people feel better. How many times had a smiling visitor greeted them at the door with the words, "I just love this house."

After dinner, Ana got ready for a meeting at the alternative school that Sam attended.

"If it wasn't for the kids, you couldn't drag me to one of those meetings," she said as she undressed. "Esther Quinn is such a lunatic! She takes some kind of sick pleasure out of arguing about every lousy point of every motion until the rest of us are ready to check into the psychiatric ward. It's excruciating."

"Community service is its own reward," Gordo said.

Ana looked at him, propped up on the bed. He had inherited his father's pink skin and blue-gray eyes. She had told him that he had a nice mouth, that she found the full bottom lip sensual. Years of sun exposure had worn the cloud of freckles on his face into a marbled patina. Only one freckle, much larger than the others, had remained distinct as he drifted toward middle age. High on his cheek, a brown reminder of the boy he had once been.

"We've got to figure out a way to get Esther off that board before she drives everyone crazy. We don't pay the teachers enough to put up with all her meddling." Ana disappeared into the bathroom. "I'm going to take a quick rinse," she said.

At the school board meeting, Ana would be spending her evening not only with the obstructionist Esther Quinn but also with the rest of the members of the board. That meant she would be with Jonathan Elliott, who everyone called Corky. Corky had a crush on Ana. Gordo was sure of that. He just didn't know how Ana felt about Corky. He was the grandson of one of the island's patrician families. Rich, but you never knew how much of—and just when—the money passed from one generation to the next. Tall and handsome with dark hair and a face that hadn't gone soft in middle age, Corky was a lawyer by training. In spite of his casual approach to practicing law, he always had two or three corporate clients, somehow connected to his family, and he tried the occasional lawsuit. He had a reputation for being good on his feet, even entertaining, in the courtroom.

Gordo usually felt some affinity for Ana's admirers. After all, he had something in common with them, and he could well understand why they found her attractive. But it made him uneasy the way Ana seemed just a little too eager to laugh at Corky's jokes. To see her grow uncharacteristically animated and chatty in his presence. And he knew that on occasion she had concealed that she and Corky had met for lunch or for drinks after work.

He probably should have just talked to her about it, but he didn't like the side of himself that was possessive and suspicious. He knew it was not endearing. If it was all harmless flirtation, he would just appear silly and insecure. If not, Ana wasn't likely to tell him much.

Ana and Corky. She didn't usually shower in the evening before school meetings. He felt something surging through his body, making him vigilant. A kind of enhanced acuity of suspicion. Moreover, the tug of jealousy seemed to change his body chemistry—to make him nervous and jumpy. A wave of fear, a burst of adrenaline, a whiff of betrayal. Something was getting to him.

Of course he was happy to have Ana involved in Sam's school. They had divided the responsibilities—Gordo had his hands full serving on his own dysfunctional board at St. Stephen's, where Jake was in the fourth grade.

In his saner moments, Gordo told himself that Corky was just being Corky, the social gadfly with an eye for attractive women. It meant nothing.

Gordo sprawled out on their old iron bed, his head drooping backwards over the side of the mattress. As Ana emerged from the bathroom, he watched her, his view upside down. She was lithe and rosy, her skin still pink from the hot shower. As she dropped her towel he reached for her and missed.

Ana rummaged the bureau. He watched her step into a pair of black panties, transfixed by her little girlish dip, knees parted, as she pulled the waistband home. There was something beautiful and evocative about that dip. He knew it was a habit, formed in childhood, that had been repeated every day of her life.

"Hey," he whispered.

She moved closer to the bed and he drew her toward him. With his head lolling off the high bed, his face was aligned for her. Gordo pressed his nose against her. He could feel spirals of pubic hair, redolent of peppermint soap, beneath the black cotton. He kissed her. In the past, this had often led to more kisses, to the peeling off of remaining clothes, and, ultimately, a postcoital search of the bedroom for her panties.

"Gotta go," she said. Ana spun away from him and disappeared into the closet.

• • •

Gordo did not have much time for stewing over Ana. Within moments Jake announced that he needed help with homework. And, after all, hadn't she been late for her meeting?

Let it go.

He was telling himself that more nowadays. Just let it go.

By the time Ana slipped out the door, Gordo was caught up in helping Jake with his multiplication tables.

Didn't even get to see what she wore, he thought morosely.

Feeling a bit of a fraud for not having mastered all the multiplication tables at this stage of his life, Gordo quizzed his son on the eights and nines. Nine times eight equals seventy-two. Right? Gordo found himself wanting a calculator—just to make sure. He was pretty sure, of course he was, but he would feel better about it with a calculator. Sometimes he wondered if he would spend the rest of his life bumping into incompletions. The twelve tables, he'd never gotten those down. A good spin serve on the tennis court—not yet. Mounting the family photos in scrapbooks? Organizing his tools in the garage? Let it go.

• • •

The boys were in the bathtub, which was full of bubbles, boats, foam bath blocks, and dinosaurs.

Sam had a stegosaurus at the helm of his boat.

"Here comes Captain Stego!" he announced.

Jake had a tyrannosaurus perched on the edge of the tub. "Tyrannosaurus Rex is the toughest!" said Jake. "He'll eat a vegetarian stegosaurus for breakfast. Attack!"

Jake pitched a bath toy toward his little brother's boat, causing it to rock wildly.

"Ja-ake," Sam pleaded. "Don't *dwown* my *dinosaw*!" Sam had just started with the speech therapist, but Ana and Gordo were already mourning the day when his charming lilt would be corrected.

Gordo scooped up some bubbles and applied a foamy beard to Sam's chin. "I believe there's a pirate in this bathtub."

"This is my *pi-what* ship," announced Sam.

"It's Stego the Pirate!" said Jake. "Attack!"

Jake hurled another toy figure at Sam's boat, capsizing it.

"Ja-ake!" Sam screamed. When he was mad, he always extended his older brother's name to two syllables.

"It wasn't me. Tyrannosaurus Rex did it," Jake argued.

Sam wasn't buying it. "You sunk my boat on *puhpose!"* He filled the boat with water and splashed his brother in the face.

"My eyes!" screamed Jake. He hated to get water in his eyes. Sam knew that. "Boys, settle down," said Gordo. Sam was scrappy, he thought. At six, he already knew where his older brother was vulnerable. These joint baths were almost a thing of the past. Jake already preferred taking showers. Gordo had them share the tub to expedite the process.

"*Whey'as* Mom?" Sam asked.

Every conversation Gordo had ever had with the boy, if it progressed long enough, ultimately reached this question.

"Remember Sam, she's at your school."

"When is she coming home?"

"She wants to come home as soon as she can. But sometimes the meetings take a long time."

"Will she be home to tuck me in?"

It was one thing for Ana to be gone for the evening. But to Sam, for her to miss bedtime was a serious form of neglect.

"She's going to try."

The doorbell rang.

"Is that Mom?" asked Sam.

"Mommy doesn't ring the bell," Jake said.

The doorbell rang again.

"You guys need to get out now so I can answer the door. Jake, help your little brother get dry."

• • •

Gordo jogged down the steps, past the stained glass window on the first landing and down to the second landing, where the staircase reversed itself and left him facing the front door. Through the glass pane in the door, he could see the figure of a tall man, although a lace curtain made it impossible to determine who it was.

Opening the door, Gordo saw the man's back. As the visitor

turned toward him, Gordo studied his face. Those glaring eyes! He slammed the door shut and locked it.

It was him! Gordo felt his heart surge. He tried to think clearly.

Gordo asked, "Who are you?" Maybe he could learn something.

Through the glass, the stranger looked directly into Gordo's eyes and asked, "Who are you?"

Then the man's arm moved forward.

Gordo saw, heard, and felt the blast. The plume of light. The explosion and the breaking glass. The punch—like a fist—to his chest.

Despite all that, he was still confused.

What happened? Something earsplitting and powerful, but what exactly was it?

He looked at his chest.

Is that a hole in my sweater?

Gordo staggered away from the door and climbed the stairs. His mind was swirling. He tried to sort out what was going on. Surely it could not be. No, there was some other explanation.

Don't blanks fire a chunk of paper wadding? But would it leave a hole in the glass? He struggled to explain what had happened.

He raised his sweater and saw a clean hole with blood.

Jake and Sam, stunned by the noise, were at the top of the stairs. They were naked and dripping from the bath.

"I think I've been shot!" Gordo shouted. Jake was jumping up and down on his toes. His mouth was wide open in a grimace. As soon as Sam heard his brother's wail, he unleashed a shrill scream.

"Jake, get me your baseball bat. I've got to call for help."

Gordo dialed 911 from his office at the top of the stairs.

“Nine-one-one emergency services. What is your emergency?”

“I think I’ve been shot,” he said.

“You *think* you been shot?” said the dispatcher.

Gordo realized he wasn’t making sense.

“What do you mean?” she asked.

“I have a hole in my chest. Blood is coming out. I need help.”

“Someone will be there in a couple minutes,” she said.

For once, there was an advantage to living in the historic district. The police station was six blocks away.

Aside from the sharp pain in his chest, he didn’t feel that bad. Maybe I’m in shock. Is this how it will end? A jolt of pain and then I lose consciousness?

No. Not now.

Where was that voice in his head coming from?

Gordo could feel his heart pounding. He could hear the wail of a siren.

“Help is coming,” he told the boys, extending his arms to them. They wrapped their damp arms around his waist, a baseball bat dangling from Jake’s quivering hand.

“They’re almost here,” he reassured them. “Stay up here until I call you. Put on your pajamas.” Gordo wiped Sam’s runny nose and grabbed the bat.

The ambulance and its crew got there first, with the police close on their heels. Gordo met them at the front door with Jake’s baseball bat in his hand—in case he confronted the man with the gun. He still wasn’t thinking clearly. His left hand covered the wound. The words “direct pressure” floated through his mind, an echo from the *Boy Scout Handbook.*

The EMS crew, a man and a woman, had him sit down on the piano bench.

Laura and Ed from next door appeared.

“We heard the shot,” explained Ed.

"Laura, go up to the boys," Gordo said. "I made them stay upstairs."

• • •

A woman in an orange jumpsuit raised his sweater. Her voice was calm and soothing.

"There's the entrance wound," she said.

Gordo was bleeding from the left side of his chest, red hole and pink nipple side by side. Wearing latex gloves, the woman gently pulled the cotton turtleneck up under his chin. So composed was her voice, she might have been examining a skinned knee. A sharp, burned metallic smell hung in the air. Cordite. The rifle range at Camp Karankawa.

Gordo pointed to the stairs. "Look over there," he told the policeman. "I saw something shiny."

A moment later, the police officer stepped over to the piano, with a small coppery object in the palm of his hand. "The slug was on the floor by the stairs. Twenty-five caliber."

"So it ended up directly behind you," the paramedic said with concern.

Pulling him forward, to examine his back, she looked puzzled.

"Now where the hell is the exit wound?"

She removed his shirt.

"It had to come out somewhere."

Then she unfastened his belt and unbuttoned his pants.

"I just need to look around. Sometimes the bullet can come out in weird places."

Gordo sat listening to this with a sense of urgency and detachment. They were talking about him—his body—but it felt like it was happening to someone else.

After a moment, the woman looked at her partner and shrugged.

"We'd better find that exit hole."

Two

Pain was beginning to radiate outward from the bullet hole. The dull penetrating soreness of having been hit very hard. He could feel blood slowly dripping from the wound.

I'm okay.

His own interior voice kept repeating the words.

Gordo was seized with the desire to round up his family and get off the island.

I'm okay.

More flashing red lights strafed the windows. Ana swept through the door. Gingerly, she gave him a hug.

"Gordo," she whispered. "Are you all right?"

"I think so."

"Was it him?"

"Yeah."

Gordo wondered what the paramedic thought of this exchange. "Him" was family code. Him was the mysterious, violent presence that had invaded their lives.

"Mommy?" Sam's voice floated down the stairs.

"Sam! Jake! Come here," called Ana.

Laura had kept them sitting on the top step of the stairs. Frightened, obedient little boys.

Jake and Sam spilled down the staircase in their pajamas. Laura trailed behind. As Sam launched off the bottom step Gordo realized that, had the boys been dressed, they would have been on that very spot during the shooting. The place where the bullet had come to rest. Jake and Sam were always a few steps behind him when he answered the doorbell. He shuddered at the thought of one of the boys stopping the bullet.

"Daddy, did you get *hut*?" asked Sam.

"Come here and give me a hug." Gordo leaned into Sam with his uninjured side, looping his arm around the six-year-old. He inhaled the freshly bathed little boy smell. Soft skin and his mother's straight blond hair. Jake stood aside, the stoic older brother. Fighting tears, Gordo reached for him.

"Guys, I'm fine," he said, swallowing hard. He didn't want the boys to see him upset.

"*Gwoop* hug," said Sam. It was his answer to conflict. The woman in latex gloves backed away as Ana joined the knot of family.

"I'm okay," Gordo repeated.

"How can you be okay with a bullet hole in you?" asked Ana.

"I don't know, but I'm okay."

Laura came in and put her arm around Ed.

"What are we going do?" asked Ana.

The medic moved back in, focused on her work.

She worked her finger into the wound.

Gordo winced.

"Strange," she said.

"Yeah?" said Gordo.

"Must be an in and out. Shallow."

"How did that happen?" asked her partner.

"Doesn't really look serious," she said. "But you better go to the hospital. They'll probably want to keep you overnight for observation. It could have bruised your heart."

"I'm sure I'm all right," Gordo said. "I can go see Lena in the morning."

Turning to Ana, she said, "Talk some sense into this guy."

"Gordo?" Ana said.

"You guys are upset," said the woman's partner. "Even if he's okay, why take the risk?"

"I just have a feeling," said Gordo. "I want us all off the island."

The policeman, whose questions had been interrupted several times, went over the description as the medic bandaged the wound.

"White male, thirty-five to forty. Six feet tall, about one hundred sixty pounds," he said. "Watch cap, flannel shirt, blue jeans. And you don't know him. Right?"

"Right," replied Gordo. "He was unshaven. About three days growth."

"I'll put out the description. See if we can find him," said the policeman. "The case will be assigned to a detective. He'll want to talk to you in the morning."

"I'll be there."

The cop pointed to Gordo's chest. "You know what I'd do if I were you? I'd go buy a lottery ticket. It's your lucky day."

Everyone except Gordo laughed. Awkward, nervous laughter. He could still feel the slow, sticky drip from his chest. He felt lucky to be alive but not in any mood to celebrate.

The woman in the orange jumpsuit snapped her latex gloves disapprovingly as she removed them.

"If you're not coming, we have to answer another call."

The officer stepped aside to bark into his hand-held radio.

Suddenly, the police and the ambulance crew were gone. Gordo was beginning to realize that they were on their own.

Ed came over to him. In a low voice, "This guy means business, Gordon." Ed never called him Gordon. "You can't stay here. You've got to get out. Just leave. He wants to kill you. And if you stay, he'll be back."

"I know," Gordo said. "I know."

Laura was talking to Ana.

"Ana and the kids don't need your help to get off the island," Laura said.

Ana looked dazed.

Gordo put an arm over Laura's shoulder, ushering her and Ed out the front door.

"You guys—thanks. But we're outta here."

• • •

Gordo didn't have much of a plan, but he knew where to go.

"Let's get some things together," he said. "Enough for a couple days. Hurry. We're leaving."

And so, there in the entrance hall of their home of thirteen years, Gordo made the decision. Over the years, he'd grown more and more attached to the place and all its eccentricities. The soft longleaf pine floors, dimpled and scarred from a century of footfalls. Their wedding china behind the imperfect, swirled glass of the built-in cypress china cabinet. Jake and Sam's breathy cadence drifting through the upstairs in the wee hours. But on this night, Gordo learned that it only took an instant to break the spell.

• • •

Leaving the house, a duffel bag swinging from his shoulder, Gordo suddenly became aware of all the deep shadows around him. The street lamps did nothing for the great clumps of darkness near the porch, behind shrubs and fences, and near the raised foundations of the old Victorian houses. Bladelike foliage of the palm trees and oleanders formed thousands of waving daggers in the cold wind. Batavia Boulevard seemed black and threatening.

Gordo felt weary but vigilant. Not bothering to open the trunk, he threw the bag into the back seat.

"*Whey'a* we going?" asked Sam, yawning.

Gordo buckled Sam's seat belt for him. "To Dickinson, Sam."

"Oh."

As he closed the car doors and walked to the passenger's side of the car, he lingered for a moment. From his vantage point at the curb, he could see the whole lovely façade of their home.

When will we be back?

Then he saw something. At least he thought he saw something. A person in shadow? Head and shoulders near the far side of Ed's house? He stood up straight and squinted into the darkness. It could have been anything. Ed's yard was a thicket of bushes and vines.

Let it go. To hell with it. Let's get out of here.

Gordo climbed into the car and quietly said aloud, "Let's get out of here."

"Shouldn't the police be out looking for the guy?" asked Ana, noting the empty street.

"Probably," he replied. "But it's Galveston." Shorthand for what they both knew. The island police were known for sloth and incompetence. It seemed like there was always a cop under indictment, if not the chief of police himself.

While Ana drove, his mind raced ahead. Where were they going? They would go to where Gordo had come from.

Dickinson Bayou. The old house.

The boys would feel protected there. They would all feel protected.

Gordo's parents had spun a cocoon of safety around him and his siblings. As an adult, he realized it was illusory, that his mother and father could not really protect them from all that was bad. But as children, Gordo and his brother and sister did not know that.

His own father had been the authority figure. Well-educated and resourceful, he had worked all his life to be able to insulate his family from harm. Everyone knew one another in the old neighborhood. If a serious crime had ever been committed on that stretch of the bayou, Gordo was unaware of it.

He and the rest of the family knew that his father kept a loaded pistol in a drawer in his bedroom. As a boy, Gordo opened the top drawer from time to time. Blue steel revolver inside an open, shallow box. Handy. At the ready. A little sign was stuck inside the rear lip of the box. His father's neat block lettering: "LOADED." They were living out in the country, his father had once said. "Good idea to be prepared, just in case."

Gordo was not sure his father ever got the hang of being out in the country. He could remember his father mowing grass in a starched white shirt. Dr. O'Connor, the Yankee cardiologist.

His mother, a timid, curvaceous beauty when married at nineteen, had, by the time of his earliest memory, expanded in stature to that of a large, assertive matron. While Dr. O'Connor's authority was rooted in his intellect and ability to get things done, Helen O'Connor was the physical presence that loomed largest in the household. She was imposing in size and manner and could generate an explosive fury in an instant. And she was only too willing to turn her powers of intimidation on anyone she viewed as a threat to her children's interests. Gordo didn't know how many nuns at Our Lady of Redemption School or Little League coaches had felt her wrath. Hers was the disposition of a large maternal animal protecting her young.

So earlier, while bleeding and trying to decide what to do,

it was only natural to return to where things had always been safe. They were going to Dickinson.

• • •

Gordo and Ana talked quietly during the drive. They didn't want to alarm the boys, who were beginning to drift off in the back seat.

"It's not like you'd expect," said Gordo. "Once I accepted the fact that I'd been shot, I felt this weird calmness. As if my brain realized that getting excited, getting emotional, was not productive. Not helpful. It was like—You're shot, now deal with it. Call for help, take care of the boys, meet the EMS. No rage. No pain. No flashbacks. Just fear and uncertainty."

"It didn't hurt?"

"Too stunned to feel anything. I've felt more pain stubbing my toe on the way to the bathroom in the middle of the night."

Not long after they crossed the bridge to the mainland, they reached a fork in the road. The left fork was the familiar path to his mother's house. The right would take them to the hospital where Gordo's father had worked for decades. Gordo was feeling a little more soreness. He knew the doctors there.

As if she could read his thoughts, Ana, who was driving, asked, "How do you feel now?"

"I'm okay. A little sore."

"We could stop."

His left shoulder was hurting. Was the pain radiating down his arm? Did that mean something?

"Maybe we should take a right."

They parked near the emergency room. Near the doctor's lot where Gordo's father parked his big Oldsmobiles over the years. Mainland Hospital. As a doctor's son, he'd always liked the sprawling red brick pile, built in the 1960s to heal the well-insured workers from the chemical plants and their families. Five hundred beds on six floors. His father's long starched white coat with his name embroidered over the chest pocket.

Martin M. O'Connor, M.D.

Cardiology

Before Gordo reached the emergency room, he saw a familiar garland of curly gray hair around a balding head.

The man turned and there he was. Alvin Mann, the abrasive heart surgeon who had been such an offstage presence during Gordo's childhood. His father's colleague and adversary.

"Al," said Gordo.

"Gordon." The surgeon nodded at Ana.

"Working late?"

"Got a patient who's not doing well. I'm trying to keep the nurses from killing him. What are you doing here?"

Gordo explained.

"Gordon," he said crossly, "what the hell have you done now?"

While Dr. O'Connor had been quiet, cerebral, non-invasive, Al Mann—ten years his junior—was a doer, a cutter, a screamer. At times, his father had called him "nothing more than an over-educated plumber." Over the years, the two of them had had more fights than anyone could count. Gordo hadn't seen the surgeon since his father's funeral almost five years ago. He'd caught a glimpse of Al in one of the pews and been surprised to see him crying.

"Let's take a look," said Al, taking charge of the situation.

"How's your mother?" he asked, as he examined Gordo in a room full of shiny equipment. Gordo could hear Ana talking softly to the boys in the corridor outside.

"She's okay. Lonely, I suppose."

"Your father . . ." Al said, his voice trailing off.

"Did you know that when he first came to Texas he asked me if most of my patients had worms?" Al chuckled, as he placed a cold stethoscope to Gordo's chest. "He really thought this was the sticks. Pissed me off right away."

And suddenly, Gordo was a boy again there at the hospital. Not being sewn up, his lip flayed open from the bamboo-shoot sword wielded by his older brother. Not with a knee the size of a melon from a schoolyard injury. No, this time he was GSW. Gunshot wound.

Al's hands were quick and facile for such a burly man.

"Look Gordo, you've got a little noninvasive chest wound and a big bruise. But I'm going to admit you anyway."

"I don't want to stay if I don't have to."

"Why not?"

"Ana and the boys are pretty upset."

"So? They should be," said Al.

"I'm on my way over to my mother's."

"Gordo, I've known you since you were a little boy. Otherwise, I'd just admit you and be done with it. But if you want to be pigheaded like your old man, go ahead. I don't think you'll have any problem. If you feel any more chest pain, call me at home and get back here right away." Al Mann wrote his home number on the back of his card.

"I'm in surgery all morning tomorrow. Who's your primary doc?"

"Lena."

"Go see her first thing."

"Thanks," said Gordo, taking the card.

Al Mann looked at him.

"I miss the stodgy old bastard. His little wry jokes."

"Me too."

• • •

Back on the highway, Gordo wondered if he was doing the right thing. But his homing instincts seemed to be in control. Which was strange, because he'd always considered that their home—the one he shared with Ana and the boys—was home.

They were slicing a diagonal path across the county, north toward Galveston Bay, which cut a sixty-mile wide scoop out of the Texas coastline. As they reached the high bridge that crossed the mouth of Dickinson Bayou, Gordo peered down at the lights of the pier at Hillman's, an ancient fish house where he'd eaten fried shrimp as a boy. A small fleet of shrimp boats was still docked there, rocking gently. The briny fragrance of the bayou floated up from the water's edge. Even in the blackness, the scene was comforting and familiar.

• • •

At the old house on the bayou, Helen, Gordo's mother, was reasonably calm. She assumed the manner of nurse on duty. It was only when Gordo pulled off the gauze patch that she shrieked.

"Oh God! It's right over your heart!" she gasped. "You could have been killed."

Helen crossed her hands over her breast, breathing hard. "I don't understand this," she said.

Gordo stood silent, allowing her to absorb the situation. In general, Helen savored action and drama in her life. This was giving her a full dose. But after she caught her breath, she reached for a cotton swab with a sense of purpose.

"Look at that," she said. "Look at where it is."

She was right. He hadn't given it much thought. Cold stainless steel rib spreaders. Surgeons with their hands inside him looking for a bullet and trying to piece things back together.

He winced as his mother cleaned the wound with hydrogen peroxide.

"You don't want this infected," she said.

"Al Mann already—"

"I don't understand," she repeated, cutting him off.

"Who did this?" Helen was in her bathrobe and shanks of hair, secured in a bun on the back of head by day, fell around her shoulders. She looked old. He thought back to her last birthday. Sixty-nine. Not that old.

"Mom, I told you. I don't know this guy."

"Who's mad at you?" she continued.

"What about Ana? Somebody must be mad about their case."

"Have any of her clients seemed upset about something?" she asked. "Has she been sued for malpractice? What about her brother who does drugs? Has he been around?"

Gordo could barely get in a word. His mother had expanded her role from that of nurse to crime investigator.

"Do you owe anyone money?"

"Mom, you're interrogating me a lot more than the police did."

She prepared a fresh gauze pad for the wound. "I'm entitled to. I'm your mother!"

• • •

Gordo and Ana tucked the boys into the double bed in Helen's guest room. Ana kissed them and assured them that all was well.

Gordo was drained, but he couldn't think about sleep.

"What's next?" Ana asked when they were alone.

"I'm not sure. We've been talking about leaving Galveston."

"That would take some time," she said. "The house. The law firm. Where would we go?"

"We've always wanted to move back to Austin."

Their college town. Where they'd met.

"Leave Galveston?"

"We could leave."

"Weird. It feels different—the thought of actually doing it."

"Well?"

"Maybe. Let's think about it," she said.

"What about tomorrow?"

"Let's get the kids back to school. Make things as normal as possible," Ana said. "Tomorrow's going to be tough on them. I just hate to think about them having to deal with the questions."

"What do you mean?"

"Their friends are going to ask what happened," she said. "Can you imagine Sam trying to explain what happened? 'Daddy opened the door and got shot.' The next question will be 'Why? Why did he get shot?'"

"Ana. I'm sorry. They'll just have to tell the truth. That we don't know why."

She put her arms around him. "It's just so weird. What does this bastard want?"

"He wants to kill me. Which is strange. To think that someone wants to point a gun at you and pull the trigger."

Gordo scoured his past for the offending moment. A confrontation, an argument, bad blood. Surely it would stand out in relief, leaving an unforgettably bitter taste. The gunman's eyes were full of rage.

• • •

Gordo had been examining his life for clues ever since the man first stepped into their lives. He'd seen the guy once before, last October, moments after he'd thrown a brick through the glass in the front door. After the thunderous crash, Gordo raced outside, where he was confronted by a tall, wild-eyed white man about his own age.

"Don't fuck with me!" the man said.

Gordo just stood there in the walkway in front of his house.

"Don't fuck with me!"

"Who are you?" Gordo asked.

"I'm your brother," he answered.

Before Gordo could say more, the man pulled out a knife and stepped toward him.

"Don't fuck with me."

Gordo went inside and called the police. But by the time they arrived, the man had vanished. An officer got a description and filed a report, although Gordo never heard from the police again. But then, Galveston was a violent place, and no one had been hurt. Who could blame them?

I'm your brother. Gordo had a brother. Ben, who lived in Dallas. The man with the knife was not his brother.

As alarming as that encounter had been, Gordo felt somewhat relieved to have seen this guy. There had been other acts of vandalism—two smashed windshields—but no one had gotten a good look at the man. Gordo knew nothing about his identity. And not knowing who the person was, not having any idea of his size or age or race or anything, seemed to make him even more threatening. But after the incident with the man and his knife, Gordo at least knew something. He knew it was not someone from his past. At least not anyone he could remember. This was not some old transgression come back to haunt him. And the man was not formidable. This was a tall, skinny, angry white guy who looked emotionally unstable.

"I can deal with this guy," he had told Ana that night in October. "I feel better knowing what he looks like. Less scary than someone who only lives in your imagination."

"Maybe you can deal with him, but what about us?"

"We're going to have to take some new precautions," he had responded. And they had. A new security system. Always an adult with the kids outside. More outdoor lighting. And they established the practice of Ana calling from her car phone when she was about to pull up to the curb in front of the house at night. These seemed like reasonable measures to Gordo. In his view, the angry man was more a nuisance than a threat.

But entwined with Ana in bed in his mother's home, Gordo knew that a burglar alarm and floodlights weren't enough.

"I thought I could deal with this guy," he told her. "I was wrong. I can't deal with a gun-shooting lunatic. I don't want to. Time to get out."

Ana held him. They were both too tired to think about the how and why.

"You're right," she said. "Time to go."

Three

Ana was seated alone at Helen's breakfast table when Gordo came downstairs.

"How are you?" she asked.

"Sore. But I'll live. Is my mother up?"

"Not yet."

She took his hand and kissed it. Gordo leaned forward and kissed her. The scent of chamomile tea and minty toothpaste swirled between them. He rubbed the muscles in her shoulders—her repository of tension and stress. He kissed her again. Her lips often had a bluish cast—the color of veins beneath translucent skin. As if she were cold. Men were always offering her their coats.

"So what do you think this guy is up to?" asked Ana.

"I've thought about it all night. What time is it anyway?"

"Getting close to six," she said. "Did you get some sleep?"

"I had some chest pain," he said. "I worried a bit."

"You should have gone—"

"I know, I know. But I probably got a lot more sleep than I would have at the hospital."

Ana nodded. "So, this guy?"

"Just about every explanation I come up with seems ridiculous. Or paranoid, or stolen from a really bad made-for-TV movie."

"Well, maybe so, but that doesn't mean we don't have to consider them," she said.

"Here are a few ideas." Gordo sat down and took a sip of her tea. "The guy's mistaken me for someone else."

"Go on."

"He has some connection to our house and something that happened there and he's projecting that experience onto me."

"A little farfetched. Go on."

"He's obsessed with me," Gordo continued. "Maybe because I remind him of someone or because I represent something painful or terrible."

He could tell that she didn't think any of these theories were very plausible.

"He's obsessed with you," he said. "And I'm just in his way."

"He doesn't even know me," Ana said dryly.

"He doesn't know me, either."

"But we don't have any evidence he's interested in anybody other than you."

"There is no rational cause for him to be interested in me, so why do we need a rational cause to explain anything he does?"

Ana didn't contest the point.

"He's observed that we are a traditional, happy family and he is the product of some awful broken home. He is enraged by any kind of Ozzie-and-Harriet sort of family group."

"He's not shooting at every traditional family in Galveston," she said.

"Okay, so we're unusually happy and that triggers his rage."

"We are?"

"We were?" he said.

"This discussion is getting weird."

"We're dealing with a weirdo."

"Maybe this could be funny," she offered, "in the right context."

"Ducking bullets is not the right context."

"No, it's not. I just keep thinking that if we try hard enough, if we remember hard enough, we'll come up with some connection that will explain all this."

"Let's keep going," Gordo said. "He's a disgruntled client of the law firm."

"I don't have any disgruntled clients."

"I know. But let's not rule out any possibilities. He's someone connected to Allen."

"Allen? He doesn't even live on the island," she said of her younger brother.

"Look Ana, I'm just tossing out ideas. We're trying to understand some very creepy behavior. Who do we know who's got creepy friends? Allen is a drug addict who hangs out with criminals. He's a link to strange people who do violent things. In fact, he's the only link I can think of."

"This keeps coming back to me," she said. "*My* disgruntled clients. *My* drug addict brother. *My* secret admirer. But look, he's not shooting at me. He's shooting at you!"

He touched his shirt, over the bandage. "I know who he's shooting at."

• • •

Ana and Gordo drove the kids to Galveston together. They needed to pick up their other car at Cooper School, where Ana had been when the police came to get her.

A small item had appeared in the Galveston newspaper,

although it didn't mention Gordo by name. He wondered aloud if someone at the paper had intervened. They knew the publisher and several of the reporters.

"One of the benefits of living in a small town," Gordo speculated.

"The grapevine is much more effective anyway," Ana said. As they crossed the causeway onto the island, the high bridge offered them a broad view of the bay, blue-green on these clear winter days, and the wafer-thin island floating before them. The scene was all horizontal lines except for the cranes at the wharves, a handful of tall buildings downtown, and the unlikely glass pyramid that housed a rainforest exhibit near the island's midsection.

To the east, he could see a winter sky of deep metallic blue streaked with pink from the sunrise.

"I wonder if that happens in the North," he mumbled.

"What?"

"The sky . . . those colors . . . in February."

"You okay?" she asked.

Then the bridge dropped them back down to earth, spilling them onto Broadway, which was flanked by decrepit cotton warehouses, convenience stores, and a cemetery. Much of the year, pink and white oleander blossoms softened this approach, but the cold months left upper Broadway stark and uninviting.

"I don't think I'll miss this part of Galveston," he said.

"It feels weird to be talking as if we're actually leaving," Ana said.

"Where're we going?" asked Jake.

Gordo glanced at Ana. She shook her head slightly.

"We're just thinking about making a few changes, son. We're not sure what we're going to do."

"Are we going to move to a new house?" the boy inquired.

"We can't do that," said Sam. "*Owah* house is *owah* house."

"We could if we wanted to," said Jake.

"Mom, we can't leave the Pilot House!" Sam, who always called it *the* Pilot House, seemed alarmed.

"Your father and I are going to figure out what's best for all of us."

"I'm not going *anywheya*," said Sam. "*Owah* house is *owah* house!"

Gordo looked at Ana. She was biting her lip.

• • •

For two people who weren't interested in organized religion, Ana and Gordo had grown quite attached to St. Stephen's Episcopal Church and the grade school that shared its name and buildings. Between schooldays, extracurricular events, church services, and Sunday school, it was not uncommon for someone from the family to be at St. Stephen's six or even seven days a week.

Gordo loved the nineteenth-century red brick church and the stucco chapel, each at one end of a lawn. The two church buildings were connected on the north side by the school and its long colonnade. A row of tall palm trees on the south side completed the rectangle. He had stood under the shade of an ancient magnolia on the green to watch the May Fête for the five years Jake had attended St. Stephen's. For Gordo, the lawn evoked dancing children, Easter egg hunts, the crowning of the queen of May, and Cub Scouts running wild on Monday nights. He served on the school's board of trustees and knew the headmistress and many of the teachers. Gordo was comfortable with his roles as slightly Bohemian writer, father of Jake, and bemused Episcopalian. A new role today—gunshot victim. He hated it.

He knew there would be questions, and he had no answers.

• • •

“Hello, Jake,” said his teacher.

Just the tone of her voice, artificially bright, told Gordo that she had heard the news. Karen Sullivan was a competent teacher. Nothing flashy, but a strong and calm presence in the lives of her students. Gordo knew her. Not well. But well enough to know that she was trying hard to seem normal. This was the teacher who picked up Jake the day he fell and hit his head on a curb on the playground. She had calmly held a gauze pad against his brow until the bleeding stopped. And she was the person who called Gordo to report that Jake was fine although he might need “a stitch or two.”

“Did you hear?” he asked.

“I heard something . . . but . . .” she didn’t finish. She looked at Gordo for help.

“Jake, why don’t you go look at the bulletin board. It looks like Mrs. Sullivan has got some new pictures up.”

Jake and the teacher stepped toward the classroom door.

“I was shot last night. I saw the man, and it’s not anyone I know. The boys were there at the house when it happened.” Short crisp sentences. Just the facts. “Jake seems okay. We’ve moved to my mother’s house in Dickinson. So Jake’s got a lot to deal with right now.”

“I’ll keep an eye on him,” she said. “Are you okay?”

He nodded and looked directly into her gaze. “Call us if you there’s anything you think we should know. A change in behavior or a problem. We’re all a little strung out right now.”

“Have the police—”

“Nothing yet,” he said. “The guy disappeared. You know the East End.”

She was from the island, and she understood.

The classroom seemed small and confining. Gordo was perspiring. And he could tell that Karen Sullivan was studying him in a new light. He was a person whose life might be more complicated than she'd thought.

Gordo grew irritated. It was as if he was being defined by a madman with a gun, instead of the Gordo O'Connor who had lived here for thirteen years.

He went to Jake, who was examining pictures of birds. Roseate spoonbill. One of their favorites. So pink that a solitary bird aloft radiated color like neon. It was the most striking of the island's birds. Gordo touched Jake's back and whispered in his ear, "Call me if you need anything."

The boy smiled and patted Gordo on the shoulder.

"In a while, crocodile," Jake said.

His typical goodbye. Gordo realized that Jake was keeping to the routine for his benefit. Intuitively, Jake knew it would be a comfort.

Gordo was moved. But he was fighting for breath in the old, overheated classroom. In an effort to avoid the arriving parents, Gordo escaped down the rear stairs and out the side door. He loved St. Stephen's, but today the old building just didn't seem to have enough oxygen.

• • •

Force of habit took him all the way home before he realized that he had a different destination. From his car parked at the curb, he examined their home. The hole in the front door's glass and the crazed areola around it was just visible. Their home was now a crime scene. The sidewalk in front was where both boys had learned to ride tricycles, then bikes with training wheels, and finally on two wheels. It was almost time to trim the hedge of pink rose bushes that ran along the front property line. Valentine's Day, his cue for pulling out the pruning shears, was about a week away.

This was home. And for some strange reason he remembered the rocks. In the backyard, beneath the bare pecan tree, a thick bed of English ivy climbed over rocks Gordo had hauled from Colorado, Idaho, and the Texas hill country. Galveston Island had no rocks. Thin topsoil covered sand and shell, but no rocks. So Gordo imported them. Large chunks of quartz, slabs of red ferrous rock hauled out of mountain streams, chalky white limestone. Wayward rocks and English ivy. Once, he accidentally left a backpack behind on a rafting trip in Idaho. The river guide—did he know Gordo was writing about the trip for a magazine?—shipped the pack to Texas. Surely he must have opened it to discover why it was so heavy. It must have posed a dilemma for him. Whether or not to pay freight for a pack full of rocks. Of course, the guide couldn't have known that rocks were a precious commodity on a barrier island. At least to Gordo.

He sighed.

Valentine's Day. Where would they be by then?

Enough. Too much to do right now. Time to go see Lena.

• • •

"What the hell happened to you?" she asked.

Lena Luchetti had an open face and Mediterranean coloring. She was pretty, but not so much so as to make him feel uncomfortable when she touched him. Which was a virtue because sometimes, as his doctor, she touched him in ways that could be awkward.

Gordo told her.

"I didn't know you were shot!"

"I told your nurse on the phone."

"I thought it was some minor accident or something. People don't usually schedule an appointment with their family doctor for a gunshot wound! Take off your shirt," she said eagerly.

"Lena, I didn't know this was going to be the highlight of your morning."

"I'm not sure we've ever had a fresh gunshot in this clinic. This is kind of a weird way to go about it."

"Al Mann looked at it last night."

"I bet he was very sweet."

But once Gordo had his shirt off, Lena grew less playful.

"Damn, look at that," she said. "Right over the heart. You had no business going anywhere but the hospital."

He told her about the aftermath of the shooting—and why he ignored Al's advice.

"What an idiot!" She was shaking her head. "The next time you get shot, you stay at the hospital. I don't give a damn about your instincts."

"I don't expect this to come up very often."

"You were not in a frame of mind to be making that decision. Al should have kept you there. I can't believe Ana let you get away with that."

"We were all pretty upset."

"Who is this guy, anyway?"

"I don't know. I've just seen him twice. The first time he had a knife in his hand. The second was last night."

"You don't live that far from John Sealy," she said, referring to the state charity hospital, which had a large psychiatric unit. "In fact, you don't live that far from all kinds of stuff."

"We moved here to live in the historic district. We never really considered the 'doctor ghettos.'" It was what people called the suburbs on the West End, where much of the faculty of the medical school lived.

"Hey, I live there."

"I know."

"Well, we don't get shot when we answer the door."

"You don't have to convince me, Lena. We're not going back."

She treated the wound, told Gordo how to take care of it, and wrote a prescription for an antibiotic. Although she had a breezy style, Lena loved to take care of people. She was patient and considerate, despite her crowded waiting room.

"I'm impressed, Gordo," she said, helping him back into his shirt. "A shot to the chest can make a real mess of things. I don't how or why, but you were lucky."

She put her hand on his shoulder. "So here's some valuable medical advice—keep away from that guy."

• • •

Gordo was sitting in a tight steel trench formed by gunmetal gray desks and filing cabinets with surfaces mottled by a thousand sweating cans of Dr Pepper. At least that's what Grover Hampton was drinking this morning.

Hampton was a large black man, a few inches over six feet in height and decades away from the last time he weighed in under two hundred pounds.

Gordo was retelling his story. Hampton and his partner, Aldo Martelli, were listening, occasionally murmuring in acknowledgment. Martelli was shorter, but just as stocky as his partner.

"And you never saw this man before?" Hampton asked.

"Like I said, I had seen him once before. The night he pulled a knife on me." Gordo reminded them of the night four months earlier. The brick and the knife.

"Right. But you don't know who it is?" Hampton asked for the third time.

Surely, Gordo thought, if he knew who was trying to kill him he would share the information with the police. "Look, until this guy showed up at my house last October, I'd never seen him before. I'm sure he's not anybody I had any dealings with."

"You'd never hired the guy to do work around the house? Maybe a former employee? Somebody who worked for your wife?"

"No, I know all the people who've worked on my house," Gordo said. "We never hired this guy. And he doesn't work in my wife's law firm."

Grover Hampton took a sip of Dr Pepper. Aldo Martelli rubbed his chin, which sounded a lot like eighty-grit sandpaper against an oak plank. The other officers called him "Tiny." Tiny Martelli.

"Now, tell me again, exactly what you did after you got shot," Tiny said. His suit, an indeterminate shade of brown, could not contain his mass, much less the bulge of the pistol at his waist. His thigh poured across the desk he was sitting on like a bag of wet cement. There didn't seem to be room for another chair in the crowded space.

Gordo explained the cascade of events once more. He wanted to help them, but he would have felt better if they'd been writing some of this down. They didn't seem to be equipped with vast powers of recall.

"You didn't go to the hospital?" Tiny asked.

"Not at first. I was pretty sure I was okay. I just wanted to get my family somewhere safe. It got kind of uncomfortable on the way over to Dickinson. I stopped at Mainland."

"You get shot and you drive in the opposite direction from the emergency room?" said Tiny. "You cross the bridge to the mainland, and go twenty-some miles before you bother to see a doctor?"

"Dr. Mann looked at me. He's a friend of the family."

"Way over in Texas City?" asked Hampton.

"It's a shallow wound. I just got grazed."

Tiny looked confused.

"And you don't know who would want to shoot you?" Hampton asked.

Gordo exhaled. "We don't get into fights with people. We pay our bills on time. We don't owe anyone money. We haven't fired any employees. I was just getting my kids ready for bed when somebody came to the door with a gun."

"You say you're a writer. Have you written anything that would get people mad?" asked Hampton.

"No. Most of what I do is published elsewhere. I cover business, health care—pretty tame stuff. And I'm a restaurant critic. But that's anonymous. I don't think anybody's going to shoot me because I didn't like their shrimp Creole."

"Some people take their food pretty seriously," said Tiny.

"Tiny takes his food real serious," offered Hampton, his voice as low as a foghorn in the harbor. It was the first evidence of humor of any kind from the pair.

Gordo managed a half smile. "How many shootings are there in Galveston?" he asked.

"What do you mean?" said Tiny.

"People shooting guns."

"People shoot guns all the time," the cop replied. "Guns are going off in the projects almost every night. Now if you're asking how many times people get shot, that's different. I think we had, what, twenty-five homicides last year. More than half, I guess, were shootings." He turned toward Grover, who nodded. "Course, not every shooting is a homicide," added Aldo.

"Like me?" said Gordo.

"Like you."

Gordo paused, waiting for them to continue.

Grover Hampton and Aldo Martelli just sat there. They were out of questions.

Something felt wrong about the interview, if that's what they called it. He was jumpy and upset but still something bothered him about the two cops.

• • •

Gordo left the dreary fluorescence of the detectives' office and stepped outside. The light was so intense he had to squint until he could pull on his sunglasses. Maybe it was the same on every island, but days like this made him feel as if he were floating on a raft in the middle of the ocean with the glare striking him from every angle. Piercing light glancing off the water seemed magnified. Amid all the brightness, Gordo was searching for someone who'd kept hidden from him for months. Someone who knew how to disappear.

In spite of everything he needed to do, Gordo went looking. Looking for a tall, thin, angry man. He drove slowly past the Salvation Army. He peered at the men killing time on the steps of the Rosenberg Library. Tiny and Grover—Gordo was already thinking of them by their first names—had made one observation that made sense to him.

"This guy probably shops at Food King," Tiny had said.

Of course. The shooter had been on foot. The East End was so compact, so densely populated, it would be easy to vanish down an alley.

Gordo found himself driving through the parking lot of Food King, a shabby grocery on his street that gouged its customers who didn't have the means of getting to the nicer stores on the West End. He studied every tall, white male he saw. What would he do if he spotted him? Wrestle him to the ground? Shout to the grocery clerks to call the police? Gordo remembered the long knife that had appeared from the man's back pocket.

But he wasn't there.

Could he still see the man's face? Hollow cheeks, thin blond stubble on his chin, glaring eyes. Navy blue watch cap snug on his head, concealing his hair. But it would be blond or light brown. Ruddy, pink skin. Maybe someone who worked outdoors. Ropy muscles and veins you could see. He'd seen the long legs and arms back in October, when the man had worn shorts.

At least six feet tall. And left-handed. A man who wielded a brick and a gun in his left hand was a southpaw. But would all this add up? Could Gordo pick him out with certainty? He thought of people who said they had problems recalling the face of a lost family member. Could he retain the image of the shooter?

Gordo could imagine a defense lawyer's question. "How long did you actually see the man who shot you? For how many seconds?"

Three. Four. Five at the most.

• • •

Gordo drove north on Batavia Boulevard until he reached his house. He had work to do. But before he got out he checked the sidewalk and the surrounding area.

It is broad daylight, he reassured himself.

He'd parked here and walked to his house thousands of times. But today was different. Gordo watched himself through the eyes of a hunter. It made him feel exposed and vulnerable.

Ridiculous!

He reached under the seat and pulled out the Beretta. His father's old .380. He stuffed the barrel inside the waistband of his pants. The steel was cold and reassuring. He knew the slide action was stiff. Cocking the pistol was tricky. He'd wrestled with it as a boy when his father had taken him shooting. How long ago had that been?

The starburst of the bullet hole in the front door's glass pane welcomed him home. Gordo slammed the door behind him and locked it.

The same spot. Right here. The left arm moving forward. The plume of light.

All of the merriment and laughter that had filled their

home for thirteen years seemed to have drained out through the small menacing hole overnight. He touched the pistol again and went to the kitchen to start a pot of coffee.

It was a familiar ritual. The rich smell rising from the grinder and the steam floating up from the pot. He usually scanned the newspaper as the coffee brewed. But the Beretta changed the character of this small, pleasant chore. Cold steel against his skin.

As he headed up the stairs, his finger traced the newel post, the heavy carved stanchion that anchored the stair railing. Gordo knew every scratch and indentation of its surface from years of caressing it as he passed. A hundred years of wear had not caused the post to budge—it was still solid as a rock.

He loved this place.

It was the house he and Ana shared before children, where Ana had been pregnant, and where the boys had entered their lives and changed everything forever. It was where they spent those early, happy years when they looked inward because the outside world could not compete with the excitement and joy of having babies in their midst. There was an innocence and an intensity about those years. The shooter had stolen their sense of security. Gordo wanted it back.

The place had survived the 1900 storm, the deadliest storm in U.S. history. Once, in the Rosenberg Library archives, he had surveyed the maps that denoted the "line of total destruction" from the hurricane that had killed 6,000 people. The shaded area extended almost to their home. He calculated that the line of total destruction stopped about 150 feet from his front door.

In his research, Gordo discovered an account of the desperate actions of the owner of his house, ship's captain Orr McManus. At the height of the storm, Captain McManus watched as his neighbors' houses were swept down Batavia Boulevard like dinghies. With the wind howling, the captain chopped a hole through the floorboards with a double-bladed ax. Black water spewed upward through the fissure like a seawater geyser. He knew the rising water would fill his home with bilge, making the house more stable on the tall brick piers of its foundation. Captain McManus used seawater to anchor his home.

After he left the library that day, Gordo went home and inspected the dining room floor. The amber floorboards of the house had vertical grain—tight, narrow bands of growth. But in the center of the dining room, open loops of grain lay side by side with the more desirable close-grained boards. The mismatched pine was not original. The story was true.

Captain McManus. Another reason why Pilot House was a fitting name for the house that had refused to budge. From the time they were babies, Jake and Sam had heard the story. When storms blew in from the Gulf they would plead, "Tell us the story of the big one."

No wonder the boys loved it so. The house was their Rock of Gibralter.

• • •

Gordo was on deadline. He had promised an article for a magazine editor who gave him lots of work. Writing was what he did, and he needed to get to it.

The article concerned the world's largest funeral home company, a Houston conglomerate that included a global network of florists, cemeteries, and even an embalming fluid manufacturer. A group of the company's shareholders was suing the chief executive and other officers for mismanagement and for squandering corporate assets on their own lavish lifestyles. The weeks of research had been fun, collecting stories of the CEO's penchant for fast cars, aircraft, and women, but it was time to put words on paper.

Gordo needed to organize his thoughts, piece together an outline, and hammer out the first draft. The next steps, editing and polishing and fact checking, while time-consuming, would be easy by comparison. After ninety minutes' work, during which he created a plan for the overall shape of the article, he fetched another cup of coffee. As he sipped, he admired the view from his second-story office. His thoughts turned to how they ended up on this island in the Gulf.

He and Ana had been living in Houston. On weekends, they took to driving down to the island to walk in the historic district, admire the Victorian architecture, swim at the beach, and eat seafood. The small scale of the island appealed to them. And they kept running into people who loved the place and shared their love with visitors. When Ana got a chance to leave the indentured servitude of a downtown Houston law firm for a job with a firm on the island, they started packing.

The idea of being near the beach and earning a living off what came out of his typewriter was attractive. He had his magazine contacts, and as long he had a fax machine and a telephone, he could work anywhere. But now, years later, he had doubts. Almost without realizing it, his working life had contracted. He had eased into a much more solitary existence, away from the colleagues he'd enjoyed as a staff writer and away from daily contact with sources. More and more of his life was lived vicariously over the telephone. And his work was drifting into more specialized areas. Managed health care, computers, corporate reports. One day, he woke up and found himself writing ad copy for a marine engineering firm. It wasn't quite what he had envisioned when he set up his office overlooking the esplanade.

Galveston was full of people who had dropped out in some way. People who'd left cities or careers or fractured relationships to remake their lives by the ocean. Interesting people. But *he* hadn't intended to drop out.

Of course, the town had plenty of productive, upstanding people. But Gordo found it curious—as well as charming and amusing—that in the course of his civic involvement, he'd encountered a number of prominent citizens who had done hard time. Arms smuggling, embezzlement, fraud. And those were just the ones he knew about. Nice people, but people with a history. Galveston was the kind of place where you could come and only share as much of your past as you wanted to.

His reverie came to an end when the doorbell rang.

Four

Gordo's heart beat faster. His breath came in shallow, rapid gulps.

Daytime. Nothing to fear.

He held the Beretta with the muzzle pointed up as he went down the stairs.

This is crazy. But so was last night.

He knew it was a man at the door, but he couldn't tell who it was. Then the figure turned and he caught sight of a bearded face through the lace curtain.

Gordo opened the door. It was Tom, his friend who lived around the corner.

Tom looked at him and the pistol. "Expecting company?"

"Last time I answered the door I got a surprise."

"I heard. I just wanted to make sure you're okay."

"Long night."

"Same guy?" Tom asked.

Gordo nodded.

Tom eyed the gun again. "You sure you're all right?"

Gordo wondered if he looked like a madman. The

hyperventilation, the racing heart, the gun. He wasn't concealing it very well.

"Fine."

Tom listened to Gordo's account.

"So what was it like?"

"Huh?"

"Getting shot. You don't have to talk about it if you don't want to."

"Different. Different from the movies. For me at least. Hurts less than you'd think," said Gordo. "But I woke up pretty sore. The whole left side of my chest is turning a weird color."

"Lemme see."

"You're serious?"

Gordo could see that his friend was indeed serious. They were close. They'd had keys to each other's homes for years. They'd ridden out hurricanes together. Gordo pulled off his sweater and his knit shirt. The left side of his chest had taken on a yellowish tint, the color of leftover chicken curry. He winced as he removed the tape securing the square gauze bandage.

Tom peered at the black, scabby hole. The lower edge of the wound was wet with a thick discharge.

"I'm coming over here tonight. Me and Siegfried and my .38."

Tom had three Doberman pinschers. All named for characters in Wagner's *Der Ring des Nibelungen*—Siegfried, Brunehilde, and Wotan. He and his wife loved opera.

"Why?"

"To stop this bastard. I'm not putting up with this."

"Tom, I appreciate the thought, but don't you think that's a job for the police?"

"This is my neighborhood. That guy comes back, he's going to get more than he bargained for. What did it feel like?"

"I wasn't sure what had happened," Gordo said. "You feel it—but then you don't feel it. I think I was relatively calm. Maybe because I didn't feel like I had the luxury of getting emotional. I tried to stay focused."

"So did you?"

"I don't know. It's still sinking in."

So how did this bullet end up behind you, without going through you?"

"Good question."

"Must have ricocheted off a wall. What did the cops think?"

"The cops didn't seem to care how it got there."

"That figures." Tom stroked his chin. "It just grazed you and then zigzagged back to the staircase."

Tom busied himself examining the walls and the ornate woodwork, looking for telltale scars, and lining up hypothetical bullet trajectories.

Armed with a practical mind, he'd often claimed he could perform any of the tasks required to restore his enormous old house as well as a professional craftsman, given some books, some practice, and the right tools. And he was usually right. Although the practice part had included a few destructive blunders.

During the last year and a half, Tom had designed forty-two compositions and etched them into the glass panes of a pair of ten-foot tall French pocket doors. One door depicted images from his family and its Texas heritage—Longhorn cattle, cactus, bluebonnets, and such. Etched into the opposite door were illustrations from his British wife's background. Samantha's family was honored with thistles, the coat of arms, some ancestral castle from Scotland, and eighteen other favorites. Gordo had been drafted to help Tom lug the doors, cypress monsters that weighed as much as he did, back and forth from the dining room to the backyard every time a few panels were ready for etching. So vile was the acid that was required to do the etching that it could not be done indoors.

"Tom," Gordo once asked between grunts as they wrestled a door down the steep flight of stairs to the backyard, "don't you intend to sell this place some day?"

"Of course," he gasped. Tom was a distance runner without much bulk—more endurance than brute force.

"Well, do you think the next owner will prize these scenes from merry old England?" asked Gordo. "What if you sell to a Chinese gastroenterologist from the medical school? Do you think he will give a damn about Samantha's coat of arms? Or longhorn steers?"

They put the door down for a moment.

"He will possess a house with character," Tom explained. "*My* character."

That was the end of the conversation. He had made up his mind and neither hernias nor sprained backs would deter him. When he took on a task, he attacked it, and he took his friends into battle with him. The good thing was that he reciprocated with equal fierceness. Tom was the one to call when you had a nasty chore at 3:00 A.M.

"You and Ana have been talking about moving to the Hill Country. As much as I would hate to see you leave," he said, "maybe you should go. This guy seems pretty determined."

"Ana and I talked about that last night," said Gordo. "She thinks it will take some time. Time to extricate herself from the law firm. Time to get rid of this place."

"Time to get killed?" said Tom.

"We're not coming back here. We've decided that."

"You're back right now. You're not twenty feet from where you got shot."

"I mean I'm not bringing the family back. We're going to find some kind of short-term place. Maybe on the West End."

"East End, West End. Gordo, it's a small island. The

school's what, five blocks away? You're here, you're vulnerable. I'd say fuck it, time to hit the road."

"Ana thinks moving the kids in the middle of the school year would be hard on them."

"Not as hard as losing their father."

Gordo wasn't in a mood to spar. "I'm in total agreement on that."

"I hate to give advice unless I'm asked for it." Tom said. "But we're friends. This guy's been buzzing around for months. This isn't just some impulsive bullshit. He's not going away. Get your stuff together and get out."

Gordo let him have his say.

"Let me know what I can do to help. Siegfried and I will be here tonight. But when I ring your doorbell," said Tom, "open the damn thing right away. You and I are about the same size. A lunatic could get us mixed up. When I find this asshole, I want to be ready for him, not standing around on your front porch."

"I appreciate the advice." Gordo reached for the shoulder of his friend. Opera lover and vigilante. "But I don't want you getting shot at on my account."

"He'll never know I'm there until it's too late," said Tom.

"This doesn't sound like a good idea."

But Gordo knew there was no changing Tom's mind.

"We may rent a place long enough to get things settled. It's the off season. Maybe we can find some place way out on the West End."

"You know you'd be welcome with us," Tom said. "But our house is too close."

"Twenty-four hours ago, could we have imagined having this conversation?" asked Gordo.

"What a difference a day makes."

• • •

While researching one of his travel articles, Gordo discovered the journal of Alvar Núñez Cabeza de Vaca. The Spanish explorer, who was trying to cross the continent, shipwrecked on Galveston Island in 1528. He and his men fought cold, hunger, disease, Indian attack, and cannibalism. Entitled *La Relación,* de Vaca's account described one early encounter with the natives:

So we got to their dwellings, where we saw they had built a hut for us with many fires in it. About one hour after our arrival, they began to dance and to make a great celebration, which lasted the whole night, although there was neither pleasure, feast, nor sleep in it for us, since we expected to be sacrificed. In the morning, they again gave us fish and roots, and treated us so well that we became reassured, losing somewhat our apprehension of being butchered.

Cabeza de Vaca endured six years of deprivation and hardship before renewing his expedition to the west. Although he ultimately befriended the Indians, the name he gave the place was *Malhado*—island of ill luck, misfortune, doom.

Gordo understood.

Malhado.

Despite his apprehension, Gordo's life plowed ahead on two disparate tracks. The mundane routine and his family's new life on the lam.

The next day, he took Jake's Cub Scout den on a trip to a blacksmith's. He had arranged it weeks earlier.

"Cub Scouts. The express train to normalcy," he told Ana.

The Scout theme for the month was history. He figured blacksmithing would teach the boys a little about an ancient craft. In reality, Gordo chose places where he wanted to go and people he wanted to see. He knew Eli McComb from around town, but he'd never been to his studio. By day, Eli was a blacksmith specializing in architectural work. The rest of the time he was a metal sculptor. His business was on the first floor of one of the old commercial buildings off the Strand.

Outside the studio, surrounded by Cub Scouts, Gordo took a deep breath. This close to the harbor, he could smell low tide. The heavy scent of salt brine and decaying fish that he never really found unpleasant. Sometimes you could forget that you were on an island, and he welcomed these small reminders.

As soon as he and the boys walked through the door, he could feel a difference in the atmosphere. Damp sea air replaced with the dry astringent warmth of an open fire. Metallic clanging resonated through the cavernous space. Something loud and violent lay ahead.

The boys' chatter began to grow louder in anticipation. The typical pushing and shoving became more intense.

"Where is it?" one of the Cubs asked.

"In the back of the building. We're almost there."

"Gross. Nick touched me with his gum!"

"Nick, gum belongs either in your mouth or in the trash."

"Daniel said a bad word!"

"Look guys, we're not going to have any screwing around inside," said Gordo. "Eli works with a really hot fire, and I don't want any accidents."

"Where's the fire?"

"How hot is it?" asked Jake.

"You'll have to ask Eli. But it's hot enough to make iron stretch like Silly Putty."

"Wow!"

"How does he do it?"

"How does he keep from getting burned up?"

Boy Scouts were all pyromaniacs at heart. Gordo knew firsthand.

"How does he keep from bursting into flames?"

"Let's go find out," Gordo said, sweeping the boys into a

chutelike passage leading deeper into the structure. He took Sam, who he included on these field trips, by the hand. Toward the rear of the building, they passed through an open iron gate and into the studio, which was busy with activity. Gordo waved to the bearded Eli, whose thick chest and broad shoulders seemed as much tools of his trade as the heavy hammer he was wielding. An iron bar glowed orange as he beat it into a curlicue.

Jake and his sidekick, Caleb, raced to the anvil where Eli worked.

"Hey! Wait up!" Gordo shouted. The other boys scampered after them.

"Dad, let's go!" Sam exclaimed.

"Let me finish this up while it's hot," Eli, all goggles and whiskers, shouted above the din. "This is going to be the railing on the balcony of an old house. But I can only work the iron for a few seconds before it cools off."

When he finished, Eli put down the work and removed his goggles. His was the brawn of heavy labor. With his burnished skin, knife blade of a nose, and high cheekbones, he looked like he'd stepped out of a Caravaggio painting.

The blacksmith proceeded to give the boys a short course on ironwork, explaining the process, demonstrating his tools, and opening the mouth of the fiery furnace.

"Let's make something," he proposed after his talk. "What do you guys want to make?"

"A suit of armor," cried Caleb.

"A go-cart," said another Cub Scout.

Eli laughed.

"A *sawd*," Sam said softly.

"Yeah! A sword," the others shouted.

Eli pulled on his heavy gloves, and grabbed an iron bar. "We can do that."

He plunged the end of the bar into the furnace and the boys watched expectantly as it changed colors from black to gray to white. From white to pink to glowing red.

"That would burn you bad," said one of the boys.

Eli beat the end of the bar around the nose of a large anvil.

"This will be the handle," he said. "Let's turn the end."

Gordo marveled at Eli's ability to give the handle a delicate taper as he hammered. Then he beat the fine end of the taper into a decorative curl.

"Now, why don't we give the sword a twist to give it some interesting lines."

After re-heating the iron in the furnace, Eli used a vice and large tongs to twist the bar like a piece of taffy, transforming the straight lines into a decorative spiral.

"Like the Maypole," said Sam.

"It's a sword," scolded Jake, "not a Maypole!"

Another plunge into the furnace and more pounding with the mallet rendered the sword whole, with a broad blade and a sharp point.

"Cool!" the boys observed.

"You could really stab somebody with that."

"You know," said Eli, "you're right. I think I'd better blunt the end a bit."

"No! No!" the boys cried.

Eli dulled the end to a crude point and dipped the sword into a drum of water. The metal hissed as steam rose from churning water.

Moments later, Eli held the sword out for Gordo. "You'd better take care of this. I don't want any injuries. Might make a good fireplace poker."

Gordo held the heavy sword. He was fascinated by the way Eli used fire, metal, and crude energy to create something of such beauty and permanence. He wasn't sure what the boys had gotten out of the visit, but they seemed to be having fun. Another Cub Scout meeting free of square knots and tourniquets.

Gordo raised the sword aloft and took Sam's hand in his. "Follow me!"

Five

"It's getting pretty strange shifting gears."

"Shifting gears?" she said.

Gordo was slicing apples. It was Sunday afternoon, and a cold front had blown in. Apple pie—comfort food for a blustery Sunday. Ana was in the kitchen to escape Gordo's mother. It wasn't that she didn't like Helen, but Ana needed a certain amount of quiet every day. Time spent reading, sipping her herbal tea, stroking her cat. Even reading to the boys had a certain meditative aspect to it. Helen, when in the company of others, had one mode. The talk mode. Full contact talking. No pauses permitted. Gordo knew she couldn't help it. It was her nature. And, after all, she was a widow. She didn't usually have people to talk to, and now she had a captive audience.

"Shifting gears from watching my back with a gun in my pocket to slicing apples and baking pie," he said. "Which life is real?"

"For the moment, they both are," she said.

"Can you get me a lemon from the fridge?" Gordo cut the lemon in half and squeezed juice over the sliced apples. "It's like I'm leading a secret life."

"You aren't, are you?" asked Ana.

"Even that damn Beretta looks like a spy gun." Gordo ignored her question. Was she serious?

"Secret agent Gordo," she said, seeming to ignore it too.

He measured a teaspoon of cinnamon to add to the sugar. "I hope she's got nutmeg around here somewhere."

"Everybody's got nutmeg."

"Everybody who cooks," he said, tossing a handful of raisins into the bowl.

And in that instant, Gordo felt sorry for his difficult mother. For him, that would be the definition of being alone—having no one to cook for.

"How are you bearing up?" he asked.

"We'd better find someplace soon."

"Is tomorrow soon enough?"

"Just."

Gordo turned the sugar-dusted apple slices into the piecrust. They might be housebound in dreary weather at Helen's, but at least the place would smell good. He cut slits into the top crust and transferred it to the hillock of apples he'd formed in the middle of the pie pan. His fingers moved quickly, surely. He never hesitated in the kitchen. As he crimped the edges of the crust, Ana's question came back to him.

"You aren't, are you?"

The smell of freshly sliced apples, cinnamon, and lemon juice wafted up from his mother's chipped Pyrex bowl.

Secret agent Gordo.

• • •

"Everybody grab something," he announced.

They were parked between a colonnade of pilings.

Jake looked out the car window and announced, "It's like we're under a pier."

"At low tide," Ana added.

"It's a *pia* house!" Sam exclaimed.

"Pier House," Gordo repeated. "I like that."

"Do you think this one could make it through a hurricane?" asked Jake, who was carrying a small cage that contained his gerbil, Henry.

"We won't be here long enough to find out."

As they climbed the stairs, their footfalls on the weathered gray boards created a vibration Gordo could feel through the soles of his shoes. He thought he could even hear an audible hum. But when they reached the deck, which overlooked the dune line and the beach, the boys were exuberant.

"We can go to the beach whenever we want to!" Jake shouted.

Sam said, "I'm going to catch a bunch of sand *cwabs*."

"I wonder if Henry would like to go to the beach?"

"Never go to the beach without an adult," Ana cautioned. She turned to Gordo, her arms around his waist. "It's a nice view. We've never lived *on* the beach."

"We're getting closer to the water," he said. "Our next move will be to a houseboat." Gordo smiled. There was something purifying about the beach on the West End. No squalor, no panhandlers, no dilapidated buildings. Of course, there were also no poor people, no black or brown people, and for that matter, almost no people at all. In February, those for whom the beach was a second home were living someplace else. Based on the number of cars visible on this stretch of the beach, only a handful of people could be in residence.

Inside, the boys explored their new home. It was worn, with a few smears of beach tar on the carpet and scarred

Formica on the countertops. But it was comfortable. A big stuffed sofa with matching armchairs. The standard wall of glass facing the Gulf, equipped with vertical blinds evocative of early eighties office decor. Three bedrooms flanked the living room, two small ones on one side and the master suite on the other. A large kitchen faced inland.

"More privacy than we've had in a while," Gordo whispered.

"I don't think I could have taken another day at Helen's," said Ana.

"This place isn't bad." He put the bags down. "I hardly remember it from when the leasing agent showed it to me. Just knew it had three bedrooms and was in our price range."

Ana eased herself onto the bed and stretched out. "Ah . . ."

Gordo joined her, spooning his body against hers.

"Will we be safe here?" she asked.

"Yes," he whispered, kissing the back of her neck. "Yes," as he kissed her earlobe, "yes."

That evening, while he was out buying milk, he picked up a mixed bouquet of cut flowers. Nothing very special, but they would add a splash of color to the bland pastels of the beach house.

"For you," he said, presenting her with the flowers. It wasn't the sort of thing he did very often, and she seemed pleased. But it made him feel like a penitent husband, guilty of some transgression. Maybe it was because the family had been forced from Pilot House on his account. However, he hadn't done anything to provoke this mess. He wondered if Ana sensed a measure of guilt in the gesture.

"Want to go for a walk?" he asked. The weather had been mild and, uncharacteristically, there was little wind.

"On the beach?" she asked.

He smiled. "It's one of the virtues of living by the water."

"What about the boys?"

"They'll be fine. We can keep the house in view the whole time," he said. "It won't get dark for a while."

"Well, okay. A short one."

• • •

Gordo had met her in college. He had been on two dates with her roommate, Elsa. Elsa and Ana. Uncommon names for Austin, Texas, of the 1970s. Elsa and Ana. *Blonde on Blonde.* Gordo and his roommate called them that after a night of too much Bob Dylan.

One evening Gordo was left waiting on the couch in Elsa's apartment while she changed clothes.

A door opened and he looked toward the hallway, where he saw the back of a pale, long body, clad only in white panties, casually stride down the hall. Ana. She hadn't seen him. But something about her narrow shoulders and hips and her small round butt stirred him. Her straw blond hair was wet, combed straight down to a spray of freckles on sharp shoulder blades. And there, halfway down her back, an interesting wine-colored splotch.

Gordo was a frequent visitor thereafter, but eventually, Elsa caught on.

"Go ahead and ask her," she said.

"Huh?"

"You keep staring at her. Go ahead and ask her out."

"Who?"

"I don't care."

Gordo thought this was way too easy. Surely he was missing something.

He played dumb.

"Not sure what you mean, Elsa."

"Fuck off. You know what I mean."

Elsa always was direct.

"Besides, I'd sort of like to meet *your* roommate," she said.

"Really?"

"Why? Is there something wrong with him?"

"No. I just thought—"

"You are such a shit. Here you are mooning over Ana while you're supposed to be dating me, and when I tell you it's okay for you to ask her out, you get jealous because I'm interested in *your* roommate. Did you ever consider that the world does not revolve around Gordo O'Connor?"

"Do you think she would go out with me? Ana, that is."

"See what I mean?" she said. "You're impossible."

"Well?"

"She might. And don't expect me to ask her for you. But she might, based on something she said."

"What did she say?"

"On the other hand," Elsa said, "she usually likes them tall."

• • •

They walked west toward San Luis Pass for about a quarter mile, casting a backward glance at the house every few minutes. Gordo had his arm at her waist. He liked the way their hips collided softly from time to time. She was two inches shorter, but with her long legs she seemed to match his stride.

She usually likes them tall. You never know.

"You never know," he said.

"Maybe I just lack imagination," she said, "but it's bugging the hell out of me that we can't figure out what this guy is up to."

Since the shooting, they could slip in and out of conversation about what he was beginning to think of as their former life and this new life they were leading. *Him.* That's all either of them needed to say.

"What about panhandlers?" she asked. "The ones who ring the doorbell."

"I've never been rude to them. Usually I just give them a dollar. The only one who ever seemed mad was the one I gave a plate of spaghetti. He asked for food but he really just wanted money for booze. *He* was pissed. But he was a little guy."

"No more spaghetti."

"The thing about all this," he said, "is that it makes me a suspect, no matter what. No matter whether the shooter knows me or not. Most people will always wonder if I didn't deserve to be shot for some reason."

"What people think is the least of our problems," said Ana.

She was right, of course.

"You indicted people," she added, referring to his service on the grand jury two years earlier.

"Everybody who's ever served on a grand jury has indicted people. Scores of them. That's your job."

"Maybe one of those creeps is back in town," she said. "Maybe he didn't like your looks. Maybe he figures you didn't give him a fair shake."

"Every one of those votes went twelve to zip. I can't ever remember any dissent. The DA's office just didn't bring a case to us unless they had the guy by the nuts."

"The suspects didn't know that," she said. "Maybe you frowned and everybody else smiled and to him, that means you're the sorry bastard who got him sent to the big house. Criminals aren't noted for their intellect."

"I got that impression."

"It's just something to think about," she said. "How else are you going to come into contact with a sleazeball?"

They turned back. The sand was damp and caked onto the soles of their running shoes. They'd only been on the beach a day, and already there was a pile of what looked like sugar-coated shoes outside the front door. Shadowy sand crabs flashed across the sand in front of them, racing sideways so fast you couldn't be sure you'd really seen something.

"Ana, I'm sorry for all this. I don't know why I'm apologizing. It's not like I did anything. But I just wish it never happened. I wish we were still at Pilot House."

"Are we expecting anybody?" she asked, looking east toward the beach house.

"No. Not that I can think of."

Gordo watched a pair of headlights slow down in front of the house. After pausing for a moment, the driver parked nearby and the headlights disappeared.

"We better go see who that is." Gordo started walking rapidly.

"Go on," she shouted. He ran ahead.

Someone got out of the car and headed for the stairs.

The dry, loose sand away from the water line made it harder to run fast. As he crossed the dunes, he saw a rectangle of light from the open door. A man in profile.

"Jake! Jake!"

Jake heard him. He walked to edge of the deck. "Dad?"

"Who is it, Jake? Who's there?"

"It's Dave. He brought cookies. Are you all right? You sound funny."

"Nothing, son. It's okay," he said.

By the time he ran up the stairs he was so short of breath he couldn't talk. Gordo bent over, hands on his knees, panting.

"Gordo—you taken up running?" Dave had a bemused expression on his face. "If so, I'd say you've got some more work to do. Sally made you guys some cookies. Kind of a housewarming present."

"Great," Gordo croaked. "That's great."

"Where's Ana?"

Dave Gunderson worked in Ana's law firm and lived on the

West End. Gordo went to the edge of the deck and called out, "It's Dave."

"Hi, Dave," she sang out, as if nothing was wrong.

Bursts of adrenaline like this can't be good for you, Gordo thought. How long was this going to go on?

Dave and Sally were only a little older than Gordo. Ana liked them both. Years earlier, Dave had seemed smitten by Ana, but then he wasn't the only one. It wasn't her fault that she was one of only two women attorneys at the firm. Everything had remained civilized.

"I'm at the club and I hear that this guy with the gun may be some whacked-out relative of yours," Dave explained. "Some guy you shafted who's now on the street and the only thing he lives for is getting revenge."

"Oh that's nice," Ana said. "Who said this?"

"Not anybody you know. Some friend of Teddy Selig."

"Teddy the weasel? I hope you set him straight," she said.

"What makes you think that we don't know Teddy's friend?" asked Gordo.

"Hotel business. Not your type. The only people you guys know are lawyers."

Dave was right. God, what a sad thought. Beyond the parents of Jake and Sam's classmates, the majority of their friends were courthouse people.

"So did you?" she asked.

"Did I what?"

"Set him straight?"

"Damn right. I told them Gordo had a bastard half-brother that you screwed out of his inheritance."

"Dave! Don't even joke about it," Ana screeched. "That's the way this crap gets started. Tell me you didn't say that." This was a legitimate question because Dave loved practical jokes and could lie through his teeth with a straight face. His partners called him Deadpan Dave.

"It's amazing how much joking has been prompted by my getting shot." Gordo had finally caught his breath. "The next time anybody gets depressed you can just shoot me, and it will raise the spirits of the whole island."

"Gordo, Dave didn't mean anything," said Ana.

"Hey, I'm sorry, Gordo. I was just joking."

"You know where this bastard child rumor is coming from?" asked Gordo.

Ana shrugged.

"Like all effective rumors, it has a grain of truth to it. A really good rumor contains a little bit of truth and suggests something scandalous that we all would like to believe is true. That's the part I don't get," Gordo said bitterly. "Why do people believe this shit?"

"What's true about it?" asked Dave.

"The shooter, the night he pulled the knife on me, said, 'I'm your brother.' That's the basis for the bastard child theory. People are taking the words of a fucking madman and jazzing them up to make a better story. And what's worse, I only told the police and a few close friends."

"Gordo, don't get upset. It's just locker room talk," said Ana.

Dave looked sorry he'd brought up the whole business.

"I know. But over time, this bullshit becomes reality. 'Gordo O'Connor—isn't he the guy who got shot by his brother in some kind of family feud?'"

"Look, it's Galveston," said Dave. "Baseball may be the national pastime, but gossip is the island pastime. You know that."

Gordo sighed. "It's more fun when the gossip is about somebody else."

"Well, of course," said Dave. "But everyone has a civic responsibility to entertain their neighbors, and now you and Ana are finally doing your part. I have to say, the O'Connor household has been seriously deficient in years past. No divorce, no criminal activity, no torrid affairs. A few tepid affairs, maybe, but they don't count."

Gordo looked over at Dave. He was smiling.

"Dave, I'm glad that getting shot has given my life meaning."

"You've always had a sense of humor," said Dave. "I think you're still going to need it."

Later, after the kids were in bed, Gordo said, "I don't understand how this all can be so scary to us and so damn funny to everybody else."

"It's not funny to the people we're really close to," said Ana. "And the others, they just don't know how to react. So they joke about it. They think it helps. And for some people, it's less awkward to laugh than to share their feelings. They don't want to believe there's any way this could happen to them. They want to believe this is some strange phenomenon like getting struck by lightning. That way they can still feel safe."

"Were you afraid when we saw Dave come to the house?"

"I got spooked," she said. "Were you?"

"I just wasn't expecting anybody."

"It'll get better."

"It seems like I'm getting a megadose of adrenaline practically every day," he said. "It's weird to not be completely in control of your body. I mean, I can tell myself that the doorbell means nothing, but I can't convince my body, which seems to be bracing for . . . for something."

"It's only been a few days."

"I am beginning to have a serious craving for normalcy," he whispered. "This place is nice, but it's not normal. It's not natural for us to be living in a house on stilts. This is a vacation house, not a real house. I just remembered that I forgot the coffee maker."

"Gordo, this is our first day here. I like this place and the kids do too. Day one is unfamiliar. Give us a little time. And there's a coffee maker in the kitchen."

"It's a Mr. Coffee."

"Gordo—"

"I can't help it."

"You survived a gunshot, you can survive Mr. Coffee."

She reached for him. Gordo loved her mouth, her blue lips. He kissed her.

"What time is it?" she asked.

"Not too late."

Ana pulled her nightgown over her head.

• • •

She rested her head on his naked stomach while he worked the muscles of her neck and shoulders. With her small breasts pressed against him, the elegant lines of her back draped across him, and her narrow hips within reach—he could stay this way forever. His hand glided over the taut muscles of her girlish ass, the inside of her thighs, and the contours between. Using his other hand, he gently pulled her hair, her earlobe.

"Ahhh." The sound exuded from her like vapor.

Gordo stayed away from her scarlet birthmark, the shape and size of a crook-necked squash. She didn't want him to touch it, drawing attention to what she considered ugly and imperfect. To him, the red splotch and its scaly, coarse texture just made the rest of her charms stand in high relief.

Lazily—intermittently—she took him in her mouth, working her tongue down the length of him. Then she planted a row of kisses upward to his navel, her tongue swirling its gnarled surface.

Entwined in this way—they formed a human pretzel. Their pretzel.

"You know me too well," he said.

"I've had some practice."

He reached for the bottle of massage oil, poured it into his palm, and plowed his hand more firmly between her legs.

They had not been too far from this position that first time together back in college. It had been early during her period, and she'd warned him that sex was not an option.

"I'm bleeding too much. I'll soak your whole bed."

So they had kissed. The ratty college apartment. He'd unbuttoned her shirt and kept peeling. Worn sheets from his childhood.

This human knot returned him to the joy and astonishment of exploring her naked body that first night. Lanky limbs, smooth flesh, glorious yellow hair. A night full of promise and good fortune, when it seemed he was at the threshold of so much that the world had to offer.

All of it, the whole dreamy tangle of past and present, washed over him like the surf he could hear out their door.

"Come inside me now," she whispered. "Fuck me."

Gordo did as he was told.

• • •

The phone jerked him from the depths of sleep. As he approached consciousness, he sucked in a huge breath as if he'd been under water a long time.

Fingers searching the bedside table. Nothing was where it should be.

No. Of course not. The beach house. But where was it?

"What . . . what," Ana murmured. Her face shook back and forth, as if a spider web had dropped over her.

There. The phone was on her side of the bed. Gordo was standing in the dark.

God, what time was it?

"Hello," he said. As he fumbled with the button of his

cheap Casio, a faint light smudged across its gray digital face. 1:17.

"Hey man," a voice said brightly. A man's voice.

"Yes."

"Hey."

"Who is this?" he asked.

"Just checking in. What are you up to?"

"Who are you?"

"You know."

Gordo heard music in the background. He tried to clear his head.

"No, I *don't* know. Who are you?"

"I bet you do."

Gordo was silent.

"How are you . . . doing?" The voice was calm, playful. The breezy, confident tone of someone in charge. Young. Twenties, thirties.

Gordo's hand moved to his chest. Was it him?

"Do I know you?"

"Maybe."

Gordo could hear his own breathing coming through the receiver.

Click. Dial tone.

"Who was it?" Ana asked groggily.

"I don't know."

Gordo was alert now. He tried to think. Who had he given the phone number to? The police. He'd called Grover Hampton to tell him they were moving to the beach house. His mother. Ana's parents. Tom.

The guy didn't call Gordo by name. But it didn't sound like a wrong number call. He seemed too sure of himself.

I bet you do.

Six

"I'm afraid this guy may know where we are." Steam was drifting off his coffee cup as Gordo stood at the window, looking out at the rolling gray surf. An offshore wind was strong enough to draw a smoky contrail of sand off the peak of the dune before him.

They only had a few minutes before it would be time to set the day in motion. The drive from the West End to the boys' schools and to Ana's office required them to shift their whole routine forward.

"How do we know it's the guy?" Ana asked.

The guy.

She was slicing a bagel, a chore that always made him wince. Ana was careless, or perhaps just clumsy, with knives. The combination of a sharp knife and a chewy bagel could easily result in bloodshed. Yet it annoyed her when he offered to help, as if she were not competent to make breakfast. It was one of Ana's paradoxes. She could swiftly disarm an opposing lawyer in the courtroom, but a bagel presented a very real threat.

“He had a real smug, wise-ass tone. Like he knew something. And I should know it too. If he’s got the phone number, then he may know where we are.”

“But how would he get either one?”

“I don’t know. I’ve only given the number to the cops, our parents, Tom. My editor. Who have you told?”

“I gave it to Sam’s teacher, in case she needed to reach us,” she said. “A couple of people at the office—Dave, Bertie, Corky.”

“Corky?” Dave was her partner, Bertie was her secretary. But Corky?

“We’re both on the fundraising committee at Cooper.”

“Right.”

Sam, wobbly and carrying his pillow, came in and announced he was ready for breakfast. Then he promptly stretched out on the couch. Ana started his oatmeal. She had an unwavering nutritional faith in oatmeal. Of course the kids would have nothing to do with her imported Scottish steel-cut oatmeal, which she laced with dried cherries and cranberries and was actually pretty good. While Ana’s public face was strong and assertive, she withheld a private fear of mineral shortages, free radicals, incompatible doses of vitamins C and E, selenium deprivation, and scores of other potential dietary ambushes. Oatmeal, she asserted, contained any number of beneficial agents that helped lower the bad kind of cholesterol or raise the good kind of cholesterol. Gordo could never keep these things straight. In any event, although the sanctity of oatmeal was never questioned, he suspected that they were but a few years away from a revolt that would overthrow oatmeal in favor of Pop Tarts.

“There’s always noise,” Sam said.

“Noise?”

“Noises.”

“What kind of noises?”

"Windy noises. Splashy noises."

"He's right," Ana said. The teakettle was singing.

"Does that bother you?" Gordo asked.

"Just *stwange.*"

"The first time I slept at Pilot House, I almost jumped out of my skin when an ambulance shot down the boulevard," said Gordo. "Now we sleep right through them. Maybe that's what's strange, not hearing sirens all night long."

"It's that annoying sound of surf and ocean breeze that's keeping you up at night, Sam," teased Ana, as she brought Sam's sugary instant oatmeal to the table.

"Well," replied Sam, carrying his pillow with him to the breakfast table, "something's *diffwent.*"

• • •

Gordo was telling Grover Hampton and Tiny Martelli about the phone call he'd received in the middle of the night.

"Coulda been anybody," Grover said, not even bothering to feign interest.

Tiny shrugged his shoulders. "Maybe a crank call."

"It seemed like the guy knew something."

"One in the morning?" replied Tiny. "Could have been some guy who dialed the wrong number and was too drunk to know it."

"Would it be worth getting the phone records? To know where the call came from?"

"What's the point?" replied Tiny. "So we get the address of some pay phone on Post Office Street. What do we do with that?"

Gordo noticed an older man stand and leave one of the desks in the bullpen. He scowled at Tiny as he crossed the room. The man was short and wiry, with skin the color of the unlit cigar that rested on Grover's desk.

"Have you got any leads?" Gordo asked, hoping to guide the conversation onto a more productive path.

"We talked to folks up and down Batavia," said Grover, "and we haven't found anybody who's seen anybody fittin' that description."

Gordo couldn't drive five blocks without seeing someone who matched the description. That was the problem, there were too many tall, skinny white guys running around on the street.

"Yeah, we're not finding anything," said Tiny Martelli. "You sure there's not more you can tell us about what happened?"

"If some guy wants to shoot me, don't you think I would want to give you every bit of information I have? I want to help you find the shooter. I've got two young boys at home. What do you want to know?"

"We were wondering if you've had words with anybody," said Tiny. "Anybody who might want to hurt you."

Gordo shook his head.

"Who do you know who might get violent? Or mixed up with violent people?" asked Tiny. "Somebody you've brushed up against."

"My wife's brother is a drug addict. But he's harmless. He gets loud when he gets strung out, but I don't think he's ever hurt anybody."

"Where does he live?"

"He kind of floats from one place to the next. Sometimes he crashes at his parents' house."

"The Colonel?"

Gordo thought he detected a flicker of hostility in Tiny Martelli's voice. Pat Hayes's name elicited all kinds of responses. It always had. People loved him. People hated him. Over the years the Colonel had represented police unions around the county in contract negotiations, extracting better pay from tight-fisted city councils. The Galveston Police Department had never asked for his help. Pat Hayes had been in law enforcement as an FBI agent. But Gordo could see that didn't mean anything to these two cops. As a special prosecutor, Pat had shut down gambling on the island. Gordo was used to getting icy stares from people who were nostalgic for hearing Guy Lombardo at the Balinese Room, people who lamented the loss of the island's old illicit sheen and blamed Pat Hayes for Galveston's decline into obscurity. As if Galveston would have become Las Vegas if not for Pat Hayes.

But cops? This was 1994. Thirty-eight goddamn years later. Gordo felt anger rising like something lodged in his throat.

Tiny propped his enormous leg on a chair.

Could these guys run if they had to? Gordo doubted it.

"The crackhead brother," said Grover. "That's good. What else you got for us?"

• • •

Gordo left the detectives' bullpen and headed for the men's room. He looked in the mirror. The close, dense air and his own rage had opened his pores and beads of sweat were glistening across his forehead. Bending toward the sink, he splashed cold water onto his face. When he reached for a paper towel, he noticed someone standing at the urinal. The little brown man.

"Those two. I don't usually talk about other cops. But those two. Sloppy work. Always sloppy work."

Gordo was weary of cops. But at least here was one saying something unambiguous.

"Something's not right," said Gordo.

"Couple a dumbasses. Thought you were faking it. Something kinky. That you were working some angle on this. I told them, 'You don't work an angle by shooting yourself in the fuckin' chest.' Only a dumb son-of-a-bitch does that, and you ain't that stupid. A fool could see that."

"Well, thanks. That makes me feel a lot better," said Gordo. What was this guy saying? What angle?

"It's the truth. I'm getting out of this dump in thirteen weeks, so I can say what I think. Not everybody here is a prick. We've got some good cops, and we've got some broke dicks who need directions to the crapper. You got miserable luck getting Martelli and Hampton. And I'm not saying that because one's dago and the other's a spade. Those two come by it naturally—they're just lazy. You know what I mean?"

Gordo was growing uncomfortable with the conversation. The last thing he needed was more trouble with the police, even if he knew just what the small man meant.

"Well, I'd better—"

"Gabilondo." The man stretched out his hand. Gordo could see a wet spot expanding on the front of his dark trousers. He only hesitated a fraction of a second before accepting the handshake.

"Hector Gabilondo."

"Gordon O'Connor."

"I know I look like an old broke-down geezer, but I used to be a pretty good cop. Back when my knees and my back and my bladder were all in working order. Thirteen weeks."

"Good to meet you."

"My nephew's on the job. Lino Gabilondo. I'll tell him we met. I don't hold nuthin' against you. Who you are."

Gordo was struggling to collect his wits, to understand what the man was trying to say, and to dry his face.

I don't hold nuthin' against you.

Why should any of these people hold anything against *him*? What was Hector Gabilondo trying to say?

"I judge people one prick at a time," said the wiry man. "If you know what I mean. Mexicans, spades, whites, the Viet Cong—all the same to me. One prick at a time."

"I understand," Gordo lied.

Hector Gabilondo turned to face the mirror. "Don't like sloppy work."

• • •

Before he returned to the beach, Gordo stopped off at Tom's. The three-story house, with its peeling iron gate, massive oaks, neglected rose garden, and Doberman sentries, seemed dark and forbidding in the gauzy morning light.

Bleary eyed, Tom answered the front door, which was at the top of a high staircase.

"How did it go?" asked Gordo.

"Not much sleep. No sleep, actually. Not as quiet as here on Ursuline. Siegfried got worked up every time somebody walked down the sidewalk."

As one of the main thoroughfares between downtown and the seawall, Batavia had foot traffic at all hours.

"Any visitors?"

"Siegfried and I were ready. But the guy didn't show."

Gordo was moved at how willing Tom was to put himself at risk.

Tom had once been an art dealer and gallery owner in Houston. His business was called the Purple Gallery. During the 1960s, he became an unofficial spokesman for the arts. As a personal statement, and as self-promotion, he wore nothing but purple clothes for five years. Purple suits, purple shirts, purple socks and shoes, purple business cards. The Man in Purple was a promoter of arts festivals, defender of free speech and controversial art, and successful entrepreneur. He was good at it because he believed in art passionately. Gordo knew that this towering nineteenth-century house had no central heat or air conditioning, but it had original work by Picasso and Miró. In this household, art was more important than heat. He was glad that Tom did not have to choose between art and food.

Mindful of all this, Gordo took his friend's shoulder. An unlikely vigilante.

"Thank you. At times like this, you learn who your friends are. But really, Tom, you don't need to stay at the house."

"I'm not," he said. "Once is enough. The night seems darker when you're waiting for a man with a gun."

• • •

That evening the phone rang.

"Heard you people have some trouble."

"Lars!"

"What the hell is going on down there?"

Lars was a friend, a widower who had sailed into Galveston harbor one day a few years earlier in a twenty-eight-foot sailboat that he docked illegally on Pier 19. A thin, sun-burnished man with intense eyes, a beaklike nose, and hollow cheeks, Lars had been on the water for months working his way down the eastern seaboard, around Florida, and across the Gulf. He'd intended to stay just long enough to refuel and buy supplies, but something about the island—the pace, the waterfront, and the ease with which he met people—caused him to stay on. Or maybe he was just tired. Gordo and Lars had met in a bakery near the harbor. After they'd become friends, Gordo regularly took the boys to the pier to visit. Having raised five children, Lars had a knack with kids. He always kept some kind of treats on board for Jake and Sam. They loved the novelty of visiting someone on a boat.

"Mom," Sam reported after his first visit, "*Lahs* has got a bike and a little boat on his big boat."

A folding bicycle provided Lars with transportation on the island. And he kept a dingy lashed to the stern of his boat. A lawyer who had devoted himself completely to family and work for the first sixty years of his life, Lars had chosen to do some serious roaming when his children no longer depended on him. After the better part of a year in Galveston, he hauled his boat out of the water and left to begin the next adventure. Gordo couldn't exactly remember where in Central America he'd been headed. But they'd kept in touch.

"Lars," said Gordo, "who have you been talking to?" A mutual friend had given him a reasonably full account of the shooting.

"Where are you?"

"Home. Minnesota. And it's cold up here. Sounds like you guys could use a hand. Why don't I come down?"

"Lars, you don't have to do that."

"I know. I want to. I'm getting cabin fever up here. I can help. I'm not afraid of that son-of-a-bitch."

"Let me talk to Ana. Can I call you back tomorrow?"

"Tell her I've already filled up the car. I can be there tomorrow night."

"Let me talk to Ana."

Gordo hung up the phone and went into the bedroom.

Ana was already sleepy. She'd been reading to Sam earlier.

"Lars?" she said groggily. "Where is he? What's he want?"

"He wants to come help us. He says he can be here by tomorrow night."

"Gordo-o-o." She closed her eyes and grimaced. "Are you serious?"

"Maybe it would be good to have someone else around. He says he'll take the kids to school and look after Pilot House."

"But it's cramped enough here," she said. "I was just getting decompressed from your mother's place. I just feel like we need to close ranks right now. As a family. Do you know what I mean?"

"He really wants to come."

"You know I love Lars, but having someone, anyone, living with you. . . . It just changes things. It's hard to relax—completely—with a house guest. At least not the way you can when it's just us."

"Lars's not your typical house guest."

"I know. He's the best house guest anybody could ever ask for. But we're under such pressure already. I just think it would be better if we didn't have someone living with us right now."

"I know you love him," he said, "and it's a good thing, too. Because he said he was leaving tonight so we couldn't change his mind. He had the car packed before he made the call."

"Oh great. So he really will be here tomorrow night."

"He's driving straight through. He said give him twenty-three, twenty-four hours."

"I feel like I've lost control of my life," she said.

"It's not just anybody. It's Lars." It had always been a source of friction. Ana needed time to herself. With the boys and with her work, she often went days without it. It wasn't that she didn't like people. She just had a gentle need to back away from the maelstrom of life for a while. Failure to do so left her drained. "But that's just it. Right now, we'll be aware of *anybody* who's with us twenty-four hours a day. It's not a good time."

"You know Lars," he said.

A fleeting half-smile swept across her face.

"That crazy Norwegian."

• • •

"Lino Gabilondo?" repeated Pat Hayes. "I don't know him. I know a Hector Gabilondo, but he would have retired by now."

"Thirteen weeks."

"What's that?"

"Hector's got thirteen weeks to go," said Gordo.

"Really? How do you know that?"

Gordo told him about the encounter in the men's room.

Pat Hayes, Gordo's father-in-law, leaned back in his leather chair. He was warming up. Transported to some other decade.

He wasn't really a colonel. Still a teenager when he enlisted, Pat Hayes was a staff sergeant in the Army Air Corps during the war. Fifty-nine missions as bombardier and navigator on a B-26. It was only years later in Galveston that someone called him "the Colonel," and it stuck.

"I'll tell you a story about Hector," he said.

Gordo settled into his seat and stretched out his legs. A big part of Pat Hayes's charm, probably a big part of his success, was that he knew how to tell a story. That's what he did in the courtroom. People didn't just listen. With his big expressive eyes and bushy brows punctuating the tale, with his little nods and inquisitive grins, and with his rhetorical questions, Pat Hayes was conducting a dialogue with his audience while the story was in motion. You couldn't just listen, you participated, as if you had been there in the flesh, and this was a private joke between you and the great silver-haired lawyer.

"Back in nineteen fifty-six, before the rackets were shut down, I had Hector arrested. I think it was for violating a court order to cease and desist gambling operations. We'd just raided a casino. Maybe the Neptune Club. Then I run smack into Hector, driving a truck full of slot machines. The standard ploy. We'd plan a raid, and somebody taking money from the rackets would tip them off so that by the time we got there, the gaming equipment was all gone. The Texas Rangers were bad. If they knew about it, everybody'd be sipping lemonade by the time we got there. The local law enforcement people were even worse. They'd have informed the casinos before you could catch an elevator out of your building. Anyway, Hector always claimed I locked him up on Christmas Eve. I doubt it. But who knows? We worked lots of odd hours back in those days.

"The strange thing was that Hector never held it against me. He said I treated him like such a gentleman that it was an honor to be arrested that way. I guess he'd been knocked around by the cops growing up in Galveston. I always tried to be civilized because it made my job easier. Back in the FBI, people rarely put up resistance. So if you were polite, it just made the whole process smoother. There were exceptions, of course. And J. Edgar Hoover was big on manners. At least in public.

"You have to understand, I knew these people in Galveston, and they weren't gangsters. To most of them, working for the Balinese Room or the Hollywood Club was no more nefarious than driving a milk truck. And the police department seemed to share the same attitude." Pat smiled at his own joke. "The local culture didn't really view the rackets as criminal behavior.

"Anyway, years later, in the sixties sometime, Hector shows up in my office. I greeted him warmly. I hadn't seen him in years, and I always liked Hector. You liked him, didn't you?"

Gordo nodded.

"It seemed that some relative, I think it might have been his own son, got into trouble with the law. I can't remember what it was. Assault maybe. Car theft? Not that big a deal, but enough to involve consequences. Hector was upset. I told him, 'Hector, I don't practice criminal law. You need a lawyer who does.' But he asked if I could help. He was insistent that no one else could be entrusted with such a heavy burden of responsibility." Pat smiled, opening deep creases in his large, weathered face.

"So I called the district attorney, whom I'd helped get

elected that year. I was his campaign treasurer, something like that. We worked things out. I can't remember the details. But Hector was so grateful, you'd have thought I'd got the boy off death row."

Gordo could see Pat taking pleasure in the memory, all these years later. He was a man who enjoyed helping people, even if it meant bending the rules occasionally. *El patrón.*

"It was nothing, really. But it was important to Hector. Not long after that Hector gets a job at the jail. Next thing I knew he was a cop."

"The gambling record didn't prevent him from getting a badge?"

"Hell, in those days, half the sheriff's deputies had been croupiers in the casinos and the other half had been bouncers in the whorehouses. It took a lot of people to run those businesses and after the crackdown, they needed jobs. Remember, every one of those guys was somebody's cousin or brother-in-law."

"But you think he's trustworthy."

"I'd say so. As trustworthy as anyone I've ever arrested." Pat laughed.

And Gordo, as countless jurors had done so effortlessly through the years, laughed with him.

Seven

"There's something we need to talk about," said Greta Radkey. "Meet me at the courthouse tomorrow."

Something in the tone of her voice on the phone told him it wasn't a social call. Greta, a large woman with a gruff voice and a sharp tongue, was a state district judge. When she wasn't on the bench, she wrote murder mysteries. She and Gordo got together from time to time to talk about writing, to gossip, or to go over some passage that Greta was rewriting.

Married while in college, she had a short career as a social worker before giving birth to two daughters. Once her daughters were out of diapers, she enrolled in law school in Houston, juggling family, a part-time job, school, and the long commutes between Houston and the island. After graduation, she established a solo practice in family law and became known for her tenacious pursuit of fair settlements for her clients, most of whom were women. Husbands who tried to hide assets or trump up reasons for meager child support terms found her to be a relentless opponent. Viewed as a hothead with a short fuse and any number of courthouse enemies, Greta surprised many by filing to run for judge of the family law court. She turned out to be a decent campaigner, and it didn't hurt that she was better qualified than her opponent. While many members of the bar expected her to become an irascible tyrant on the bench, she seemed to grow into the job. They respected her egalitarianism. She gave people hell in her courtroom, but she dished it out equally.

Gordo cut through her charmless outer office. The county had torn down its lovely old courthouse in the 1960s, in favor of a contemporary replacement with all the grace of a bus station.

"How's your chest?" Greta gave him a hug.

Coming from a person so well known for harsh words and blunt manner, this small gesture seemed amplified.

"Fine. My whole left side is turning a wicked color, though, something like an old eggplant."

"Really? Tell me about it."

"Greta, I'm not material for your fiction."

"I know, it's just that mystery writers are supposed to know about this stuff. And not many of my friends—."

"Right. Not many of your friends have been shot."

"Well, it's true," she said.

"Is that why you called? Am I here to give you a seminar on the physical descriptions of gunshot wounds?"

"I'm just curious."

"So why am I really here?" he asked.

"I heard something that bothered me," she said. "Something about you."

"I seem to be the talk of the town."

Greta took a sip of coffee from a styrofoam cup and paused. As if she was trying to decide where to begin.

"I was talking to a cop. A guy who was in here to testify. During a recess, I asked him how the investigation was going in your case. So he tells me, 'There's more to it than you think.'

"So I say, 'Yeah, what?'

"And he says, 'The O'Connors aren't telling us the whole story. We think they know the guy. The shooter.'

"So I said, 'Who is it?'

"He tells me, 'Some old employee. A client who's pissed off. Maybe somebody they owe money.'"

"Where did they get that bullshit!" Gordo exploded.

"Calm down," Greta said, with a sidelong glance to the room outside her chambers. She got up and closed the door.

"He said you hadn't reported some earlier contact with this guy," she said. "That things didn't seem to add up. That the investigating cops didn't buy your story."

"What's not to buy? I get shot. I call the police. There's a hole in my front door and a hole in me. It seems pretty damn straightforward."

"Look, I don't know what's going on," she said. "I told the cop I knew you, and that you'd told them everything, but he wasn't budging. That's why I called you."

"But why do those boneheads—"

"I don't know. As soon as he realized you and I were friends, he shut up. You know cops."

That was part of his problem. He didn't know cops.

"Who is he?"

"That's another thing. It wasn't just a cop, it was the chief of detectives. His name is Kolata. Curtis Kolata. I think you need to talk to these people. Get a meeting with the chief and find out what these guys are up to. Because if they're talking that way to me, they're talking that way to other people. And if they feel like you are not being straight with them, you can bet they're not busting their asses to find the shooter."

"Curtis Kolata."

"You know him?"

"No. But I guess I'm going to get a chance to."

"Call the chief and let me know when and where the meeting is," Greta said. "I'll come."

"You will?"

"If I'm not there, Kolata will deny the whole thing. He'll say this is just a big misunderstanding." She cocked her head and gave him a knowing look. "They're cops."

"Greta, I really appreciate this."

"I think this is serious," she said. "The nut with the gun is still out there. You need to get the cops on your side. Or at least not working against you. It's time to call in your chits. You know the mayor. Give her a call. I'd call the district attorney. You know Steve. The cops need to understand that they can't just blow this off."

Gordo was stunned. Dealing with the shooter seemed like a big enough task. This was ridiculous. He was going to have to marshal all the influence he and Ana commanded just to convince the police to take the case seriously. He felt overwhelmed.

"I have to be in court in a few minutes. If you can set up a meeting, leave me a message on my answering machine here at the office." Greta rose and came around her desk.

"How's Ana bearing up?" she asked.

"She's all right. She's not going to like this business, though."

Gordo got his second hug of the day from Judge Radkey. He was sure that didn't happen very often.

"You should call the Colonel," she said softly.

"He's not going to like this either."

"Call him."

He drove straight to the police station. The chief's secretary seemed skeptical about scheduling an appointment for the following day. But when he mentioned that Judge Radkey would be on hand she said she thought 9:30 might work after all. No one was eager to cross Greta Radkey.

Gordo went down to the second floor to the records office. He knew his way because back when his car windshields were broken, he had to get copies of the police reports for the insurance company. For four dollars each, Gordo purchased copies of the reports he'd filed. The two vandalism incidents and the episode in which the stranger had threatened him with a knife. Kolata had told Greta the detectives were suspicious about the earlier events. It had taken the clerk less than five minutes to find the paperwork. He was willing to bet that Grover Hampton and Tiny Martelli hadn't made the effort. By the time he'd finished his business in records, Gordo was livid. He was tempted to drop in on Grover and Tiny, but decided to save his ire for the meeting with the chief.

• • •

Gordo rarely felt tired during the day. But this day, so fraught with disturbing news, with a few minutes peace, he could have fallen asleep in the big stuffed chair in Pat Hayes's office. The Colonel's secretary had installed him there, in the old building overlooking the Bishop's Palace, a grand Victorian across the street. Back in the 1960s, Ana's father had bought the two-story building for $15,000. He'd then poured thousands into bringing the old structure back to life. Constructed of rubble from the 1900 storm, the Colonel's stucco building was the creation of an immigrant British mason. Augustine Perth built a Mediterranean apartment house with balconies that bore oddly organic shapes and masonry balustrades that looked like fingers of coral. Gordo loved the old building and considered Augustine Perth a self-taught genius. Through the massive arched windows facing Broadway, he could see Sacred Heart Church, which had been erected upon the site of the original church destroyed in the same storm. Scores of bodies had been pulled from the wreckage of Sacred Heart. It was from that broken pile that Perth had drawn the raw materials for the structure that would become the offices of Hayes & Jackson. During the nineteenth century, generations of the faithful received the sacraments and sang Gregorian chants within walls made of the masonry surrounding Gordo. People had perished under the weight of these consecrated bricks.

Pat Hayes burst into the room. "Damn, I'm sorry to keep you," he said.

The Colonel shook Gordo's hand at every coming and going. Always. Gordo stood when his father-in-law approached. It was the human contact that the Colonel sought out. Pressing the flesh. Pat Hayes believed in the power of human connection. His large paw wrapped around the extended hand of each person he met while his left hand worked their shoulder or their forearm. A pulsing grasp, as if its firmness was reinforced with the Colonel's every heartbeat. He must have been a terrific campaigner.

As Gordo told him about his conversation with Greta Radkey, Pat remained grim-faced and silent.

"I've got a damned hearing tomorrow at nine o'clock," he said. "Do you think we could get the meeting rescheduled for later in the day?"

"I'd like to have you there, Pat. But I think it's more important that Judge Radkey be there."

"You're right. She's got to hold their feet to the fire. I don't like the sound of this. I've always found that police can be the most unreliable, most inscrutable people in the world. You never know what kind of hijinks may be going on. When I was in the Chicago office of the Bureau, I had to deal with all kinds of police corruption. But I'm looking for their angle here. What's in it for the cops to make these accusations? Why would they sandbag the investigation? Maybe we do need

Hector Gabilondo. I know the local agent-in-charge. Maybe he can help."

"The FBI? It's not a federal case."

Pat Hayes reached for a glass. "Scotch and water?"

Gordo shook his head.

As the Colonel pitched a handful of ice into his glass, several cubes skittered across the top of his credenza. He ignored the mess.

Pat had always stayed aloof from the island's social hierarchy. Partly because he was viewed as an interloper. Islanders considered him someone from the mainland who had barged into their party, turned up the lights, and sent everybody home.

Even when Pat's law practice had grown successful and he started representing all kinds of clients, people knew him first as a plaintiff's lawyer. He never sought membership in the Artillery Club, where he might forge social connections that could undermine his effectiveness in the courtroom. He represented men injured, burned, or blown to bits in the refineries and the chemical plants. He didn't want to be sipping mint juleps with the lawyers defending Union Carbide or Monsanto. Pat knew he was more dangerous on the outside. And on some level, he still resented the island's establishment for voting for his political opponent forty years earlier.

Gordo could see the Colonel was upset. His mind seemed to be leaping from one idea to another, instead of clamping down on something solid, as was his habit. He wondered if the old man had realized that, for all his resourcefulness, his influence, and his skill at dealing with adversity, there was nothing he could do that would guarantee the safety of his daughter's family. Not until they found out who the gunman was. Pat Hayes was a solver of problems. But how could he fix this?

"You folks would be as welcome as the flowers in May at our house."

"I know. We're okay out at the beach. We've just about decided it's time to get off the island."

"I hate to think of that. But I want you all safe. I'll have the district attorney on the phone before I leave for the night," he said.

"I think Ana's already called."

"I can get out my old .45. I'm not sure I can hit anything with it, but it makes a hell of noise when it goes off."

"Pat, we'll be all right."

"I think I should let the agent-in-charge know."

"We don't need to call in the cavalry, we just need to get the cops off their asses," Gordo said.

He could tell this was eating at Pat. Then the old man brightened up.

"Did I ever tell you about the time I used the .45 to pump lead into some slot machines?"

Gordo smiled. He 'd heard the story before, but he couldn't remember the details.

"Tell me."

"We'd raided the Balinese Room and the Turf Club and come up with snake eyes. Then we got a tip to go out to the old Hollywood Club, which had been closed for years. Lo and behold, we found two thousand slot machines. A few hundred more were hidden in an old bunker at Fort Travis on Boliver Peninsula. Of course, we were keeping the Houston newspapers abreast of all this, trying to win public support for closing the rackets. Somebody tells us that if we did something dramatic with the contraband, a photographer for *Life* would come shoot pictures for the magazine. So we loaded the machines on a barge and took them out near Pelican Island, where we smashed them with sledgehammers and hurled them into Galveston Bay. I hated to do it, because they were made of exotic wood and were really beautiful machines. I wish I'd set one aside for myself.

"Anyway, the whole time we're staging all this drama, the photographer is shooting pictures left and right. Here's this image of the bay full of slot machines—the end of corruption and gambling in Galveston.

"The hell of it was that the damn machines wouldn't sink! We waited for hours thinking that eventually they'd slip under water. Finally, I pulled out my .45 and started shooting holes in the wooden cases. No effect whatsoever.

"The next day the mayor accused me of endangering navigation and threatened to have me arrested. And to top it off, *Life* never ran a single photo." The Colonel laughed in earnest at the memory.

The story had helped distract Pat for a moment. From the police, from the court hearing the next the morning, from the unfamiliar position of not knowing exactly how to help.

"You go on home to your family," said Pat. "I'll make some calls."

It wasn't uncommon these days for the old man's eyes to be red and watery. But now the Colonel looked to be in danger of spilling tears.

"You tell Ana and the boys I love them. And be careful, Gordon. Take care of my daughter and my grandbabies."

Pat Hayes, the old bombardier, G-man, and prosecutor, was giving Gordo something important. He was giving him responsibility to defend three of the people he loved most.

• • •

Gordo had jokingly called it his year of living dangerously. It was that first summer—the first with Ana—back when they were still in college. He moved into the gardener's cottage of a mansion near the campus in Austin. With its fluted limestone columns, neat row of gables, and elegant rooftop balustrade, the mansion made an unlikely, if elegant, rooming house for students. But the cottage at the rear of the property had been ignored for decades, plunging into charming decay. The iron claw-foot bathtub seemed poised to crash through the floor-boards and the kitchen always smelled of an elusive gas leak. But the rent was an enticing ninety-five dollars a month.

"They don't make bargains like this any more," he'd boasted the June day he moved in.

"Some night this whole place is going to explode," Ana said, looking over the shack with distaste. "And I'm not going to be here when it does."

"That's not very sporting."

Ana made good on her promise. She did not spend many nights at the cottage, forcing Gordo to cross town to her more genteel apartment for the pleasure of her company.

One Saturday night, he hosted her for dinner.

"I'll just step outside when you light the oven," she announced.

After a meal of chicken cacciatore and chianti—"Who needs vegetables?"—Gordo filled an aluminum bowl with strawberries, raspberries, and plum slices. He added a dollop of whipped cream.

That summer Gordo was sleeping on the screened porch, an appendage that seemed to have begun life as a potting shed. Ana lay on his bed, surrounded by windows, as he fed her berries one at a time.

She extended her long neck toward a plump strawberry topped with a tuft of whipped cream.

"Shirt," he said.

Ana unbuttoned her shirt, spread her full lips, and bit the berry in half. A fine mist of red berry juice sprayed across her bottom lip. Gordo kissed her.

She cocked her head toward the windows.

Gordo raced around the room, fruit bowl in hand, closing the canvas blinds.

Ana removed her shirt.

He raised a plump raspberry to within biting distance.

As she reached for it he whispered, "Shorts."

She unfastened her shorts, drove her shoulders deep into his mattress, and lifted her hips off the bed. He released the berry into her open mouth and helped her wriggle out of her khaki shorts.

Two berries later, she was naked.

Slowly, he painted her nipples with whipped cream. He squeezed raspberries and filled her navel with juice.

"Dessert," he said with a voice full of anticipation. He licked the whipped cream and sucked the berry juice out of her navel. Then he handed her an amber crescent of plum.

"Put it inside you."

"What?"

"Inside."

"Inside?"

She looked at him disapprovingly. Then she took the plum slice from him.

Gordo was intoxicated by her shape, her feel, her taste. He found the plum with his tongue and took it into his mouth.

Ana's breathing was slow and deep. With his head between her legs, he stabbed blindly for the fruit bowl with his free hand, returning with a strawberry. More exploration.

He muttered something Ana could not understand.

"Wha—"

He raised his head slightly. "Blessed is the fruit of thy womb."

In an airy voice he would remember years later she said, "You're so sacrilegious."

"Altar boys are always sacrilegious. It takes years of training." He returned to his task, where her thighs were beginning to tighten about his head.

"You were an altar boy?" she said dreamily.

"Yes," he said, pausing. "But it's hard to do this and have a conversation too."

"Then maybe we shouldn't talk."

"Ummm."

He drew her legs open wider and thrust his tongue deeper.

"Our Lady of Redemption," he panted minutes later, coming up for air.

"Huh?"

"The name of the church."

"Were you redeemed?"

He traced a row of kisses up the inside of her thigh.

"Tonight . . . I . . . am . . . redeemed."

"You Catholics . . ."

"Confiteor Deo omnipotenti . . ."

"Are you talking dirty to me?"

"Beatae Mariae semper virgini . . ."

"My Latin lover," she said.

"Perducat te ad vitam aeternam."

"I'm surprised you're not burning incense."

"Good idea."

"No more talk," said Ana.

"No more talk."

He opened his mouth wide to stretch his tense jaw muscles and reached for another berry. Drunk on the commingled taste of Ana, plums, and strawberries, Gordo was lost to everything but the universe that existed between her legs. Smooth taut flesh and the rhythm of her femoral pulse. Glistening pink and straw and scarlet. And the sound of her racing breath.

Finally, one long shudder followed by a delicious gasp.

She kicked the bowl. A rainbow of berries floated across the room and the metal bowl clanged like a bell as it landed—spinning upright—on the splintery floor.

"Blessed is the fruit of thy womb."

• • •

Gordo was making chili, and Ana was baking cornbread. He had just finished crushing comino seeds, and the air was full of the scent of cumin and frying onions when they heard the low tremulous hum of someone coming up the stairs.

"Is that *Lahs*?" asked Sam.

"It's someone climbing the stairs with a full head of steam," Gordo said.

"That would be Lars," said Ana.

"Gordo, my friend!" Lars thundered. Hugs all around. He was all sharp edges—elbows, shoulder blades, high cheek-bones, and a nose like a flint arrowhead. In spite of his sixty-seven years, Lars exuded vitality. It was as if the twelve-hundred-mile drive had just got him warmed up.

"I am here to protect and serve," Lars offered. "No crazy son-of-a-bitch is going to harm any of you as long as I am on this goddamned island! And I brought a friend. Come out and meet him."

Ana looked skeptical as they filed out onto the deck.

"A dog," screamed Sam.

"A big dog," said Jake.

"That's the biggest dog I've ever seen," said Ana.

"He's a pussycat," said Lars.

"Then why does he look like a wolf?" asked Sam.

"Because he *is*." Lars laughed enthusiastically. "Half wolf, half Siberian husky. And very well behaved."

The dog, in spite of being in the company of four strangers, had not moved.

"His name is Skoll, boys. You can pet him."

"Why would you call a dog Skull?" asked Jake.

"Not Skull. Skoll!" roared Lars. "In Norse mythology, Skoll is the wolf who devours the sun at the end of the world."

"That's a lot of dog," said Gordo.

"Skoll." Sam was petting the dog behind his ears. Skoll's coat was thick and deep, especially his enormous ruff. His gray fur was tipped with silver, like frost, and his eyes were yellow. In a flash, he turned his muzzle toward Sam and licked his face.

"Did you see that?" Sam asked.

"You've made a friend," said Lars.

Ana stroked the dog's neck.

"He's so gentle."

Soon, they were all in the kitchen, with Skoll curled up in the corner of the living room. Ana smiled as Sam hung from Lars's forearm, as if he were a human jungle gym. Gordo was relieved. For the moment, they were all happy to be together. There was more gaiety in the kitchen than there had been in a long time.

The chili was sharp and pungent. He thickened it with fresh tomatoes from Mexico and clumps of tomato paste. As it simmered, each bubble rose through the mixture and broke the surface with an explosive pop, turning the stove top into a splattered red palette.

As Ana cut thick slabs of yellow cornbread from a cast iron skillet, the conversation tapered off. They fell on the food with predatory zeal, working chunks of butter and spoonfuls of red plum jam into the hot cornbread. Even Sam understood the importance of getting it buttered while hot. Gordo slapped a steaming bowl of chili at each place and fetched a beer for Lars. For him, however, there was nothing like a tall glass of cold milk for washing down cornbread.

"Can't get chili like this in Minnesota," said Lars through a mouthful.

"Fresh peppers. Fresh spices," said Gordo.

Cold salt air and all the walking they were doing on the

beach made them ravenous. Jake wore a milk mustache on his upper lip and the corners of his mouth were dusted with crumbs.

"Sam, you can't just eat cornbread," Ana urged. "Try the chili."

"Why not?" he asked.

"Yeah," said Lars. "Why not?"

"Because cornbread's not a balanced diet."

Using his finger as a fulcrum, Jake made a teeter-totter out of a wedge of cornbread. "It looks balanced to me."

Sam's face pinched closed, eyes tightly shut, shrieks of laughter escaping in an outburst of silliness. Jake cackled, and Lars's booming belly laugh filled the room.

Gordo studied Ana. For a moment, the worry lines between her eyebrows were gone. This might work out.

Ana had feared the intrusion of someone outside the family. Maybe what they needed *was* someone from the outside, to bring some humor inside. To distract them from the shadow of fear that seemed to hang over the household.

At the stove, serving second helpings, Gordo touched Ana's hip. She ran the back of her hand down his cheek. He pushed a pale lock of hair away from her face. Old familiar gestures.

After dinner, he and Lars stepped out on the deck. Skoll followed them The air was cold and pure. Gordo blew on his hot coffee. "Why'd you come, Lars?"

"Sounded like you guys could use some help."

"Everything okay back home?"

"Everything's fine. The kids have the normal crises now and then. But they're adults now. Still miss their mother, of course."

"How about you?"

"A little restless, I suppose. Long winter up there. Been in one place too long. But I intend to make myself useful around here. Ana's all right about it?"

Gordo nodded. "You know Ana."

"I won't be under foot, I'll—"

"Lars," Gordo cut him off. "That's not what I meant."

He knew that before she died, Lars's wife had suffered from depression. That he'd been the public face of his family all those years. What Gordo didn't know was what kind of demons chased Lars during his wanderings.

"I'm glad you're here," said Gordo. "With this deadline of mine and all the other chaos, we're stretched pretty thin. And I don't mind having another person around. Sometimes it gets a little spooky way out here on the beach."

"My kids—I did the best I could," said Lars, returning to the subject of his five children. "Elise was good with them, but she had her problems. Alcohol. Depression. But the young ones—Martha, Katherine, David—they counted on me for an awful lot. Sometimes I think they're better off if I'm not right across town. They may be tempted to get old Dad to solve problems they'd be better off solving on their own. You understand?"

Gordo nodded.

"They're all educated. They've got jobs. They're more competent than they think."

"You miss Elise?"

"All the time. I don't miss the struggle." Gordo could see these things were difficult—painful—for him to discuss. But Lars seemed willing to talk about them. Maybe he needed to.

"And I've done lots of things that I would never have done if she were still alive," he said. "The travel. The boats. But I miss her. The kids knew more than we thought. There is some bitterness. There was a lot of denial in the house, and they resent it today. We were just doing what we thought was best."

"Parenting should come with a statute of limitations."

"You're damn right. A statute of limitations. Once the statute has run, you damn well better take responsibility for who you are." There was a sharpness to Lars's words that

Gordo rarely detected when he spoke of his family.

"Well, you're welcome here."

"Besides," Lars added, "there are worse moves you can make than leaving Minnesota in February for an island in the Gulf."

Gordo sipped his coffee. He was getting cold.

"Ana's okay?" asked Lars.

"Hanging in there. It's a little surreal. The sort of thing that happens to somebody else. The victim on the ten o'clock news. And people act weird about it. I can only imagine what people are saying out of earshot."

"You just take care of your family. To hell with everyone else! What time do the boys have to be at school? Tomorrow they'll have a chauffeur."

• • •

When he joined her, Ana was already in bed. She'd been reading, and he could tell she was drifting in and out of sleep by the way her reading glasses were askew against the pillow.

"Asleep?"

"Reading."

"Reading with your eyes closed again?"

"I guess," she said drowsily.

"Maybe I just needed a wakeup call."

"Yeah, wake me up at five-thirty. I've got to get an early start."

"No, I mean the shooting," he said. "Maybe I wasn't living as consciously as I should have."

"Conscious of what?"

"Of what was happening around me. Of all the richness in my life. In our corner of the world."

Ana didn't say anything. But he knew she was listening. Her breathing was no longer the deep, relaxed breathing of a person on the threshold of sleep.

She was never quick with advice, never eager to offer unsolicited solutions. Maybe it was from being a lawyer, from being in the advice business.

"Hmm."

"Well, I was just wondering if somehow the universe spots somebody not paying attention—and so things happen. 'Hey! You with the freckles! Wake up!' What do you think?"

"You think God shot you?"

"Maybe things just unfold in ways that give you a nudge."

"Unfold?"

"Happen."

"How many bullets do you suppose God has?"

"I guess that means you don't like my theory?"

"I don't think unconscious living got you shot," she said.

Now she was awake, and Gordo was sorry he'd roused her so completely.

"And what makes you think you're any less conscious than the next person?" she said. "If you ask me, you seem pretty aware. Can an unconscious person be a keen observer of life? And isn't that what you do? Observe things, ask questions, collect opinions, inform people. You even get paid to eat consciously."

"Observing is not the highest form of experience. Maybe it's the worst because you end up distancing yourself. You don't engage, you watch. You pick things apart. Questions, questions, questions. Bitch, bitch, bitch. Food is a good example. I've been a restaurant critic so long I could imagine the meals and write the reviews without getting out of bed."

"Well, I don't care what God thinks, Gordo. It's time to get some rest. Even God needed to take a breather on the seventh day."

Ana kissed him and rolled over, tucking the covers under her chin.

Eight

The next morning, Ana, Greta, and Gordo filed into the office of the police chief, Ernest Rossini. Curtis Kolata, chief of detectives, was already there, looking worried and uncomfortable.

Chief Rossini was effusive in getting Greta seated, ordering her coffee and creating the impression that the meeting was the high point of his day. Rossini was the size of an adult bear. He'd gone soft in middle age, but in his fine Sicilian profile you could still see the good looks he'd inherited from his father. Ernie's dad, Tony Rossini, had started out as a bouncer in the Maceo casinos, later moving up the hierarchy to one of Sam Maceo's trusted lieutenants. Ana's father had indicted Tony's boss, but that was ancient history. Water under the bridge.

This connection returned to Gordo as he was taking his seat.

God, this place had too much ancient history. Maybe they did need to get out of here. How long had Tony been dead? Fifteen, twenty years?

After the rackets were shut down in the 1950s, Tony Rossini went on to become a successful restaurateur on the Seawall. Antonio's. The Colonel had been a good customer. He never let Tony's nefarious past stand between him and the grilled red snapper. "Best on the island," he always said.

When Ana and Gordo had gotten married, the rehearsal dinner had been at Antonio's. Tony was gone, but his widow had kept the place going. The son, Ernest, had worked there when he was younger. Gordo had never had any dealings with Ernie, although he'd heard the police chief had a bad temper.

Today, however, he was turning on the charm. Ernie Rossini could just as easily have been wearing a white dinner jacket and welcoming them to Antonio's Restaurant.

Just one big happy family. Ana had called Steve Schneider, the district attorney. The DA said he would contact the chief, to make sure he understood that the O'Connors were good citizens, pillars of the community, whose account of events should be treated as fact. Schneider wanted to get reelected, and he was not eager to alienate the Colonel. Ana had left a message with the mayor. Gordo figured Rossini was beginning to recognize that he had a problem. That their problem would soon become *his* problem if he didn't straighten this out.

He was amazed at how the chief's transparent gestures had a disarming effect. Gordo even found himself wanting to get along with these people, to believe that there had just been some innocent miscommunication. But the police were putting Ana and the boys at risk. He and Ana needed to apply some heat to give the cops a bigger stake in finding the shooter.

"Tell me what I can do to help," Rossini said.

Gordo drew a breath and started. "Ana and I are very concerned about statements Detective Kolata made about us to Judge Radkey. That we are concealing information from the police, that we have not reported earlier incidents with the suspect, and that we know the identity of the person who shot me."

"We want to make it absolutely clear that these statements are false," said Ana. "Not only are they slanderous, but they indicate that the investigation is being conducted with inaccurate information. We want an explanation and—"

"If I could just say something," Kolata interjected. He didn't want a recitation of his blundering remarks to the judge. "I think I can help clear this up." Kolata collected his thoughts. "I'm not going to argue about anything Judge Radkey said about our conversation."

Gordo wondered what the odds were that he'd be saying that if Greta Radkey weren't in the room.

"But I think we need to look at those comments in perspective," Kolata said. "The detectives working the case—they're old-line police officers. They tend to go by their instincts and their experience. We had twenty-six homicides on the island last year. We solved twenty-five of them. In every case, the victim knew the perpetrator. Something about the interview led them to question Mr. O'Connor's account. Now that's not right. I've straightened them out. But in crimes like this we have to look at the people around the victim."

"You've never heard of random crime?" Gordo asked.

Ana shot Gordo a knowing look. She had warned him not to be too confrontational. "You want them to think you're a calm, rational person," she had cautioned. "Not some hothead who gets pissed off all the time. You don't want them to look at you and say, 'Yeah, I can see why somebody would shoot him.'"

"It wasn't random," replied Kolata. "There was a pattern of activity."

"That still doesn't mean the shooter knows us," Ana said.

"I'm just telling you how the detectives saw it."

"What about the prior incidents?" asked Ana. "The police

reports about the broken windshields and the night he pulled a knife on my husband? We brought copies of the police reports."

"We've got those reports," he said.

Of course he didn't say *when* the reports had been added to the file. Gordo was willing to bet they had been added within the past twenty-four hours.

"Could I see the file?" Ana asked.

Reluctantly, Kolata handed it to her.

"Now I'm not saying the detectives did everything they should have," he said. "Frankly, I'm concerned that they didn't take a signed statement from Mr. O'Connor. And I don't understand why they didn't have a composite sketch of the suspect made. We will do those as soon as possible."

"Wait a minute," Ana said. "Under status, they've checked the line for 'Inactive.' How can the investigation be inactive if the shooting took place only a week ago?"

Kolata seemed flustered. "That just means that the file remains open until there are additional leads or a new development. That's standard."

"A week-old attempted homicide is classified inactive? That's standard?" Now Ana was getting confrontational.

Chief Rossini cut in. "We've reassigned it to a different team of detectives. The investigation is active. Very active."

Kolata looked rattled. "Anyway," he said. "I do want to apologize for . . . for what's . . . for any misunderstanding. I was talking to Judge Radkey in her official capacity. Some of the information was off—but we've taken care of that."

"So let me get this straight," said Ana. "The officers blew off the investigation because their instincts told them Gordo was lying, even though they had no evidence of that. Did they even ask anybody if we were reliable people? I can't imagine that if they'd asked anybody at the courthouse, or in the community, that they would have heard anything that would lead them to suspect that we were withholding information. They didn't bother to get a written statement or a good description or make an artist's rendering of the suspect? Who are these guys?"

"Couple of veterans," said Kolata. "Old school, you might say."

"I guess we should be grateful they're not rookies," she said. Ana looked like she was ready to give Kolata a tongue-lashing.

Then it was Gordo who made a point of meeting Ana's gaze.

Back off, girl.

"Do you make a point of slandering all crime victims?" Ana was just warming up.

Greta had remained silent, but her presence seemed to lend a certain gravity to the meeting. Gordo's transactions with the police, whatever the outcome, would be transitory, but Judge Radkey was a constant factor in their lives.

Greta cut in.

"I just want to make sure we're all in agreement. There's no reason to think the O'Connors have been anything but absolutely truthful in their account of what's happened?" Kolata nodded. He was leaning forward in his chair, forearms on his thighs. Rossini sat far behind his desk, an innocent bystander to this scolding.

"There will be no more false accusations about the O'Connors by the police," Greta continued. The word *false* had a directional force aimed squarely at Kolata. "New detectives have been assigned to the O'Connors' case. The police intend to actually conduct an investigation and get a full description and a signed statement from Gordon. And they'll have a sketch made of the suspect. Is that correct?"

"That's right, Judge," said the chief. "I'm glad we've had a chance to sort things out. We've got hundreds of cases going at any given time. Sometimes things fall through the cracks.

That's not an excuse. But we're all human, and we make mistakes, just like everybody else." Chief Rossini, despite his folksy homily, looked eager to get the group out of his office.

"Ana, Gordon—call me if I can help in any way," said Rossini, offering a farewell handshake. "I'm sorry about what happened at your home. The East End—what can I say?"

Spoken like a man who lives on the far West End, thought Gordo. He'd known cops who just shook their heads when responding to calls in the historic districts, implying that the middle-class people who lived in those neighborhoods were lacking in good common sense.

"Judge, it's always a pleasure," said Ernest Rossini warmly, as if they'd all been his guests for dinner at Antonio's.

• • •

"Kolata's probably going to get an earful," said Greta, as they walked down the linoleum corridor. "But at least somebody will have to get off their ass. I still don't understand this. I've seen plenty of stupid cop stuff, but this is more than stupid."

"Old-school bullshit. That's what it sounded like to me," said Ana.

"You were starting to get in that guy's face, Ana," said the judge. "That's not what we want. The cops still have a thousand ways to screw you. You want to give them a push, but not hard enough that they feel obligated to push back."

"Greta, I appreciate this," said Gordo. "Most people don't want any hassles with the police. I know you have to work with these guys all the time, and that what you're doing may complicate your life."

"It's nothing. Think about it. You guys are part of the establishment. You've got political connections, you know people, you're out there working in the community. If *you* can't get help from the police when you need it, who the hell can?"

Three men strolled by them. Gordo figured two of them to be plainclothes cops. The third was in uniform. Something about the man in the middle, the one in uniform. He looked directly at Gordo as he passed.

Familiar face. But from where?

Suddenly, Gordo stopped. He looked back over his shoulder in disbelief. "I could have sworn I just saw Norman Zweiger. In a uniform."

"You did," said Greta.

"Who's Norman Zweiger?" asked Ana.

"Bad cop," Greta whispered. "You know him?"

Ana studied her husband. "What's the matter?"

"I was on the grand jury a few years ago."

"The child abuse case," said Greta.

"How did he get reinstated?"

"Jury acquitted him."

"What are you guys talking about?" Ana asked. "What jury?"

"Let's get out of the police station."

Nine

"Norman Zweiger was a cop who got charged with sexually abusing his stepdaughter," Greta Radkey explained. "At trial it was a pissing match between Zweiger and the girl. His wife was a nurse, and the girl, who was only about fourteen—"

"Thirteen when it started," said Gordo.

"Okay. Thirteen. Anyway, she says the cop is having sex with her while Mom's working the late shift at the hospital. This goes on for a few years until the girl's little sister hits puberty. The victim figures it's only a matter of time before her stepfather starts on her little sister. So she tells mom. Zweiger says the girl's just an imaginative teenager who wants some attention and doesn't like her stepdad. The jury has to decide who to believe. Zweiger brings in some of his fellow cops, his high school teacher, people like that, to tell the jury he's a real Boy Scout. No physical evidence. Jury acquits."

"The girl wasn't lying." Gordo had taken an oath to keep secret all evidence heard in grand jury deliberations. He didn't know the protocol here—if Greta, as a judge, would frown on him saying more. "How do you know all this?" he asked her.

"Courthouse grapevine. And later on, of course, the mom and Zweiger got divorced. If a guy's a real asshole and he's married or has children, sooner or later he ends up in my court. It's almost enough to turn me into a lesbian." Greta paused a half beat. "Almost."

"The other cops," said Gordo, ignoring the joke and gazing out into the parking lot, "they were afraid of Zweiger. His boss had an extra pistol strapped to his ankle while all that was going on."

"Oh, I'm not surprised. Zweiger's a real piece of work. Has that edgy Vietnam look about him."

"He's a vet?" asked Ana.

"He's a vet all right," said Greta. "But I don't believe all that Vietnam crap. I used to be married to a vet. Guys went to 'Nam had their problems just like everybody else. The place may have amplified their problems. But in the end, people are who they are. You ask me, send an asshole to Vietnam—what you get back is a bigger asshole."

"I can't believe Zweiger's back in uniform," said Gordo. "That's ridiculous."

"That's the civil service."

• • •

"Tell me about the girl," Ana said later that night.

"I'll tell you, but don't tell anybody else. A lot of this must have come out at trial, so the facts are probably out there, but I don't want anybody to ever quote me. Girl's name was Esperanza. I still remember. Very pretty. Hispanic, long dark hair, big brown eyes. Petite. She was sixteen, maybe seventeen when all this broke. The mother worked the night shift at John Sealy Hospital. From the age of thirteen on, after the little sister was down for the night, Zweiger took the girl into his bedroom. She said that the bedroom had a sliding door. She said

Zweiger drilled a hole in the door frame. He'd insert a nail to lock the room from the inside."

"This story is starting to give me the creeps."

"It's a creepy story. When I was on the grand jury, most of the cases had some element of humor to them. The suspects were usually such fuck-ups. If they hadn't screwed up, they wouldn't have been there, right? Occasionally, the stories were sad. Things gone wrong, lots of pain all around. But this one, something about it just put everybody in that room on edge. The way the girl described Zweiger, you could *feel* him. Then he shows up. You could also see right into the guy's mind. Here was a girl with this childlike beauty. Vulnerable. He knew she could be intimidated from the word go. Every person in the room could see it. And the fact that it was so obvious, that she was so helpless, made it even more disgusting.

"When that girl spoke, it was all matter-of-fact. No drama whatsoever. As if her emotions had been shut down. Listening to her, you got the impression that there wasn't one scrap of information that could be wrong. She was resigned to these things. She was full of this awful knowledge. And if there was anything human in you at all, you could not question what she said. That girl would just start talking and the truth would pour out. She had lived every word of it. She had paid for every word of it with her innocence. Tough for a girl whose name means hope."

"How did the jury acquit him?"

"I don't know. You're the lawyer. They must have found a way to introduce reasonable doubt. Maybe she got rattled in the courtroom. I never thought Zweiger would get his badge back."

"He sounds like an animal."

"At one point, Esperanza said Zweiger told her he was going to give her a break. He'd have sex with her three nights a week and two nights a week she'd get off easy. She'd only have to perform oral sex on him. He was at her five nights a week. I guess the mom was home the other two."

"Did you see the mother?"

"She was a wreck. The girl had a kind of resignation about it all. It had happened. She couldn't change that. She didn't like talking about it, but she could when she had to. The mother—well, you can imagine. It was new to her, knowing what Zweiger had done. She looked like she'd just stepped away from a car wreck. Some part of her must have not been working when all that was going on. I mean, to not have known something was wrong. But I came away with the impression she was not a bad person. A good nurse. Single mom. Overwhelmed. When she met Zweiger, she probably figured she'd finally found someone to take care of her. Her savior. That he'd keep her and her daughters safe."

"What was he like?"

"Tall, lanky. Kind of a dead look in his eye. Definitely seemed capable of violence. The other cops thought so, or they wouldn't have been strapping extra guns to their ankles."

"Who told you that? About the guns?"

"Ernie. Ernest Rossini. He told all of us. In the grand jury room. He wasn't chief back then. He probably doesn't remember that I was there. One face in twelve. He was pretty jumpy that day. And he told us he wasn't the only one."

"And they let Zweiger back in."

"They must not have had any choice," he said.

"Must have been a little tense around the water cooler."

• • •

That night Gordo was awake.

The character of his sleep had changed. When the boys were little, Gordo had learned to sleep so lightly that a slight shift in the rhythm of Sam's breathing would cause him to get up and check on him. He was so finely attuned to the nocturnal sounds of the household that once, when he heard the splashy torrent of Jake's peeing stop suddenly in the middle of the night, he leaped up and raced to the bathroom. Jake, fast asleep, stood in front of the toilet, spraying the adjacent wall with his errant stream.

There hadn't been any sleepwalking in the last couple of years. With no little ones to fall victim to sudden infant death syndrome, he and Ana were beginning to slip back into deep, less vigilant slumber. Until the shooting. He'd done all right at Helen's house. But being back on the island had elevated his sensory awareness. The wind howling off the water. The creaking of the timbers beneath the house. Birds arguing on the roof, despite the plastic owls hanging from the gables and the rubber snakes someone had flung up there to discourage them. And the low vibrato of a person climbing the stairs to the house. Especially that. Sometimes a hum of any kind—the flutter of louvered storm shutters in the wind—jerked him from the depths of slumber as effectively as a fire alarm. And in that state, he knew exactly how many steps it was to the drawer with the Beretta.

He didn't want to live this way.

He missed Pilot House. With Ed and Laura next door. Tom around the corner. Here, he was seventeen miles from the police station. Unless there happened to be a car patrolling the West End, it could take a long time for the dispatcher to get help to their stretch of beach.

He was thinking about his conversation with the Colonel. The slot machines and his .45-caliber pistol. So many stories, so much life. Even living in hiding with a homicidal maniac on his trail, Gordo felt his own life was bland by comparison.

Last summer, he and Ana had taken the boys to Washington, D.C. During the trip, Ana's parents flew up to meet them. The Colonel took them all on a tour of the FBI headquarters and some of his other old haunts. But the moment that stood out for Gordo was at the Smithsonian Air and Space Museum. A bomber, a B-26 named *Flak Bait* that Pat Hayes had actually flown in for several missions, was on exhibit. The plane flew more missions than any other bomber during the war, sometimes returning to England with an engine ablaze or its hydraulic system shot out. By the end of the war, the plane was like Swiss cheese, with more than 1,000 holes from enemy fire. Painted on the fuselage, just below the cockpit, was a red bomb for every mission *Flak Bait* completed. Gordo touched the rows of bombs, representing more than 200 forays into the sky. The red paint was crackled and peeling.

Holding each boy's hand, Pat showed them the seat he had occupied as navigator and bombardier.

"It was the safest seat on the aircraft. They put armor plate around the bombardier—not to protect me," Pat said, laughing, "but to protect the instruments."

Then he took Jake and Sam past the cockpit, into the nose of the plane.

"I manned the nose gun, a .50-caliber machine gun, when we were en route," he said, pointing to the narrow plastic-enshrouded nose gunner position.

It was hard to picture the Colonel, the great bulk of him, shimmying up into the clear plastic nose cone of *Flak Bait*. But of course, Pat had been a wispy teenager then. Closer to Jake's age than to Gordo's. Was Jake, a mere eight years from now, capable of climbing into a bomber, crossing the English Channel, and attacking the Germans? Gordo couldn't imagine such a thing. Hard to imagine sending Jake off to any war.

Much of the fuselage had been cut away for the exhibit, so Gordo exited the plane like a crash survivor, stepping through a hole in its flank. He went around to the nose to watch the boys inside. As they took turns sitting in the gunner seat and playing with the machine gun, Gordo rapped on the Plexiglas nose cone with his knuckles, creating a thin and insubstantial thump. A quarter-inch of plastic was all that had separated Pat from the sky above and the earth below. All that separated him from exploding flak and firing Messerschmitts. A quarter-inch of plastic had gotten him to Germany and back all those cold gray mornings. He must have felt terribly exposed inside this plastic shell with nothing for protection except the .50-caliber machine gun between his legs.

And if Pat hadn't made it? There would have been no Ana, no Jake, no Sam. Gordo's constellation. Sam laughed as Jake pretended to fire the gun, complete with sound effects. Gordo steadied himself against the plane and swallowed hard.

God bless the inventor of Plexiglas!

• • •

Gordo padded around the silent house barefoot. He poured himself a glass of milk and reached for the saltines. Milk and crackers. The perfect midnight snack. He could put away quite a few without even thinking about it. He refilled his glass, spilling a milky pool onto the counter. Reaching under the sink for a sponge, he discovered a cockroach party in progress. They scurried from the light.

"Great," he said, slamming the cabinet door shut. "Just me and the roaches."

They reminded him of a passage from the journal of Cabeza de Vaca. While marooned on the island, the explorer observed the natives eating insects—and worse.

> *Their principal food is roots of two or three kinds, for which they search throughout the land. The roots are very bad—*muy malo*—and cause people who eat them to swell up. Those people are so hungry that they cannot do without them, and go two or three leagues looking for them.*

Sometimes they kill deer, and sometimes they catch fish. But this is so little, and their hunger so great that they eat spiders, ant eggs, worms, lizards, salamanders, snakes, and poisonous vipers. They eat dirt and wood and whatever they can get, as well as deer excrement and other things I will not talk about. My observations lead me to believe that they would eat stones if there were any in that land.

Gordo finished off the glass of milk. He was beginning to think he could hear sand being blown under the threshold of the door. A gusty, gritty, scratchy sound. He was beginning to crave solid earth, a place with stones.

• • •

The next day, Gordo and Lars returned to Pilot House. Lars the solo mariner. He wanted to get their wok so he could make them all shrimp stir-fry.

"You drive the kids to school," said Gordo, "you pick up the mail, you cook for us. You know what Ana said last night?"

"I don't like the sound of this."

"She said it's like having an *au pair.*"

Lars laughed. His big, generous laugh.

"A male Norwegian *au pair.*"

"I told you I would make myself useful."

"You have. And we're grateful to you. You and Skoll."

Lars pulled his Jeep into the alley. In addition to the wok, they loaded the juicer, the blender, and the espresso machine. All deficiencies of the beach house kitchen. Gordo brought more clothes from Ana's closet to replenish the lawyer wardrobe she needed. Then Gordo lifted the tongue of the boat trailer onto Lars's hitch. He ran his fingers along the smooth lines of the gunwales and remembered building the boat. The day Ana, wearing a respirator, caught sixteen-foot strips of fir as they peeled off the table saw. As he fed the blade, the majority of the sawdust blew toward the rear, covering Ana with a layer of pale sawdust. Later he and the boys started gluing the fir strips along the edge of the hull to form the gunwales.

"Dad, the wood is *stwaight* and the boat is *cuhved*." Sam informed him of this fact as if the folly of the task was perfectly clear.

"That's the magic of it."

"What's magic about wood and glue?"

"We're going to start out with four long, thin, straight pieces of wood. And we're going to clamp two pieces to each side of the hull, starting in the middle. And as we work our way fore and aft, the wood is going to follow the curves of the hull."

"This is *nevuh* going to *wuhk*," Sam said with resignation.

"Well, I've never done it before, but I'm going to have faith."

"Dad, are you sure you read the directions?" asked Jake. "I don't think the wood will bend enough."

"If you're right, son, we're going to have a hell of mess on our hands."

Clamping off the fir strips every twelve inches or so, Gordo, Jake and Sam negotiated the boat's beautiful curves. The red-veined fir looked handsome against the mahogany hull.

"Magic," Gordo said, stepping back from the boat.

"No magic. Somebody *figuhed* this out," said Sam. "They knew what would happen."

"Somebody besides us?"

"*Wight.*"

Gordo remembered the conversation as he spotted blisters of the epoxy that had dripped on the concrete floor of the garage. He stubbed one of the cloudy globs with the toe of his shoe. It had cured as hard as cement. How many nights had he spent out in the garage that year as they were building the little sailboat? Late at night, listening to broadcasts of old radio mysteries like "The Shadow" and "Dragnet." Standing at his workbench, back turned to the alley, and the radio obscuring the sound of approaching footsteps, he could have been killed. If the shooter had walked up in the blackness, his life could have ended right there in the garage, as he was building a sailboat for his boys. Ana would have found him the next morning.

They christened the boat *Shark Bite*. Gordo didn't need it at the beach in February, but it was the only way he could figure out to transport the last item. He and Lars went to the corner of the backyard where, beneath the brown, brittle leaves of a clump of banana trees, they lifted the rabbit hutch off its frame and hauled it to the alley. The hutch, with its potent smell of ammonia, was too big for the Jeep.

"Lars, I'm sorry about the rabbit shit. No way to handle the thing without getting it all over your hands." Years of Petey droppings had been strained by the wire mesh on the bottom of the hutch. Their hands were soon encrusted with the sticky, greenish residue.

"Don't worry about a little rabbit shit. Let's get moving."

As Peter Rabbit hopped around in a state of confusion inside, they eased the hutch into the hull of *Shark Bite*.

"Damn hutch is going to scratch up your varnish job. That's a shame."

"Can't be helped."

Petey started thumping his rear paw in alarm. He had never been moved this way, and he was panicked.

"I know, Petey, I know," Gordo said.

There was something final about moving Petey out of the yard. He and Lars had been returning to feed the rabbit and pick up mail. Gordo knew visits to Pilot House would be less frequent now. He rubbed at an ugly yellow scratch in the brightly varnished floor of the boat.

After they climbed in the car, he sighed and punched the remote control and the garage door slowly descended, closing a chapter in his life. *Shark Bite*, for all its handsome lines, looked ludicrous with a rabbit hutch in its stern.

Gordo felt like he was leaving a piece of his life behind. It would have been easier to accept if they were just leaving rather than being driven from the place they loved. His throat tightened, and he steeled himself. He didn't want to be wiping away tears with hands redolent of rabbit droppings.

The O'Connors were now officially on the lam. Headed west, with their ridiculous load, Gordo thought of the von Trapp family. But they weren't crossing the Alps to safety. They were headed for a house on stilts. A house with a roach problem, that shook in the wind.

Ten

"I've never seen a boat being towed down the road with a rabbit at the helm," said Lars. "And I never expected to be doing the towing."

"The Carrots of Wrath."

"By Joad, you've got it! The Carrots of Wrath."

"Well, we *are* heading west," said Gordo, smiling a little at the awful pun.

One of the benefits of having Lars around was that it kept things upbeat. Gordo couldn't get too mad, too upset, too despondent, too whatever. He shouldn't care that much about revealing his emotions in front of others—especially with Lars—but that was just him. The way I'm wired, thought Gordo.

Lars drove. In his travels, dealing with all kinds of unfamiliar people, he had developed a sense for when silence was the most constructive link between two people. Lars had learned how to be around people in a way that let them establish the boundaries of privacy.

On the seawall, Gordo observed a woman riding a bicycle on the Gulf side of the road. He took in the shape, the convexities of her bottom, its upward tilt accentuated by her grasp upon the inverted handlebars of her ten-speed. He noticed the auburn hair. Without thought, he silently identified the woman from the gym at the medical school where he often worked out. Neither her ass, pleasantly taut above the narrow saddle, nor her hair was exceptional. As they passed, he turned back for confirmation.

Bingo.

He didn't know this woman, and he had no interest in her beyond an appreciation of her appearance. Yet somehow, without effort, he had memorized the shape of her ass and the exact shade of her dark red hair.

Was this normal? Was this what was called "a roving eye"? What would Ana think, he wondered, if she knew he committed to memory the contours of strange women? This redhead, who was concerned about her thighs. Who spent an inordinate amount of her workout on machines that tormented the muscles of her legs and buttocks. Useless minutiae from other people's lives. A waste of good memory cells and the food it took to support them!

Let it go.

They were driving into a winter sunset. Here on the West End, away from the buildings and the lights, the island seemed reduced to its most basic elements. Water, sand, sky. A blue norther was due and the sky, the color of blue porcelain only hours earlier, was now a pink and gray smudge above the horizon. Roseate spoonbill pink. Gordo watched seagulls motionless in the sky, effortlessly held stationary by a twenty-mile-an-hour wind. Brown grasses lashed back and forth as cattle casually worked their way toward barns north of the road. Rusty strands of barbed wire whipped past like airy bars of music on a page.

On the Gulf side, brackish choppy surf was breaking on a beach littered with tidal debris. Gordo kept looking behind him, checking on the boat. Asymmetrical and ungainly with its load, *Shark Bite* seemed to buck against the wind in protest. He patted Skoll's damp muzzle.

"Years ago—you ever feel heavy from the weight of taking care of so many people?"

"With five kids? Hell yes! Felt like I weighed 300 pounds. Sometimes I could hardly get out of bed in the morning. I didn't know how I was going to pay for all those shoes and groceries. I felt it every day for at least twenty years. Never seemed like I could make enough money. I remember one year I had to borrow money to pay for Andrew's college tuition. All I could think of was, I've still got four more to go!" Lars said, glancing at him. "You're under a lot of pressure now."

Gordo wasn't sure if his last statement was an observation or a question. Maybe this was what was meant by active listening.

"For me, it's more primal," he said. "It's about protecting the family from harm. You can't travel light—move fast—with little children. If it was just me, I might go back to Pilot House and wait for this guy. I'd like to ask him some questions. I wonder how he'd feel about looking into the barrel of a gun. But I can't afford that."

"Ana and the boys can't afford that," said Lars. "Besides, it would be stupid. This guy's sick. You need to stop thinking about him like he's just another person. You can't ask him questions. If he had the answers then you wouldn't have this problem in the first place. Crazy people *are* different. I've dealt with them and I know."

Lars had taken an interim step on his flight away from the demands of private practice. Before he'd taken up full-time wanderlust, he'd spent twelve months as a public defender in a small town near the Canadian border. During that cold, lonely year he'd represented the poor, the mentally ill, the criminal, and those who were all three.

His advice to Gordo: "Try to avoid getting tangled up in the criminal justice system. You want to put as much distance between you and the shooter as possible. And don't put too much faith in the police and the courts."

"The police have made that part easy."

"Frankly, Gordo, you're probably better off if they don't find this guy. Just make sure he doesn't find you. Let him have a chance to fixate on somebody else. You don't want a nut for a lifelong enemy. If they ever tried the guy, he'd end up knowing everything about you, and he'd never forget. Do you really want some violent lunatic stewing about you for years in a prison or a psychiatric hospital? Sooner or later they'll let him out."

"You're saying we don't want him arrested?"

"I'm just saying that the system—the criminal justice system—could leave you more exposed," said Lars. "Less secure. More vulnerable. I may be jaded. But that's the way it is."

Just then, a strong wind hit the Jeep and seemed to suspend their progress. Gordo turned back toward *Shark Bite*. The hinged roof of the rabbit hutch rose 45 degrees, as if to tip its hat at the whole crazy enterprise, before falling shut.

"Damn, we almost lost the top of Petey's hutch in that gust," he said. "That would have really freaked out Petey."

"Not as much as it would have freaked out the guy in the Chevy behind us," said Lars. "Can you imagine having that roof sail through your windshield?"

"Good thing we're almost . . . there." He was about to say home.

"I like the beach house," said Lars. "But I like any place on the water."

• • •

Gordo was back home, pulling pizza dough out of the food processor when she called from her office.

"Lars and I got the Cuisinart, the espresso machine, the rabbit hutch—all the modern conveniences," he said.

"Great," said Ana. "That should improve your disposition in the morning."

"I'm making potato pizza with goat cheese and red onions. When will you be here?"

"That's why I called," she said. "I've got a meeting with a client. A little fire to put out. I'm not sure how long it's going to take."

"You're going to miss some good eating."

"I'm sorry. You and Lars and the boys have fun. I'll call if I'm going to be late."

"All right. Get someone to walk you to your car."

"I know."

For once, everyone turned in early, even Lars. Because he was so robust, Gordo tended to think of him as being middle-aged even though he was sixty-seven. After they renewed their nightly cappuccino ritual with the machine brought from Pilot House, Lars went to his bedroom to read. Could he be tired from all the lifting and hauling they'd done? Physical vigor was part of Lars's identity, just as his penchant for taking long and strenuous voyages. But he could not change the fact that he was getting old.

Gordo descended the stairs to check on Peter. On Batavia Boulevard, the hutch had been protected by the fence and the banana trees. Here, under the piers of the beach house, Petey was exposed on all sides. Gordo raised the hinged roof. The rabbit was huddled in a corner of the hutch, looking nervous and watchful. He had been reunited with Henry, the gerbil, who was burrowed into his roommate's fur.

"I know how you feel, guys. This is just temporary," he said, stroking the rabbit's brown coat. "You won't be here long."

He scanned the road for Ana's Volvo. It was late. Sand danced across the driveway in a dervish and he shivered back up the stairs. Had she told him the name of the client? Not that he could remember.

• • •

Gordo waited up for her. At about half past midnight, he heard her light footfalls upon the stairs. He'd been trying to read without much success.

"You're still up," said Ana, sweeping her hair out of her face. "Damn wind."

Gordo nodded. "Did you get everything squared away?" he asked, striving for casual interest.

"Well, not everything. But I think I picked up a case." She turned from him, removed her coat, and stepped out of her heels. "Those shoes have been killing me for hours."

Was she trying to change the subject? He couldn't let it rest.

"So what's the deal?"

"Accounting malpractice. At least that's what it looks like. Could be some serious money in it."

"Who's the client?"

"The Elliott Foundation."

"Corky?" He knew there was nothing casual in the way he said it.

"He *is* vice-chairman of the board."

"Did you have a good time?"

"Gordo, relax. It was work."

"All work?"

"It's never all work with Corky. You always have to hear about what he's interested in. He's big on real estate right now—renovating the Sheridan Building on the Strand."

"Lot's of stories. Good sense of humor. You had a good time?"

"I suppose so," she conceded. "He told me some crazy tales about his family. You know they came to the island the year after the Civil War."

"A night away from the safe house?"

"Well, it has been a little tense around here lately."

"Circumstances beyond my control," he said.

"I know. I'm not blaming you. It's just nice to get out and laugh a bit."

"I'd be more entertaining if I didn't have a homicidal maniac stalking me."

"It's not your fault."

"Does this merrymaking have to be in the middle of the night?"

"I told you. He's got a legal problem. The foundation has a cause of action against their accountants and their regular lawyers have a conflict of interest. It could be a good piece of work for the firm. Corky told me all about this case first, and then we just started talking about other stuff."

"Such as?"

"Such as everything. You know Corky. He's all over the place."

"That's the problem. I know Corky."

"We were just having a drink."

"And just where was this legal consultation taking place?"

"At the Tremont House."

"Of course."

"Gordo, please don't be an ass about this. It's business."

"Is it that important that you reel in new clients for the firm right now?"

"Corky brought it up a while back. I know it's not a good time. But I promised I'd talk to him about it. I thought you and Lars could get by without me for a few hours. Please don't be mad."

"I just don't see why you have to do your rainmaking with

Corky. You know what he's like. And I don't understand why you have to do it at midnight."

"You know the job isn't over at five o'clock. My working late hasn't bothered you before."

"Corky gives me the creeps."

"Maybe we should just go to bed." She hooked a finger through the straps of her shoes and padded into the bedroom.

Gordo listened to the wind howl. Would he feel less threatened if he made more money? Ana was generating more than three-quarters of their income. She never seemed to resent this. She never seemed that interested in material things. At least not beyond having a comfortable house and a little travel now and then. Did she want more? Or did she just crave frivolity right now? He could understand that. He could understand it all. He was a man on the run with a chest wound and very little income. Not exactly the alpha male. He hated this in-between life—without a fixed household, without a known destination, and replete with so many uncertainties.

Ana was somebody in Galveston. A partner in an established firm, nimble navigator of the courthouse, school board member, and daughter of Pat Hayes. Did she really want to flee to a new life of anonymity?

Eleven

Lino Gabilondo had said to meet him at the Phoenix Bakery, a strange choice for a cop. The Phoenix was half a block off the Strand and located in an old hotel building that had nearly burned to the ground a few years back. The developer saved a wall or two, and in doing so, qualified for some historic preservation tax breaks. The exterior of the restored structure was a copy of the old hotel, now used as an office building. The bakery, located on the first floor, had a beautiful courtyard that opened onto Tremont Street. Gordo liked the coffee, but the baked goods were more edible art than food. That didn't stop the tourists.

He was early, so he got a cup of coffee and took it outside. He found a sunny table in the courtyard, which was surrounded by flowers.

One minute after ten o'clock, a man he took to be a lawyer from the large law firm in the building approached his table. Gordo studied him carefully. Olive skin, dark hair, heavy eyebrows, large eyes. Elegant gray suit and a green foulard tie. The law firm was primarily in insurance defense, and it seemed to recruit handsome lawyers, the kind who appealed to female jurors. It was their lot to defend employers against their accident-prone workers who happened to get maimed or killed in the county's refineries or at sea. The Colonel often opposed them in court.

Gordo tried to remember meeting this man. Had Ana introduced them? She was always introducing him to new lawyers.

"Hey," he said, withdrawing the chair opposite Gordo.

He read the confusion on Gordo's face.

"Lino Gabilondo. Hector's nephew?"

"Of course. I guess I need more coffee to wake up."

Lino raised his dark eyebrows slightly.

"I hear you're having a hard time with Grover and Tiny," he said.

"You don't look like a cop."

Lino remained silent.

Gordo sensed that he had said the wrong thing. He didn't mean it as a compliment or as criticism. He'd just said it. Something he'd been doing ever since the shooting. Just saying what was on his mind. As if the shooter had blown away tact and diplomacy.

"Hector asked me to look into this."

"Your uncle told me he knows Pat Hayes," Gordo said.

"Pat Hayes arrested him—on Christmas Eve." Lino didn't sound at all nostalgic about it.

"Before you were born."

"Look, I don't know the whole story. I just know my uncle said to do what I could. That things had gotten messy." There was a slight Hispanic lilt to his voice.

"With Grover and Tiny?"

"Right."

"So have you been assigned the case?"

"No."

"Are you even a detective?"

Lino shot him an ugly look and rolled his eyes.

"All right," Gordo said. "Sorry about being so punchy. I haven't had many good experiences with the police so far."

"Maybe I can help explain things," said Lino.

"You can?"

"Not yet. I'll see what I can find out. Try to figure out what's going on. Maybe give you some news from time to time."

"I'd appreciate it," Gordo said. "Thank you. And Pat Hayes thanks you. Ana is his only daughter."

"I understand."

"And this goes back thirty, forty years?" Gordo asked.

"What can I say? My uncle never forgets a friend."

"Especially those who lock him up on Christmas Eve?" Gordo said.

"I told you, I don't know the whole story."

"Who ever does?" Gordo took a sip. "Well, anyway, what *do* you know?"

"I'm going to get some coffee." As Lino headed for the building, Gordo noticed the handsome drape of his suit. Most cops wore suits that looked like sacks with arms sewn into them. While Lino was short, his suit accentuated his broad shoulders and trim waist. And when he returned, his jacket fell open, revealing a burgundy lining. A clotheshorse.

"First," said Lino, "this is just between you and me. That's important. I know you've got a problem, but I've got to work with these guys all the time."

"Got it."

"Grover and Tiny blew it off. I'm not sure why," said Lino. "They told other people in the department they didn't buy your story. Like you seemed to be hiding something. Very suspicious of the fact that you didn't go straight to the hospital. That you just high-tailed it off the island."

"Can you really ignore an attempted homicide just because you think the victim should have made different plans?"

Lino shrugged. "It's a small department. Detectives can go their own way so long as somebody doesn't raise hell."

"So then what did they do?"

"They classified the investigation 'inactive' the very next day and headed for Snapper's."

"The bar?"

"Lot of cops hang out there."

"And that was it?"

"That was it until Judge Greta begins to make it interesting," said Lino. "Maybe they took you for somebody who was banging somebody else's wife and got what you had coming."

"So if we were just a couple of law-abiding citizens who didn't know our way around the courthouse, absolutely nothing would have come of this?"

"Nada."

"That restores my faith in law enforcement."

"It's the way it works. You weren't seriously injured. They have other cases."

"It's the way Galveston works," said Gordo. "You went to Ball High School?"

Lino nodded.

"Afterward?"

"University of Houston."

"What did you study?"

"Political science."

"Law school?"

"I thought about it. I got married. We've got a little girl. Not going to happen anytime soon."

"So where do things stand now?" Gordo asked.

"Jerry Peyton is working the case, but it's pretty cold. We've had two new shootings since yours, and those people are pretty bad off. One's dead. It shouldn't make a difference, but you walked away. Without the chief's involvement, your case wouldn't have gotten top billing anyway. Jerry Peyton gets a call from some victim's widow; he gets a call from you out at your beach house. Whose case is he going to jump on? It's human nature. At least unless something else happens."

"So I shouldn't count on the police at this point?" said Gordo.

"Well, that's where I come in."

"Yeah?"

"I'll call you when I learn something."

"What do I have to lose?"

"Your life. You should be careful."

Gordo sat back in his chair, not sure what to make of Lino Gabilondo.

"Hey, why did we meet here?" he asked.

"Because no cop would be caught dead in this place."

"Damn, the phone's dead—again!" Gordo slammed down the phone. "I've talked to Ma Bell more times than I've talked to Ma since we got here."

"First it was the salt corrosion," said Ana. "Then it was the humidity. What will they blame it on now?"

"Vermin. I think they will blame it on either mice, roaches, buzzards, or Henry," he said. "It's bound to be our gerbil's fault."

"Sand crabs. I'm betting on sand crabs."

"This must be the tenth time the phone's gone on the blink," he said.

Gordo hated the phone trouble. They were already too isolated out at the beach. It was Saturday, and he told the phone company he couldn't wait until Monday for repairs. They needed a phone, he tried to explain. But there was no easy way to do that. To explain why they had to have phone service at all times. Why the absence of a dial tone made his blood pressure soar.

He started to try, saying, "We need this phone. For safety. We've got two little boys . . ." But it was too complicated, too messy. "Just get somebody out here as soon as possible."

Ana had a phone mounted in her car, but cellular service didn't extend out to the west end of the island.

Hanging up, Gordo screamed, "Goddamn phone company!"

Getting shot had opened a small gulf between Gordo and every other person who had not been shot. People who had never heard the loud report, felt the heavy impact, seen the blood. Gunfire had become so trivialized, portrayed countless times on television and in movies, that everybody thought they knew all about it.

Easy. Point and shoot.

On Saturday night, Gordo and Ana were at a party for the trustees of St. Stephen's. Not long after they arrived, Joe Clayton, a banker and one of the board members, approached Gordo.

"There's a guy in the alley back there with a gun looking for you," Joe said.

Gordo felt his whole body stiffen. Glass in hand, as partygoers swirled around him, he quickly sifted through a mental checklist. He knew there was an alley in back. They were within walking distance of Batavia Boulevard. This was all within the realm of possibility. A split second later, Gordo realized that this was Joe's idea of a joke. People laughed. Gordo laughed, hoping no one had noticed his initial reaction. It was funny, actually. A way to raise the subject without walking on eggshells.

Gordo held back. He felt like asking Joe Clayton if he knew what it felt like to be shot. But clearly, the man had never seen real violence.

He didn't hold it against the banker. A lot of people were unsure of the facts. The newspaper never returned to the story of the shooting. But Joe Clayton had no idea how the joke made him feel. The jolt of fear and adrenaline. The joke at his expense. How could Joe have known? On the other hand, how could he have thought that getting shot made for good cocktail banter?

• • •

Sunday evening, as dusk approached, Gordo closed the blinds and lowered the shades. The kids were watching TV, and Ana was in the bedroom reading. Lars had gone into town. The stairs outside began to reverberate.

"*Lahs*?" asked Sam.

"Maybe," replied Gordo.

There was a loud knock.

Sam walked over to the door, the glass of which was obscured by louvered blinds.

"Sam, get away from there. I'll get it."

The shade had caught before it reached the bottom of the glass panel in the door and Gordo could see through the lower section of the window. The porch light illuminated a pair of heavy work boots and blue jeans. The man was pacing back and forth.

Black work boots. Blue jeans. Nervous pacing. Gordo froze. The louvers revealed the faintest outline of the man. He was tall.

Skoll studied all this from his corner, the giant head raised and alert.

Gordo could not bring himself to get any closer to the door. He raced to the bedroom and grabbed the Beretta.

Skoll started barking wildly. It wasn't Lars.

Gordo snapped the slide action back, loading a bullet in

the chamber. His heart was pounding. That nervous movement—the black work boots. Sam said something, but Gordo ignored him.

"Dad," Sam called.

"You boys, go to our bedroom."

"Who is it?" Ana called.

The boys raced to their mother.

Gordo approached the front of the room, staying clear of the door. He wanted to look through the glass door, but in doing so, he would be exposed. He didn't know what to do. Skoll's teeth were bared, and saliva flew from him with each savage bark.

"Who is it?" he shouted above the barking.

The reply was muffled.

Gordo drew back the slide just far enough to check that there was indeed a bullet in the chamber.

"Who is it?" he said louder. Another reply.

"Phone company!"

Gordo pressed the cool metal of the Beretta to his cheek and took a deep breath. His shoulders relaxed. Drawing the blinds aside, he saw a large black man wearing a tool belt and an irritated expression on his face.

Gordo was about to open the door.

"Dad." It was Sam, who was peering around the corner.

"What?"

"The gun."

"Yeah."

"Shouldn't you put the gun away?" said his son.

"Right."

"Just a minute!" he shouted.

When Gordo finally unlocked the door, the phone man eyed him carefully. Not sure if he wanted to come inside. Gordo held Skoll's collar. He and the dog were both panting. The phone man was trying to size up the situation.

He probably thinks he's walked in on a lunatic asylum, Gordo thought.

"Sorry, we've had some trouble lately," he explained, thinking it would be a lot more awkward with a gun in his hand.

Thank you, Sam.

"We're careful about strangers. We weren't expecting you. Come in."

"My supervisor asked me to stop by during my shift," the man said, but his expression showed he wished he hadn't bothered. "To make sure your phone was working."

Fear seemed to hang in the room like wisps of smoke. Sam and Jake looked at him curiously, as if they were seeing some strange incarnation of their father. Someone they did not fully recognize. They had never seen their father afraid.

"We got our dial tone back yesterday afternoon," said Gordo.

"I'll just check the phone line and get out of here," said the man.

Later, after the telephone repairman had left, Gordo tried to put the best face on his behavior.

"I was just trying to make sure that if it was the guy, he wasn't getting past the door." In the family lexicon, they all knew who "the guy" was. "I'm sorry if I upset you."

"Dad, I told you the man was black," said Sam quietly.

"What? No, you didn't," said Gordo. "Did you know he was black?"

"I told you he was black," Sam repeated.

"No way. I didn't know he was black. If I had, there wouldn't have been any reason to go through all that."

"He did," Jake said.

"Huh?" Gordo couldn't believe it.

"Sam told you he was black."

"Really?"

"You didn't listen," Jake said.

"How did you know?"

"I saw him through the gap," said Sam. "I saw him when he *fuhst* walked up. I told you he was black."

Gordo sighed. What was there to say?

"So you guys knew all along that it wasn't the shooter?"

They nodded.

"Shit!" he said with disgust.

Gordo could feel the shame on his face. He had made an ass of himself in front of the boys. He hated the shooter even more. He had been shot. He had been driven from his home. He was living in hiding. But until now, at least he had not been humiliated in front of his sons.

"I'm sorry," Gordo said. "There's nothing I can do about that now. I was focused on making sure he didn't come inside. If it was the guy from Pilot House, I was ready the put six shots into anybody who tried to get through that door."

"Dad, maybe you should try to calm down," Jake said.

Gordo studied his oldest son. The boy was trying to be helpful. *Try to calm down.* Jake walked over and petted Skoll, who had returned to his makeshift bed.

"I didn't know, boys," said Gordo. "Skoll and I didn't know."

Twelve

Monday morning, Gordo returned to Pilot House to collect mail and to pick up a toner cartridge for his printer. Once inside, he reached for the burglar alarm keypad. The normal beeping was silent. The familiar blinking lights were still.

Odd, he thought.

When he flipped the hall light switch, nothing happened.

No power.

Gordo pulled out the Beretta.

Without knowing why, he was sure someone had been here.

He moved cautiously through the house and back to the kitchen. Ana's cookbooks, usually a neat row on the counter beneath one of the rear windows, had been shoved aside. Two were on the floor, covers splayed.

Then he saw that the window had been forced open, stripping the latch screws from the wood sash in the process.

Damn!

He'd always meant to add a stronger latch to these windows,

which weren't visible from the street. One more thing he'd never gotten around to.

Then it occurred to him that whoever had broken in might still be inside.

Gordo listened.

Hearing nothing, he moved toward the stairs. The only sound was the grinding of his left knee and the gentle creak of the old staircase. He inspected his office, the boys' bedroom, the family room, the bath, and finally, the bedroom he shared with Ana. No one. But he discovered that it was their bedroom that had held the intruder's interest. Drawers were ajar, the closet was open, the cluster of photographs on the old bureau had been moved.

His heart sank. Ana's jewelry would be gone. His father's gold watch. The strongbox with other valuables. He should have removed it all. How could he have been so careless!

He checked the back of the drawers, the top shelf in the closet, Ana's dressing table. It was all there. Nothing missing. Someone had examined their things—touched them, held them—and left.

Gordo's relief at finding their possessions was tempered by the fact that he now knew who had broken in. Someone motivated not by greed. But by the desire to pry his way into their lives. To rattle them. And he was doing just that.

Gordo left the bedroom and returned to the kitchen to call the police.

While on hold, waiting for someone to track down Jerry Peyton, he noticed something on the refrigerator door. At the bottom of a shopping list, the list they would have used if they had not fled the house the night of the shooting, was a brief message written in angular scrawl.

There, between school photos of Jake and Sam and an invitation to the Cub Scout banquet, were the words:

Sorry I missed you. Catch you later.

• • •

“Inside our house?” Ana was fuming.

“He tripped the breaker,” explained Gordo. “No power, no burglar alarm. Then he broke in through the back window.”

“When?”

“Clocks stopped at 2:37.”

“A.M. or P.M.?”

“Don’t know for sure. A.M., I would think.”

“What did the cops say?”

“To put a padlock on the breaker box,” he said.

“What did they say about evidence? About finding the bastard?”

“They took some prints,” he said. “But they found talcum powder on the window frame.”

“So?”

“He probably wore gloves. Disposable gloves are dusted with talc.”

“This guy’s not stupid,” she said. “How did he know about the alarm?”

“We’ve got decals on the windows, remember? We wanted people to know there was an alarm.”

“Nothing’s missing?” she asked.

“Not that I could find.”

“All that trouble—“

“Just to look at our stuff.”

“He’s sick.”

“We knew that.”

“He’s really sick,” she said. “Tell me what he wrote again.”

Gordo recited the message.

“‘Catch you later,’” she repeated.

“Son-of-a-bitch.”

Ana shivered. “It gives me the creeps knowing he was

going through our things. Our home! When is all this going to end?"

• • •

Tuesday afternoon Gordo made the drive to the East End to pick up the boys. One of the few dads in the carpool line at St. Stephen's, he brought the newspaper to read while he waited. Some of the well-heeled moms climbed out of their Suburbans and Mercedes station wagons to join friends while waiting for the queue to begin to move, creating a kind of coffee klatch on wheels. He always felt a little awkward here, not wanting to seem antisocial. But at the same time, not eager to be taken for a househusband.

He usually just kept his nose buried in a book and waved agreeably to anyone he recognized. In the mild afternoon sun, he left the car windows open. The palms that lined Church Street next to the school wore skirts of dead fronds, old foliage that needed to be trimmed. He'd mention it at the next board meeting. Another thousand dollars we don't have, he thought. Every year, some board member expounded that it was a waste to pay a tree trimmer when lots of parents had ladders and chain saws. But no one ever volunteered to prop a thirty-foot ladder against a towering palm and jerk a heavy chain saw to life.

"It sounds like a job for someone who doesn't place a high value on their arms and legs," said Gordo. "Not to mention the risk of being catapulted into Church Street." That usually resulted in Gordo calling the tree trimmer, a Salvadoran man with several helpers of uncertain nationality. Small men who scampered up the ladders with nonchalance, their skin matching the color of palm bark.

The last time, Mimi Lehmann, who had married into the southern branch of the investment banking family, had said to Gordo, "Perhaps you can get your man to give us his non-profit discount?"

Your man?

Irritation swelled in his chest at the thought that they had become *his* palm trees that needed trimming and that *his* man needed to do it, in the same way that the St. Stephen's gala and auction was *her* party.

"I'm not sure that Pasqual Gutierrez understands the distinction between profit and nonprofit organizations," Gordo explained. "To him, I suppose, a broken neck is just as broken either way."

He saw Mimi's Range Rover three cars ahead. Of course Mimi had abandoned it to gossip in someone else's car and would probably hold up the whole queue once kids began spilling out of the building. Mimi was probably comparing notes on the snow conditions in Aspen, he thought, while I'm worried about tracking down Pasqual Gutierrez and his machete crew. If only the public schools were better.

"Isn't it awfully late in the day to be reading the paper?"

Lisa Pierce. A freelance photographer, Lisa worked with him on magazine assignments from time to time. She was about thirty, and he enjoyed her company. Her work was first-rate.

As Lisa's head dipped inside the passenger side window, he couldn't help admiring the curve of her breasts, held in check by a black bra beneath her loose sweater. She had always been thin, but she was well into pregnancy and from what he could see, her bra wasn't going to do the job much longer.

"Getting pretty curvy there, Lisa. You lean over much farther and you could cause palpitations in some of the dads."

"I know, isn't it great! I've always wanted breasts." She pressed the sweater against her chest. "But I only see one dad around here."

Lisa smiled, and Gordo, who had always found her attractive, considered her rosy blush, her frisky smile, and the afterimage of her engorged breasts.

"Lisa, I believe you are a magnificent example of a person with 'that pregnant glow.'"

"Glowing, huh? Is that what's going on? Well, I wish someone would tell my lower back that it's supposed to be glowing too."

"You'd better tell Eric to get on with the massage therapy at once."

"Not any time soon, I'm afraid. Eric's in Honduras."

"Honduras?"

"Tropical disease research. He has some collaborator down there. Or as he puts it, 'better bugs.'"

"Back soon, I hope?"

"Ten days. Say, I have the photos for your travel piece. Do you need to see them before they go out?"

"The editor had a couple requests. Let me check my notes. I could drop by tomorrow."

"Just give me a call. I've got a bunch of darkroom work. Be there most of the day."

"The darkroom . . ." His voice trailed.

She gave him a disapproving look and sighed. "Just come look at the photos." The school bell rang and then she ambled away, leaving him to study her in the rearview mirror.

Pregnant women move differently. He just couldn't decide how it was different. Maybe it was that the pelvis and stomach, normally free agents, seemed to move together as a unit. As she turned to climb into her car, her dark hair gleamed in the sun.

That pregnant glow.

There in the carpool line, he was transported back to his last encounter with Lisa Pierce. Just before the shooting, he was working on a piece on a wetlands preservation controversy for *The New York Times*. Gordo mentioned Lisa's name to the national desk at the paper, and she got the photo assignment.

Shots of environmentalists in the marshes, protesters at

public hearings, and birds. Lots of birds. She asked Gordo over to her house to help identify some of the people in the photos before she submitted the prints. He always resented how photographers could get in and out of an assignment much more rapidly than he could.

"About the time I've slogged through all the research and reporting," he told Lisa, "just when I'm headed back to the office to start the first draft, the photographer is merrily handing his film to Federal Express and celebrating with a cold beer. By the time I've polished the piece and checked the facts, the damn photographer will have recovered from his hangover *and* gone out and finished the next job!"

"Well, I'm not sending my film. I don't get published by *The New York Times* every day. I'll do my own darkroom work."

• • •

One day not long after the shooting, she was still printing when he arrived at her home. Gordo knocked on the door to the darkroom that she'd had built in her garage.

"Hold on!" she called out. "Almost done."

Gordo went inside to the kitchen and studied the photographs hanging on the walls. Photos of Lisa, her husband, Eric, the tropical disease specialist, and their son, Cody. Lots of lush green jungle scenes and beaches. Lisa, with her dark mane and fair skin looking sunburned while Eric and Cody were tanned like natives.

"Hey," she said, entering the kitchen. "Swiss Family Pierce."

"They're beautiful. Where is it?"

"Costa Rica. Two years ago. Cody was just three. You can come inside if you like. I've got one more print to make." He stepped through a door just inside the garage with black plastic sheeting stapled to its edges.

"I'm saving up for a revolving darkroom door. So I can come and go without screwing up what I'm processing," she explained.

One side of the darkroom had large rectangular trays of solutions. On the other was a workbench with her enlarger. Somewhere a fan seemed to be circulating fresh air, but the smell of acrid chemicals was strong. It took a moment for Gordo's eyes to adjust. He watched her compose an image on the easel of the enlarger. It was unseasonably warm, and Lisa was wearing a sleeveless shirt, jeans, and an apron. Her hair was pulled back in a ponytail resting on her shoulders. He watched her slender fingers adjust the knobs on the enlarger and crop the image.

Smokestacks and refineries appeared on the the easel. As her hands moved through the path of the light, the image was projected onto her white skin. Then he saw what she was after. In the foreground, balanced on one leg as if holding a pose, stood a Great Blue heron in the marsh. Beyond the bird, the skyline was defined by an industrial landscape, an ugly tangle of burning flares, towers, and oil tanks spanning the horizon. Lisa had captured the essence of the story in a single frame.

"Were you holding your breath, hoping the heron wouldn't fly away?"

"I didn't waste any time getting a few shots off."

"It's very good."

"I like it," she said. "Just need to get the contrast right. *The Times* is on newsprint, so if I don't get it right, the heron will get lost in the midtones of the marsh."

He watched her move a piece of cardboard with a hole cut into it between the lens of the enlarger and the easel, painting the area around the bird with light.

"That should do it." She removed the photo from the easel and dropped it into the developing tray. With her hands behind her waist, she arched her back and stretched. "I'm ready to get off my feet. What time is it?"

"About two. When's the baby due?"

"Not for a few hours, at least."

"No really, when's the due date?"

"Lots of questions. Sometimes it makes you weary," she said. "The loss of privacy. You wouldn't believe what people ask. About the baby or my swollen feet or whether the baby is riding high or riding low or if I know whether it's a boy or girl. I've been reduced to this human stroller, going around answering questions like some sort of maternity tour guide."

"Sorry, I just wondered how much longer—"

"Oh, don't mind me." She laughed. "I'm just talking. Baby's due in May. I'm just getting grumpy and feeling sorry for myself. Eric says he's got to get all his research travel in before the baby comes, so he's going off tracking down exotic viruses for the next couple of months."

"You mean no one's massaging your feet every night? Drawing you hot bubble baths and giving you pedicures?"

"Pedicures? I'm lucky just to shave my legs these days. Pretty soon I won't be able to *see* my legs."

"You develop the picture and I'll work on your shoulders." He lifted her hair and draped it across her collarbone. Then he began to work the cords of her neck.

"I could have used you in here for the past three hours." An egg timer rang. "Time to move down a tray," she said.

He moved with her, drawing his thumb and forefinger down the muscles that spilled into her shoulders.

"Mmmm." Her head rolled back.

Gordo looked over her shoulder at the print in the tray. "I see."

"See what?"

"You did something that made the bird pop out of the picture."

"Pop out, huh? That's exactly what I was trying to do."

Her work was just as solitary as his. And she liked having someone take an interest in it, enjoying the simple pleasure of sharing her craft.

"Time to move to the next tray."

Their two-person conga line moved sideways, his thumbs now kneading either side of her spine. Amazing, he thought, that this knobby stack of vertebrae could add up to such loveliness.

"This would definitely make darkroom work more bearable. Can I call you the next time I've got to spend an afternoon on my feet in here?"

Gordo didn't reply. He just kept his thumbs moving in small circles on either side of her backbone, one vertebrae at a time. As he grew closer to her waist she arched her spine like a cat.

Lisa rocked the tray slightly, keeping the chemicals circulating around her print. The timer chimed again and she deftly removed the photo with plastic tongs and dropped it into the wash and turned on the water. A bubbling sound filled the room as the water flowed into the tray. Gordo stayed with her, his fingers deep in her hair, massaging her scalp.

"You are quite a lab assistant," she said, turning to face him. Bathed in red light, he was still touching her and it seemed that her hands were on him, but between the darkness, the close, chemical-laden air, and his anxiety, he wasn't sure. She leaned toward him. The press of her splendid stomach. Lisa Pierce kissed him gently on the mouth. They both inhaled. Gordo could feel a delicate moisture on his lips.

Finally, after an excruciating moment, he felt her tighten her grasp and he took a long, searching drink. He could feel her smooth skin, the weight of her ponytail on his arm, and the fullness of a thin woman heavy with child. Her tongue was sweet and probing. They were panting like horses. A phone rang.

"Leave it," she said.

But the ringing, four insistent screeches before the answering machine interceded, jerked him back.

"This is a garage," he gasped.

"Yes it is," she said, covering his face with light kisses.

"We are married."

"That's right," she whispered.

"You are not a little pregnant."

With that she landed, feet flat on the concrete floor.

"But gloriously so," he added. And then he held her stomach as if it was a fragile basketball. "You are gloriously, irresistibly pregnant. Van Eyck couldn't have painted a more beautiful mother-to-be."

"A mother-to-be with raging hormones," she said wistfully. "You must think the worst."

"Not at all. It's my fault. All that touching. You're just so . . . touchable, really. I mean, who wouldn't want to massage your scalp and watch you slog through toxic chemicals? Especially in that green apron. You vixen!"

She laughed. Her laughter was surprisingly low and earthy. Much different from her speaking voice.

"We probably shouldn't take this too seriously. A little harmless fooling around by a lonely pregnant woman and one very kinky man."

"That's what I get for trying to be gallant."

"Is that what you were doing?"

"Not exactly."

"I guess we should be grateful for the phone," she said.

"I suppose."

"You're sure?"

"No."

"Really?"

He staggered away from Lisa's house, full of trepidation, confusion, and perhaps a tiny bit of euphoria. The weight of all he was coping with seemed to ease for a few fleeting moments in the darkroom. Bathed in that accusatory red light, he forgot that he was being stalked, and he forgot the hole mending in his chest. But by the time he left, he understood that he had not jettisoned an ounce of tension or anxiety. No, he had just added a few more boulders atop the yoke he wore across his shoulders. One more thing that could go awry. One more thing that would go awry if he were not careful. What was he thinking? He wanted to blame it on stress. Surely he was entitled to that. But he knew better. God, he hoped Lisa was level-headed about all this. All he needed was a weepy phone call at midnight to make his life even more complicated. In fact, his life was far beyond complicated. His life was swerving down the road as if a drunk were behind the wheel. He needed some coffee. He needed to sober up.

Thirteen

When Gordo reached for the phone, he couldn't get a dial tone.

"Damn!"

He needed to ask his editor some questions. Deciding to press on, he spent the morning finishing the first draft of his magazine article. He sketched out a simple outline and let the words fly. Just keep putting words on the page. He'd done more than enough interviews and had plenty of material. Get it down; clean it up later. Always better than you think it is when the words are hitting the screen. Four hours of work without distractions. He ran a word count. Right on the money.

Then he drove to the convenience store at Eight Mile Road to call the phone company. The store, which had a small meat market in back, looked as if it had been built of driftwood. The unpainted planks of various sizes that clad the exterior had aged beyond the silver gray of weathered wood to a dull, salt-pocked black. Standing at the outdoor pay phone, Gordo inhaled the sweet scent of beef jerky and Cajun tasso snaking around from the smokehouse in back. His stomach growled as he asked for a manager at the phone company and was put on hold. The balky phone service seemed like one more sign of their troubled existence at the beach.

They needed a goddamn phone that worked!

He could see waves breaking in the distance. This far west, you could see both the flat watery horizon south over the Gulf and the bay to the north.

What were they doing here? Probably not more than twelve feet of elevation on this stretch of beach. A long, narrow sand spit that nature never intended to stay put. So why should they? Waves were beginning to curl as they passed over a sandbar.

Three bars ran parallel to the island's Gulf shore. He knew them well. Seventy-five yards out, the first lay firm and rounded like the back of a sea serpent in repose. A pleasant swim beyond was the second. In the summer, standing atop it exposed your chest and shoulders to the warm breeze. He liked the feel of it, a soupy mixture of river bottom from the Mississippi, Sabine, and Trinity mucked together with Gulf sand—molded around the soles of his feet. When he reached the third bar, he was past the breakers. Warm buoyant water caressing his body. He loved to stand on the third bar, schools of fish passing by. The delicate scrape of fin upon his ankle.

Stepping off the seaward edge of the third bar, he never knew what to expect. Could he stand? Or would the bottom fall away?

For Gordo, the third bar was always a watery step into the unknown.

A voice returned. The phone company would get right on it. Gordo gave the woman a little extra hell for good measure.

With his legal pad whipping in the wind, he talked to his editor in New York. Then he made one more call.

He knew he should not go. It was clear to him that this was a bad idea, an idea that was rife with ways to render what was left of his life into a maelstrom of betrayal and harm. Lisa Pierce had asked if he wanted to see the photos for the travel article. There wasn't a valid reason to go. Not to identify people in the photos. Not to help select images to illustrate the piece. That was the photo editor's job. He could contribute little to the task at hand.

"You can see what I've got," she said.

Those words might have haunted him even more if Lisa's stomach did not resemble the prow of a small sailing vessel. Surely nothing would come of it. She was twelve weeks away from delivery. He remembered the tautness of her stomach. The strength of her grasp. The texture of her tongue.

Lisa wasn't wearing the chemical-stained green apron when she met him at the door. The top two buttons of her white cotton blouse were open. What had she said? She always wanted breasts? Now she had them. The placket of her shirt extended just below her sternum, where pleats enabled the fabric to fan out across her magnificent stomach.

"You're late. I've finished in the darkroom. No wrestling with the human cannonball today."

"I'm leaving."

Her throaty laughter seemed to be an audible expression of her bulk.

"Always surprised by your laugh," he said.

"I know, I know. Two voices, one body. One big body."

He paused, not knowing where to go with her comment. He didn't want to be put in the position of defending the loveliness of her body. Not today.

"The photos," he said. On with business.

"Oh."

He sensed disappointment in her expression. Those brown eyes were unsettling. Gordo found himself admiring her thick mane. Carefully brushed, her forelock drawn back and held in a silver clasp.

He sat down on the sofa as she spread the photos around the coffee table. Handsome pictures of boats in the harbor, iron-front buildings on the Strand, the Bishop's Palace, a child on the seawall. Nice work, but photos she'd taken many times. They'd both worked on more Galveston travel articles than they cared to remember.

"Hey," Gordo said, picking up the seawall shot, "this little boy looks familiar."

"Don't tell." She flashed a smile. "We took shrimp poor boys to the seawall that day. Of course, Cody wanted to throw bread to the gulls."

In the photo, the Holy Spirit, in the form of a white sea gull, was about to descend on four-year-old Cody. The child looked beatific, a bright look of wonder on his face as the bird hovered above.

"I like this one best," he said.

"Me too."

"I just can't seem to find the tongue of flame above Cody's head."

"The what?"

"You weren't raised Catholic, were you?"

She looked at him quizzically.

"The Holy Ghost."

"Yeah?"

"He's usually depicted as a white dove hovering above the head of one of the saints," said Gordo. "He liked to buzz the apostles a lot."

"Saint Cody," she said.

"Right."

"That's what I'll call this photo. Saint Cody and the Holy Ghost," she said.

"Well, whatever you call it, I predict that it'll get published with the article."

"Thank you for steering so much work my way," she said. "I appreciate it. I don't know most of these photo editors. The jobs would probably end up going to photographers in Houston."

"It's in my own self interest. I want my articles to look good. You do good work."

"Have you been thinking about that day in the darkroom?" Lisa asked.

"Oh, I suppose I've thought about it a time or two."

"I just want you to know I don't make out with every visitor to my darkroom. That was an aberration."

"You make me sound like a mutant," he said.

"A pleasant aberration."

"Well, I suppose it's time for this pleasant aberration to move on. I can see that you have captured the charms of our lovely island and successfully hidden away its squalor."

"You know this place," she said. "Gorgeous Victorian architecture, tacky tourist traps on the seawall, ghettos. I don't think the editors in New York want the whole scene."

"I don't think they'd buy your photos of Magnolia Terrace."

Another lovely smile.

"You know Magnolia Terrace started out as temporary housing for soldiers in the Forties," he said. "But it lives on thanks to the Galveston Housing Authority."

"So, you have to leave?"

He studied her gaze.

"You okay?" he asked.

"Oh, I thought . . . I could put on a pot of coffee."

"How are you doing?" he asked. "Sleeping all right?"

"Yeah, when I'm not getting up to pee."

"Eric back soon?"

"If he can pull himself away from his tropical germs. He says he's found a terrific new viral strain."

"I'm happy for him."

"You know, tropical medicine was a way for Eric to combine his interests. Research and travel and Latin America. He's really happy bouncing around the jungle in a Jeep. When we were younger, we traveled together a lot. But nowadays, it's Eric's trips, Eric's conferences, Eric's grants. I'm just the baby factory."

"Well, you do love kids. And he can't carry the babies. These days you really wouldn't want to be squatting in the forest every twenty minutes, would you?"

"No, but that's not the point. I'm saying that the things we used to do together, the things that made life interesting, are now just Eric's big adventure. I know that's the way it has to be right now, but that doesn't mean I have to like it."

Gordo kept his counsel.

Lisa leaned forward, as if to stand, and he got another view of her new winter-pale maternal curves. Halfway to her feet, she plopped back into the sofa.

"My back is killing me." She turned away, presenting her back to him.

"Where?"

"Down low."

And so, his hands were on her once again, working the flat surface of the small of her back.

"This smooth cotton shirt. It's kind of—"

"Put your hands underneath," she instructed.

He felt a hard, tense layer of muscle to the side of her spine. He examined the squareness that had replaced her waist, a straight plunge from ribcage to hips. Did he know Lisa well enough to be learning these things about her body?

"Eric used to massage my back when I was pregnant with Cody. Before I became a germ widow."

"I did Ana's back when she was pregnant, but what she really liked was to have her feet and legs massaged."

"That would be so wonderful. I haven't had my feet rubbed in ages."

She stopped short of asking him. But the possibility hovered there on the sofa, like a third person.

Why did he do what he did next? Gordo had a fundamental desire to please others, attractive women not excluded. She was sore and uncomfortable. Beyond that, the individual physicality of women was intoxicating. A tactile vocabulary of shapes and textures. An entire universe of the unexplored.

Finally, the powerful allure of not knowing where his actions might lead. Not knowing the response he might elicit. Crossing the third sandbar. It was that mystery that prompted him to take Lisa's hand, lead her to the carpet in the center of the room, and help her onto the floor.

Fourteen

Gordo started with the ball of her foot. He pressed his thumbs deep into the thick pad of flesh that cushioned the bony joint, then followed the outer edge of the sole, avoiding the arch where she might be ticklish, until he reached her heel. He worked carefully, attuned to her breath, listening for any sign that he was applying too much pressure. Lisa was lying on her side, with her back and upraised soles toward him.

Stillness, breath, touch.

Thin leathery calluses on her heel and the pads of her foot.

"You go barefoot," he said.

An affirmative sigh.

He studied a knobby enlarged joint.

"Dancer? Runner?"

"Cross-country. High school."

Gordo had seen her running on the seawall. Good stride, light on her feet.

He kneaded the pad of each toe with the concentration of

prayer. Then he drew back each toe until meeting resistance, just shy of pain, before curling it forward. An arc of motion. His fingers moved to the webbing between her toes. Each tuft of flesh explored as he searched for an axis running through her body. Her heel more than a sinewy cable behind her ankle. A pathway to a reservoir of pleasure if he could find it. Gordo took his time.

He moved up from her heel to her calf, crosshatching the large muscle with his fingers. Dissipating tension. Lisa's breath was slow and deep.

Her denim skirt seemed to drift upward, exposing her thighs and the confluence of her legs, her broad bottom, and a white cotton crescent.

"What are you doing to me?" she asked with a husky voice.

"What do you want?"

"Never mind."

Propped on an elbow, Lisa turned toward him.

"My feet. That should be illegal."

He slid up to meet her face, kissing her chin, her cheekbones, and her forehead. She touched his face, drawing his mouth to hers. He felt the smoothness of her tongue, tasting of coffee, and inhaled her escaping breath. Gordo touched her exposed collarbone and the hollow beneath it.

"You are a small woman magnificently enlarged."

"Magnificent?"

"These delicate little bones supporting all this wonderful flesh."

"What is this? An anatomy lab?"

"I am a student of your anatomy."

"You are taking advantage of an emotionally deprived, pregnant woman," she said playfully.

He released the third button of her shirt and kissed the curve of her breast exposed above her bra.

"I think you have outgrown your underwear."

"Really?"

"I think you need to be liberated—"

"You're wicked."

"—in order for me to minister to your neck and shoulders."

She rolled away from him. If she had not been six months pregnant, she would be lying on her stomach, but instead, she lay on the relatively flat plain between her hip and the side of her belly. With some effort, she reached behind her back and unfastened her bra. Gordo pushed the straps off her shoulders and plied the muscles of her shoulders. He traced the cords of her neck into her hairline. Plunging his fingers deep into her hair, he massaged her scalp.

"Ahhh."

He tugged on the ridge of her ear, as pink and delicate as a seashell.

"You're ruthless," she whispered.

After he finished her back, she raised her hip as he pulled her skirt down and off. She was still turned away from him, clad only in her white cotton panties.

"The schoolgirl look," he said.

"Big enough for two schoolgirls. Maybe three. Maternity panties—you get your choice of white or white."

"Your ass is opulent. Probably just a narrow boyish ass before now."

"I wouldn't have put it that way."

"More womanly now."

"I'm ready to get my old ass back."

"Not so fast." And Gordo slipped his hand inside the waistband.

Later, she rolled toward him, and he kissed her. Her breasts were full with skin so translucent that he traced a blue vein with his fingertip. He kissed her again.

"Now what?" she asked.

He wasn't sure what she wanted. He examined her stomach, taut and assertive. She was beautiful.

"What do you want?" he asked.

"I'm not sure."

Gordo could picture himself taking her from behind, his hand on her breast.

A child's voice, shrill and unintelligible, pealed from the street. What time was it? He was suddenly conscious of passing cars, stray noises, and the muffled churning of the furnace. Conscious of the fact that they were close to the point of no turning back.

"I should go," he said.

"Is that what you want?"

"I want lots of things," he said. "But I can't have them all."

"You're so odd."

"Not sure if it's the hormones or the planetary alignment or the phase of the moon that got us here," he said. "But I don't think you really want to go on."

He watched her unreadable eyes.

"I'm having trouble figuring out what I want," she said.

"Fair enough."

He kissed her and handed her shirt to her.

"Glorious," he whispered.

Two different jolts, two weeks apart. The raw, livid fear of the gun muzzle, and the gnawing, conflicted trepidation of infidelity. These things could shorten your life, he told himself.

Living on the edge.

Go home!

• • •

Slightly out of breath, Jerry Peyton scaled the stairs of the beach house.

Are any of these guys in shape? Gordo wondered.

Peyton had called first. The cop who had taken over the investigation from Tiny Martelli and Grover Hampton.

"I'm letting you know I'm coming cause I don't want to be shot," he said over the phone.

"Good idea," said Gordo. "You don't want to be shot if you can avoid it."

"You're the expert now."

Peyton cleared the top step and sized up the house and the view.

"How come there's just one of you to replace Martelli and Hampton?" asked Gordo.

"I make half as many mistakes. That means it takes half the time."

"They're that good?"

"You got the gun right now?" asked Peyton.

"Not now."

"Good. Where's the coffee?"

"What's with it about the gun?"

"Don't like guns."

"A cop who doesn't like guns?"

"This job, you see what can go wrong."

Gordo poured coffee for the detective, whose close-cropped hair and boxy head put him in mind of a high school football coach. Junior varsity.

Why had the chief assigned him? Peyton didn't appear to be terribly competent. But so far, he seemed like a straight-forward guy with transparent motives. That was worth something.

"I brought some pictures," Peyton said, placing his cup on the counter and sliding onto a barstool.

"Bad guys?"

"See if you recognize anybody."

"Who are they?" Gordo asked.

"Guys who match the description. Some who like a .25."

"Popular gun?"

"Not especially. But in the right hands, it'll do the job."

Peyton held out photographs mounted in paper sleeves that each held five mug shots. Men with bloodshot eyes who needed a shave. Photos made at booking in the middle of the night.

"Some of these guys look like they could be the shooter's brother," said Gordo. "But they're not him. Hollow cheeks and angry eyes. That's what I remember."

"I'm going to toss out a couple names. You tell me if they mean anything. Juventino Campos?"

"I think I'd remember that one."

"Jason Morrow."

Gordo shook his head.

"It was a long shot," Peyton said, pushing his cup away. "Just gotta keep doggin' this thing 'til somethin' breaks."

"I appreciate anything you can do," said Gordo. "We've got children."

"We're doing our best."

"That's what I need. Your best."

Fifteen

The treasure hunt birthday was Gordo's idea.

"We can do it at the beach. It will be fun. It may be the last time Sam will have his friends over. We can have a map and buried treasure."

"But now?" Ana seemed troubled.

"If we leave, there won't be another opportunity."

"We can have a party," she said. "The four of us."

"That's not a real party. Not with buried treasure."

"Gordo, this isn't going to change things. A great birthday party is not going to change the fact that some lunatic has been trying to kill you. And that the boys were there when you got shot. That they could have been killed. The best party in the world isn't going to change that."

"Two hours. After school on Friday. Three-thirty to five-thirty. The kids are out of here by nightfall. You were the one who wanted to maintain an aura of normalcy. It's not normal to skip a seven-year-old's birthday party."

"Nothing about this is normal. I've given up on normal. I'm ready to get the hell out."

"Two hours. Lars will be here. We'll call your dad. He'll get a special agent from the FBI if you want."

"Oh, great," she said quietly.

He knew she was softening.

"Okay," she said, "two hours."

"It'll be good for Sam. The weather's been beautiful. Pirate hats, eye patches, shovels, sunset. I don't want all our memories of this time to be bad."

"Is that it?" she asked.

"I'm not willing to hide like a criminal," he said. "We didn't do anything wrong."

"But we are hiding. We're hiding because this guy wants to kill you."

"I want a treasure hunt."

"You are stubborn," she said. "Stupidly stubborn."

"We'll invite the boys in his class, plus Matt and Eduardo. A real band of pirates. This is going to be fun."

She touched his shoulder. "The last party."

He thought of their Mardi Gras parties, planned and spontaneous. All the parades that passed down Batavia Boulevard, filling Pilot House with friends who used their house as a base of operations. They invited people from the mainland and from Houston, who had to arrive hours early because of the traffic jams. Parties that went on for hours with lots of kids and friends and extended families.

"The Psychedelic Ghostbusters," said Gordo.

It was the year a group of graphic designers from Houston brought paper jumpsuits, spray painted them on the beach, and showed up at Pilot House in uniform, high on paint fumes and drugs. They were so inflammable that Gordo thought they might spontaneously combust.

She smiled. "Remember the time Taylor brought his teenage daughters, their friends, his mother, and his grandmother?"

"Four generations of a family we hardly knew."

"I got to know them pretty well by midnight," Ana replied. "You were out in the street going crazy. Meanwhile I was trying to keep the grandmother from falling off the balcony."

"Really?"

"Of course she was too loaded to have felt anything if she had."

"I don't remember this," he said.

"That's because you were out in the street, whooping it up with some drunk woman who crashed the party. Everybody was whooping it up except Nurse Ana, who was in charge of the geriatric crew."

"They weren't all old," he said. "I remember somebody's teenage girls throwing beads off the south balcony. I look back at the house and I see a horde of young guys trampling the roses. The kids are yelling and jumping and laughing, trying to get the two girls on the balcony to throw them some beads. I figured any minute the girls were going to invite the boys inside."

"The worst part," Ana said, "was when one of the boys started throwing beads up to the front balcony where the mom and granny were. I thought the old lady was going to break through the railing trying to catch them."

Long nights. The first few years the Mardi Gras parades had been all fun, all night. A party for two hundred thousand people in your front yard. Open the front door, and your guests had the best seat in town.

The morning after the Grand Parade the boys would leap out of bed to sift through the oleanders for plastic beads and doubloons, which retained their value for a few more hours. Gordo would walk with them the length of the esplanade in front of their house, with Sam on his shoulders to reach beads caught in the magnolia branches. After they'd had their fill of rummaging among the broken bushes, cigarette butts, beer cups, and other trash, Jake and Sam would bring their treasures into the kitchen to count them. By then, Ana would be up and have breakfast ready. At school the next day, with their friends equally burdened by beads and doubloons, the value of the trinkets evaporated.

After a few years, the prospect of a house full of drunks grew less enticing. Sometimes the crowds killed small trees in the esplanade. But the parties were part of their shared history in the house. A part of their unrecoverable past.

The last party.

Gordo sighed. Parties would never be as grand and excessive as they had been on Batavia Boulevard.

• • •

Josh did not come to the party. He was Sam's closest friend at school. But Sam accepted the excuse without question.

"What did Josh's mom say?" Ana asked.

Gordo had taken the phone call.

"She said they had some conflict. That Josh wouldn't be able to come," he said.

"But she didn't say what it was?"

"She was kind of vague."

Ana bit her bottom lip. She looked as if she might cry.

"It's okay," said Gordo. "Sam's fine with it."

"But it's his best friend."

"Look, we don't know Josh's family that well. All they are likely to know is that I was shot under mysterious circumstances. I understand why they might be reluctant to send their seven-year-old to our home. Or they might actually have a conflict. It may be nothing."

"Josh told Sam he was coming," she said. "He told Sam all about the gift he was going to get. He said he was getting him a light saber."

"Something might have come up."

"I don't see why people have to take it out on Sam. The party's fifteen miles from where the shooting was."

"Josh's dad is at the medical school. He's not from Galveston. They probably have no idea where we live. All they know is that something spooky happened and they don't want their son mixed up in it. Let's not blow this out of proportion."

"I hate that son-of-a-bitch," she said. "I hate him."

Him.

Their code.

"I saw Lisa Pierce at the store when I was buying supplies," she added.

"Really?"

"She saw all the paper plates and cups and candy and stuff and said, 'I know what you're up to.' So I told her about the treasure hunt, the last party. Cody seemed interested, so on impulse, I invited them. Sam seems to get along with Cody, even though he's younger. Lisa said she'd bring her camera. We could get some great photographs out of this. The pirates in action!"

"Great," he said.

"Is something wrong?"

"No. There's always room for more pirates."

"I'm glad we're doing this," she said. "It'll be a pain in the ass, but Sam will love it."

• • •

Gordo always steeled himself for the boys' birthday parties. The hyperactive children, their metabolisms surging on sugar, seemed to take on the jerky movements of the inhabitants of a freshly crushed anthill. Kids racing back and forth from one sensory magnet to another. Presents, cake, piñata, ice cream, party favors, games, jugglers, balloons, squirt guns.

Today, he felt more intense and more detached. A lot of

kids and a lot of ground to watch. They'd need adults on the beach and at the house. They'd have to keep an eye on children crossing the dunes. Thank God for Lars. Gordo wanted the party to go well. He might well never see some of these people again. When it was over, it would really be over.

The chorus of voices was growing in volume and intensity as Gordo gathered the pirate hats and the toy spyglasses he'd bought as party favors. Where was that treasure map? As he was searching, Lisa Pierce walked through the door.

"Hey," she said. "Ana told me I had full bathroom privileges."

"Mi baño es su baño."

Lisa's face was flushed.

"Those stairs are kind of hard on a pregnant woman," she called out as she headed for the bathroom.

"You can always just go in the dunes."

"Too many pirates," she shouted through the door.

After he heard the toilet flush, Gordo put down the hats and met Lisa in the hall.

"You look . . . healthy," he said.

"Is that the best you can do? Cows look healthy, too."

"You look *mahvelous.*"

Lisa put her arms around him and kissed him on the mouth.

"I know that's wicked," she said. "Here in your own home. Surrounded by children."

"And wife," said Gordo.

"And wife. I just wanted to do that. Must have been some hormonal surge. After six months, I'm ready to feel *mahvelous.*"

"I'd really like to bite your bottom lip. To nibble on your earlobes. But I've got a treasure hunt to get underway." He was amazed at how easy it was to slip into this kind of talk. But then, he knew it was only talk. He had been to the precipice, shrouded in a fog of lust and temptation, and turned back.

"That's the worst excuse I've heard in some time. But at least it doesn't involve tropical diseases."

Lisa leaned into him, her firm stomach pressed against his, her presence both girlish and maternal. He studied her full bottom lip and remembered her white cotton panties.

"Too wicked," she growled. "I don't know what's wrong with me. Go to your pirates, Blackbeard!"

"Gordo!" Ana called out. "The natives are getting restless."

He jerked away from Lisa as Ana turned the corner.

"Oh, there you are, Lisa. You found what you were looking for?" Ana had Skoll with her.

"Yes. As a human bowling ball, the stairs were quite a challenge, but I made it. Gordo says I have permission to squat in the dunes next time."

"Of course, I do it all the time."

"I love this neighborhood," Lisa said.

"Got to put the wolf away," said Ana. "Matt's little brother was terrified when he saw Skoll."

"That's not a dog. That's a horse," said Lisa.

Ana led Skoll into Lars's bedroom. "Gordo, you'd better get down there with that treasure map before we have a riot on our hands," she said.

"Blackbeard is on his way."

"Lisa, there's something I wanted to ask you."

Despite his curiosity, his need to know what Ana had on her mind, Gordo collected the map, the paper hats, the spyglasses, and plastic shovels, and headed for the beach.

Gordo was in the throes of the treasure hunt when suddenly, in the corner of his eye, he spotted something bright. A tricorn hat festooned with brilliant yellow and green feathers. Magnificent feathers. And a black eye patch.

Who the hell?

“Look, a pirate!” one of the boys exclaimed. They started running toward the newcomer, who, Gordo noticed, was also wearing a heavy double-breasted burgundy coat with gold epaulets.

“Stand back, ye scurvy dogs!” the man shouted, “or I’ll spear your gizzards.”

Then he withdrew a long sword from the silver scabbard hanging from his belt, producing a metallic zing, just like Captain Hook.

“A real sword! A real sword!”

Removing his hat with a flourish, he crossed his body with the sword and bowed elegantly from the waist. For Ana. She responded with the slightest, almost imperceptible wave. A signal meant only for Captain Hook.

Corky. Corky Elliott.

“I didn’t know about this *paht*,” said Sam, smiling at his father.

“It’s a surprise,” said Gordo, as if the pirate’s appearance was just one more *paht* of the treasure hunt. But he was thinking of Ana’s little private wave. Upraised fingers swept in a truncated, conspiratorial arc. A wave that told him that she knew Corky would be here.

Now Gordo was the only one left by the water. A breaker crashed on the packed sand, and a thin sheet of cold, foamy water ran over his feet. With the treasure hunt brought to a standstill, he walked over to join the group milling around the dashing pirate.

“Corky, I didn’t know you were in the Knights of Columbus.”

“Just a get-up I have for the Krewe of Lafitte,” Corky explained. “Thought it would be the uniform of the day for treasure hunting.”

The Krewe of Lafitte. Of course.

Lafitte was the Mardi Gras krewe for the members of the

island's social hierarchy, men born on the island to established families. Like all the krewes, it existed solely to throw lavish parades and parties the week before Lent. The Krewe of Lafitte was made up of bluebloods, with a sprinkling of hard-toiling achievers to lend a democratic patina to the group, along with a few interlopers who had married into the right families.

"Hope you don't mind my crashing the party," said Corky. "Ana told me about this affair, and I just couldn't resist getting involved. I'm always on the lookout for buried treasure."

"Well, of course, who could resist?" said Gordo, trying to conceal his irritation. "The more the merrier. I know Sam would agree."

Gordo eyed the ornate engraving on Corky's sword: *The Royal Krewe of Lafitte.*

"Do you want something to drink?" Ana asked.

"That's a stupid question," said Corky, releasing a peal of resonant laughter. It started deep and then rose in volume and pitch. He seemed to exhale mirth like cigarette smoke. If you heard him without seeing him, you'd expect the laughter to be produced by a man of great bulk. But here was Corky, six feet four inches of trim elegance.

A person could go far just on the strength of that laugh, thought Gordo.

As Ana and the visitor walked back to the house to fetch a drink, he watched them side by side. The top of Ana's blond head barely reached his gold epaulets.

Gordo understood that jealousy exerted its death grip most effectively upon those who knew temptation. Here he was, flush with the taste of betrayal—the taste of Lisa—watching his wife and an attractive man disappear together. He kicked the loose gritty sand, which the wind swept back at him.

"The *twesha*!" Sam was shouting. "We've got to find the *twesha*." He waved the map like a flag. Then the boys raced back toward the water, with Lars and Gordo bringing up the rear.

Under the circumstances, it was going to take every bit of his concentration to find the damn treasure. The boys, who had forgotten the number of steps they'd taken from the last landmark, needed his help. Now the whole enterprise seemed stupid and tedious. Maybe he should just go find the X and help them dig it up. But he couldn't. Surely that was some kind of failing. Not long ago he had had his tongue down Lisa Pierce's throat. But he would play it straight. They would use the map. The part of his being that compelled him to brew the coffee to stain the paper, to char its edges, and to add meticulous serifs to the lettering on the map required him to see it through. In the midst of chaos, Gordo—altar boy, scoutmaster, father—was clinging to structure. Memorize your Latin, obey the Scout Law, follow the map. Reassuring structure of any kind.

• • •

After much confusion and backtracking, the boys finally got pointed in the right direction for the final one hundred pirate paces. They spied the X drawn in the sand and the whole procession broke into a sprint. Devon, one of Sam's classmates and a fellow Cub Scout, tripped on the way and began to cry.

Gordo helped him up, impressed with the boy's ability to shed tears instantaneously.

"Pirates trip on the beach all the time, Devon. It's a professional hazard."

Within moments, however, Devon grew absorbed in the excavation.

"I want to dig," he muttered.

The flexible plastic shovels soon became catapults, flinging sand into the wind. Devon thought this was hilarious.

Gordo could feel grit between his teeth.

"Hey, real pirates concentrate on the buried treasure," he said.

"This isn't real treasure," replied Devon. "You buried it."

"I see something!" Gordo shouted excitedly. He was ready to bury Devon instead.

"It's red," one of the boys observed.

"It's the treasure chest!"

"No, it's not," Devon insisted.

Fortunately, the other boys ignored him. Maybe that was Devon's problem in life.

Sam fell to his knees.

"I get to open it," he shouted.

As Sam fumbled with the clasp, the box popped open, launching scores of chocolate doubloons wrapped in gold foil onto the beach.

The boys dove after the coins. Lisa's son, Cody, who had remained largely passive, jumped onto the dog pile.

"Guys!" Gordo cried. "There's enough for everyone. You don't need to fight for them."

"We like to fight!"

"Pirates fight," said Devon.

"Yeah!" Cody agreed.

"Okay, fight," Gordo muttered.

He felt exhausted. He turned toward the beach house to look for Ana, who was nowhere in sight. As his eyes continued their sweep across the dunes and out over the water, a wave broke 150 yards offshore. Like a row of church pews, the three sandbars. Cabeza de Vaca's boat crashed on one of the sandbars the day he was shipwrecked. *Malhado.* The explorer's way of expressing six years of bad karma.

Maybe this party wasn't such a good idea after all.

• • •

Lisa Pierce, Ana, and Corky were laughing as Gordo led the pirates up the stairs. Ana and Corky were drinking beer from unrecognizable bottles.

"Happy hour," Gordo said. "I'm ready. What are you drinking?"

"Fat Tire," Ana laughed.

"Fat Tire?"

"Microbrewery in Colorado," Corky explained. "Fat Tire Brewery."

"Ah. Well, I think we have some hungry pirates here. Who's ready for cake and ice cream?"

"Before you do that," Corky said, "I've got something for the birthday boy and his mates."

Corky went inside and soon emerged with a giant plastic Wal-Mart bag. It looked as if it weighed forty pounds. Gordo could see multicolored candy wrappers through the white plastic.

"This is what's called a last-minute piñata." Corky had cinched the top of the bag with cord, making it look like a large plastic onion. Standing on a chair, he tied the other end of the cord to a rafter.

"You guys can whack this thing with your shovels until it explodes."

"Cool!" one of the boys exclaimed.

"Me first!"

"It's my *buthday*," Sam cried.

Gordo looked toward Ana. She shrugged.

"I think I need one of these designer beers," he said.

Sam went first, pummeling the swinging Wal-Mart onion repeatedly, to no effect.

"Hit it! Hit it!" the boys screamed.

Sam, soon out of breath, gave way in favor of his friend Daniel, who was much bigger. Daniel whacked the bag repeatedly, but the toy shovel didn't have enough mass to tear the plastic. Another boy stepped forward.

"I'm afraid your improvised piñata is too much like the real thing," Gordo said. "Never seen a piñata that didn't have to be cut open with a machete."

Corky stepped forward. "I think it's time for more drastic measures. Who's ready to find out what's inside that piñata?"

"I am!"

"I am!"

The children were in a fever pitch.

"I want you all to stand back," Corky proclaimed. Then he drew his magnificent sword and handed it to Sam.

Sam's eyes grew wide. He looked toward Ana.

"Be careful, Sam," she said. "Is this safe?"

Sam was beaming.

"Gordo, is this safe?"

"Is it safe to have a seven-year-old swinging a sword in the middle of a bunch of glucose-crazed kids?" said Gordo. "Let me give that some thought."

Sam grabbed the sword with two hands, wielding it like an ax, and delivered a heavy blow. The bag burst immediately, and a torrent of candy spilled out upon the deck. Corky grabbed the sword from Sam as the children dove after the sweets.

"You must have bought all the candy at Wal-Mart," Ana shouted.

"The clerk did give me a strange look. I just told her I had a sweet tooth."

"The moms are going to kill me," said Ana, "when they see what we've sent home with their kids. But we'll be out of here soon—so what can they do?"

And then Gordo heard something he had not heard in a long time. He heard the delicious trilling of uncontrollable laughter from Ana, punctuated by little explosive bursts of air from her nostrils. He loved her laugh, and it had always been a balm for the family. The boys made fun of these noisy outbursts, but they loved them too.

Standing there, in the midst of the chaos, he took a deep

breath and looked out toward the Gulf. Corky had made her laugh. Gordo could hear the wash of the surf beneath the excited voices of the kids. The sun was beginning to redden the sky, and even the sand, brackish under the harsh inspection of the sun, was taking on a sugary paleness with the approach of dusk. When were they leaving?

"We want cake," one of the boys shouted.

"They want their cake," said Lars. Even Lars, the indefatigable wanderer, was beginning to look frayed.

"I'll get the plates," Ana said.

"I'll help," said Corky, following her inside.

"I think she can manage a stack of paper plates," Gordo said to no one. Realizing he didn't have matches, he went into the kitchen.

More laughter erupted from Ana. Corky seemed to hover over her as she stood at the sink. The plumage in his tricorn hat bobbed as he whispered in her ear.

"Matches," Gordo announced.

Ana jumped. "I've got to grab a towel," she said, skirting around Corky, leaving him alone with Gordo.

"I came in here for something," said Corky.

"Paper plates."

"Ah, yes," said Corky.

Lisa burst in. "Devon's looking pretty green," she reported. "I think he's already eaten all his chocolate doubloons."

"Serves him right," said Gordo.

"Where would I find those paper plates?" asked Corky.

"Try that door," Gordo replied with a wave.

Corky walked over to the bedroom door with his loose, cavalier gait that seemed to suggest that he owned the world. He opened the door.

Gordo heard a roar and then Corky's scream.

"Ahhhh!"

The door slammed.

"Goddammit!"

Ana and Lars came running. All the boys peered inside, as if they were missing something good.

Corky looked like he'd narrowly escaped death.

"What the hell is that?" said Corky, hyperventilating.

"You met Skoll," said Lars.

"It almost took my arm off! That thing looks like it belongs in a cave painting."

Gordo chuckled. "Skoll can't stand men who wear feathers."

• • •

Gordo was exhausted when he finally climbed into bed that night.

"Sam loved the party," Ana said. "Thanks for all the work on it."

Her back toward him, he leaned over her shoulder to give her a kiss, palming her ass. "Corky and his getup were a big hit. Especially the sword."

"And the makeshift piñata."

"You like him, don't you?" he said.

"He can be fun. Don't you think so?"

"I guess. I see the way he looks at you."

"It's nothing," she said.

"Good."

"You and Lisa seem to be on good terms."

"I love pregnant women."

"I remember," she said.

"But Lisa didn't dress up in a ridiculous costume and buy forty-five pounds of candy just to impress you."

"Did you think that was seductive?" she asked.

"I don't trust Corky. He's never been denied anything in life. He takes, then he moves on."

“Look, we’re almost out of here. Let’s not fight,” she said. “Let’s make the most of the time we have left.”

“When can we leave?”

“I need a couple of weeks to get things squared away at the office. I’m meeting with the partners on Monday to talk about it. But where are we going?”

“I don’t know,” he said.

“Time to make some decisions,” she said.

“Even though we’re not living at Pilot House, I still feel connected to it,” he said. “It’s ours. It’s home. It will be strange to cross the causeway knowing we’re not coming back.”

“You’re getting awfully nostalgic for someone who’s being stalked by a madman.”

“I know.”

Sixteen

Monday Ana met with her partners to explore her options for leaving the firm. Gordo, eager to talk to her about the discussion, tried to call during the afternoon without success. If they were going to move, they would need the money from the sale of her stake in the partnership. Late in the day, she called to remind him that she was going to a meeting of the fundraising committee of Cooper School.

"I'm buried here at the office. I'll just work late and go straight to the meeting."

"Fundraising for Cooper is not the highest priority right now."

"I've got to give a report."

Ana took volunteer work seriously, as if it were one more client.

Gordo fed the boys, helped with the homework, and got them ready for bed. Sam protested that his mother was not home by bedtime.

More weary than tired, Gordo couldn't sleep. His

thoughts kept returning to Ana. And Corky. He'd exercised enough self-control to not ask if Corky would be at the meeting. But Gordo knew that he would.

That morning his shaving cream had been gone from its place in his drawer. He found it, as he usually did, in the shower. Ana's hair was so fine and so fair that she didn't need to shave very often and never bought her own can—she just borrowed his. When Ana wanted to look her best, when she wanted to look sexy, she shaved her legs and wore a black push-up bra and matching panties. He went to her bureau drawer. Several black bras lay nestled amongst her underwear. He could see Ana's pale shoulders beneath black straps. To him, at that point of undress, with the gentle curve of her breast dipping beneath black lace, she was irresistible. The thought did not give him any comfort.

This restlessness was driving him crazy. Lars had turned in for the night. He and Skoll were there for the boys. Gordo grabbed his car keys and scrawled a note.

Gone out. Back soon. G. 11:45.

He quietly padded out the door. Casting a glance toward the water, he could see shadowy blurs of motion. Sand crabs skimming across the sand, as if they needed to keep moving in order to stay alive.

I know just how you feel.

He knew it was wrong to go. To spy on her. But he could not help himself.

Finding her silver Volvo was easy. It was just down the street from the Tremont House. The space in front of it was occupied by a black Mercedes. The blocky letters on its personalized license plate: CORKY.

Gordo drove around the block and parked up a narrow cross street in the shadow of a tree growing through the sidewalk. The tree trunk passed through a metal grating shaped like the spokes of a wheel. Candy wrappers and trash had become tangled in the grillwork, as if the town's overall shabbiness was eating away at the edges of the fussy downtown historic district. Half a block from the tourist promenades, empty wine bottles lined the sidewalk like bowling pins.

Slouching in the car, he felt a knot in his stomach. Fear of what he might discover, and shame from how he might learn it. His jealousy was an elixir that he couldn't resist. What were they doing? Were they talking intimately in the bar, his finger tracing her long forearm? Or had they gone upstairs? He would not go inside the hotel. He would wait. As he did whenever he came to the East End, he had slipped the Beretta under the seat of the car. In the past, he had viewed the gun as a precaution. Tonight it seemed an extension of his whole edgy frame of mind.

Christ, you are supposed to be the sane one!

Nervous energy and all the coffee he'd swilled forced him out of the car. Gordo ducked down a nearby alley to pee. On his way back, a large black man approached him on the sidewalk. Seeing the color of his skin, Gordo felt more secure. He knew this man was not carrying a gun for the express purpose of killing him. More secure than if it had been a tall white man. For Gordo, who had lived in a biracial, high-crime neighborhood for more than a decade, this was a reversal.

As they passed, Gordo looked directly at the man and said hello. He saw the man's spine stiffen. He eyed Gordo suspiciously.

Of course.

Gordo resumed his vigil, thinking that what he was doing could push his relationship with Ana to a place where he might not want to go. If this encounter were to go badly, he might not be able to restore things. Maybe he should let Ana sort this out by herself. He should be home with the boys.

His fingers were on the ignition key when he saw her.

Lamplight glancing off her straight blond hair. Corky walking with her. Close, but not touching. She unlocked her car door.

Get in!

Corky touched her shoulder, turning Ana toward him and putting his arms around her. They kissed.

Gordo reached for the door handle.

Enough!

But Ana backed away. She seemed to be smiling—wagging her finger at him.

Enough intimacy to touch and to kiss. But she was applying the brakes.

Gordo was frozen. Watching.

Corky gestured theatrically, imploring her to get into his car. Ana tossed her head back in laughter. She opened the door of her Volvo.

Get in, Ana!

Corky still gesturing. He wanted her in his Mercedes.

Then Ana said something that ended the conversation. Corky hopped into the black Mercedes and headed west. Ana followed.

Gordo started his car. His old Toyota too distinctive for him to tail her closely, he stayed back, avoiding the pool of light at the upper end of Batavia, their old street.

Only after Ana was well ahead did he turn toward the Gulf.

He followed her as she crossed the island, her tail lights an echo of those of the Mercedes. At Broadway the light turned yellow.

She accelerated through the intersection, but Gordo was too far behind.

Damn!

Caught at Broadway, he watched Ana's taillights recede in the blackness.

Ana, go home! Just go home!

• • •

Why is it so hard to find what you're looking for on this scrawny island?

The shooter. The truth. Now his wife.

Give me a prairie, he thought, where you can see. He turned his car west toward their shaky home on the beach.

At the beach house, Gordo couldn't sit still. He just wanted Ana home. Pacing the room, he spied a videocassette on top of the TV. He pushed it into the maw of the VCR and turned down the volume. Old grainy film flickered on the screen. Blocky lettering: Hayes for Congress. He'd brought the tape from Pilot House to show Lars. Black-and-white footage of the Colonel making a speech in the 1950s. Pat Hayes as a young man—younger than Gordo was now. Pat with dark hair slicked back, a square jaw, and no jowls.

Then the picture cut to the steps of the federal building on Batavia Boulevard. The candidate with the missus and kids. Gordo fixed his stare on the six-year-old girl—board-straight hair and delicate features. White pinafore and dark round hat. Red, she'd told him. Blue collar and trim. Patent leather shoes. Ana in red, white, and blue.

Pat would have had his vote.

Ana hated being on display back then. But you'd never know from the image on the screen. She smiled and waved to an unseen crowd. She was a dazzling little girl and Gordo loved her. Fourteen years would pass between the filming and the day they met in college, but he was entranced. Ana in red, white, and blue.

• • •

When she came through the door at one-thirty Gordo was sprawled on the couch.

"I didn't expect you to be up," she said.

"I wanted to wait up for you."

"Well, after the meeting, some of us went out for a drink."

"Elizabeth Booker maybe?" Elizabeth Booker was a stout woman in her late forties whose husband was the pastor of First Baptist Church. Her daughter had a learning disability; otherwise she would never have attended an alternative school. The Bookers were not alternative people.

"No, not Elizabeth."

"Corky, I suppose."

"Gordo, it's too late for this," she whispered.

"Those committee meetings go on and on."

"We just went out for a drink."

"The meeting broke up at what? Nine-thirty—ten o'clock?"

"I'm not doing this. I worked hard today, and I'm getting ready for bed."

"Ana, it's after one-thirty."

"I know what time it is."

She left him standing in the kitchen.

Gordo wanted to confront her. But he was loath to disclose that he had spied on her. It felt wrong. He scoured his memory of them together. What could he discern from those few minutes of watching them? She had broken their embrace. But where had they gone?

Had the shooting prompted Ana to question the life she had chosen? Was she looking for something different?

Gordo brushed his teeth and washed his face. The shock of cold water knocked away what little drowsiness remained. Maybe it would help clear his head. He entered the closet for the flannel boxers he slept in. But he couldn't keep from nosing around, looking at her things. Hanging from a hook on the back of the closet door was her black bra. He touched it and could feel her warmth.

She wanted to look her best. She wanted to feel sexy.

He went back to the couch to sulk. He felt that some strange permutation of his character had emerged, completely beyond his control, as a result of what had happened since the shooting.

How long ago?

Less than a month.

So much had happened, and so much more had to happen before they could get past this. They could be gone by summer. If she really wanted to leave. He would never get to sleep until he talked to her.

She was in bed, and her reading lamp was off. She almost never went straight to sleep, no matter the hour. Bedtime reading was her soporific.

"I'm sorry I was so late," she whispered. "Did everything go okay with the boys?"

"They're fine."

"Good."

She closed her eyes.

But he could not leave it.

"So you went out for a drink?"

She sighed. "Right."

"Where?"

"The Tremont House."

"Did you go anyplace else?"

"Please Gordo. I need to get some rest."

"I need to get some answers!"

"You don't have to shout," she said. "You'll wake the boys."

"Where have you been?" he demanded.

"I just told you."

He grabbed a book from the dresser and hurled it across the room. The book's pages billowed in flight before it crashed into the wall near Ana's nightstand. It struck the hollow wall like an insect splattered on a windshield. Ana's reading lamp rattled.

“What’s wrong with you?” she said.

“What isn’t wrong?”

“You need to calm down.”

“I think I’ve been too calm,” he said. “Maybe that’s the problem.”

“I don’t know what’s going on, but throwing things isn’t going to help.” Ana bristled with irritation. “Waking up Sam and Jake and Lars isn’t going to help.”

Gordo picked up the book. It was the heavy volume of *The Once and Future King*. Sam’s favorite. The book’s spine was broken.

“Shit!”

“Why don’t you come to bed,” she said, her voice softening. “We can talk about this tomorrow. Let’s get some rest.”

Gordo stood over her. He could hear himself breathing. Too weary to press her, he crawled into bed beside Ana, furious but leery of confrontation. It would be impossible to extract what he wanted to know without revealing his own dubious conduct, of which he was ashamed.

There had been such change in their lives since the shooting. The tectonic plates of his existence had twisted and buckled into rubble. He thought he had always presented to the world an interesting and attractive persona. A writer—albeit of magazine articles. Not bad looking. Likeable, at least to the people he cared about. But since they had gone on the lam, his own identity seemed wounded. He knew the rumor mill was circulating his name, and if other people’s perception of him had changed, was it possible that Ana’s had too?

The writer Larry L. King had once quipped, “The world rates the freelance writer on the socioeconomic scale somewhere between busboys and rodeo clowns.” Ana had never held this against him. She’d always seemed content. But now?

The wind was up, and as he lay there, he could feel the

house sway and hear its timber emit the soft groans of a ship under sail. Things were moving.

Always moving—but most of the time change was nearly imperceptible. Now, each day seemed to bring upheaval. He longed for the terra firma of their earlier life.

Why would someone shoot Gordo O'Connor?

He needed to figure it out. Fast.

Too many images for sleep.

The gunman. His glowering eyes.

Ana.

Ana and Corky.

An innocent, waving girl in red, white, and blue.

Seventeen

The next morning, Lars announced that he was leaving to visit friends at Aransas Pass, a channel in the barrier islands near Corpus Christi. When Lars was ready to move, he moved suddenly. It was his way. He might stay for weeks and then announce he was leaving at the breakfast table and be gone by lunch. Gordo wondered if the beach house had become too much of a pressure cooker for his friend. If Lars had sensed some craving within Ana for a house without visitors. Or maybe he just had a lady friend down the coast.

"Looks like things are pretty calm around here," Lars said. "I'll be gone a few days. Do you mind if I leave Skoll?"

"Your dog's as welcome as you are."

"That's always been the case, wherever I go."

After Ana and the boys got off for the day, Gordo made Lars a thermos of coffee for the drive south. "Too bad you're not a birder. I think this is the high season for exotic feathers at Aransas."

"I am a birder. They've provided me with a great deal of

companionship over the years. I just seem to befriend the common ones. Don't have much use for fancy birds."

Lars gave Skoll a farewell rub behind the ears and hauled his duffel bag down the stairs. The air was warmer and heavy with moisture. A combination of sea spray, dew, and dried salt left the windows of the Jeep barely translucent. Gordo turned on the spigot and hosed down the windows as Lars warmed the engine. The wipers worked back and forth like a metronome.

"I'll see some friends, do a little fishing, be back early next week."

"We'll look after Skoll."

"You look after yourself." Then he put the Jeep in gear and roared away.

• • •

He couldn't bring himself to talk to Ana about Corky. But he also couldn't stop thinking about it. The way they were so comfortable together. She came home early and started helping him fix dinner. They both knew it was a gesture, her leaving the office earlier than normal, but to mention it would force them to deal with the reason for the gesture. Instead, he asked about her meeting with her law partners.

Her expression told him it hadn't gone well.

"Jack's got definite ideas about what the assets are worth."

"He's got a very good reason the assets are worth a whole lot less than what you paid for them, right?" Jack was Gordo's least favorite partner at the firm.

"It's not that bad," she said.

"The piranhas smell blood."

"It's not that bad."

Gordo felt a pang of guilt when he said ugly things about lawyers. After all, his wife and his father-in-law were lawyers, and lawsuits put bread on his table.

"Jack senses weakness, and so he's got to go for the jugular," said Gordo. "Force of habit. The fact that you're his partner doesn't faze him. He knows we're under pressure to leave. He knows some crazy bastard is shooting at your husband. So what better time to put the squeeze on you? He's such an asshole."

"Look, I don't know what the building's worth," she said. "I don't know what the computers and the law library are worth. And under the partnership agreement, it's really worth whatever a majority of the partners say it's worth."

"What does Jack want to pay?"

Ana mentioned a figure that was a fraction of her share of the capital in the firm.

"The firm spent half a million on the building expansion last year and you paid your share. And the financial statements will tell you what you've got in the equipment and the library."

"We've been depreciating the equipment as fast as we can." Ana looked like she was about to crumple. The shooter, the law firm, the house, the move, and now, the tension that had built up between them.

Gordo was mad, but he wasn't sure he had a right to be.

"I don't want to put you under any more pressure than you are already. I'm not criticizing you about this. Jack's just being a prick."

"It feels like criticism," she said. "It feels like you think that if I were tougher, I'd be driving a harder bargain. But in the end, I'm just one vote. They're going to do what they're going to do. What's the alternative? Take them to court? The others will try to be fair. In the past, we've all benefited from Jack being a professional asshole. That's why people hire him. He's made money for the firm because of his take-no-prisoners approach. He's made money for this family, our family. For years, it was to our advantage. Now it's not."

Gordo knew a part of his anger had nothing to do with the law firm. He was mad about Corky. But now, with so much around them falling apart, he wasn't going to open a fresh wound.

"Okay. You're right, the prick's made himself useful before. I guess we knew Jack was going to be tight about buying you out. It's a lot to deal with right now." He put his arms around her. In his bitterness and jealousy, he hadn't touched her much lately. He missed the touching, the small grace notes of daily contact. He ran his hand up the small of her back.

"We'll get through this," he said. "We'll come out of it fine."

"This isn't how I ever imagined us leaving," she said. "There's just so much to do. It's not just moving. It's like we're evacuating before some big storm hits. No farewell parties, no hugs. We've been cut off from so many people. When was the last time we just went out and had fun? We might as well be in some awful witness protection program. But we're not witnesses. We're not criminals. I'd shoot that son-of-a-bitch if I had the chance."

Gordo held her tighter. She had the capacity to get weighed down. To lose emotional altitude, to fall into a descending spiral. So did the Colonel. Her father covered it with a false ebullience that didn't fool the people close to him. Ana couldn't disguise it. Gordo always considered it his job to pull her out of the spiral. It was one of the countless things he had done for her in their life together, just as she had done countless things for him. He needed to let go of his jealousy and help her. He took a dishtowel and wiped away a single teardrop, high on her cheek, below the small crow's feet etched into her pink wind-burned skin. He kissed her.

"A place with rocks. Big ones," he said.

"I could plant a garden."

"Cactus and hills and a creek in back."

"A stone house next to a cliff."

"We'll find it," he said.

• • •

That night Gordo was working on a health care article in his office as Ana read to the boys in the next room. *The Once and Future King*. Passages seeped into the room like sand carried by the wind.

Thank God for the aged, sings the poet:
And for age itself, and illness and the grave,
When we are old and ill, and particularly in the coffin,
It is no trouble to behave.

Gordo could listen to Ana's clear, high reading voice all night. He knew Jake was snuggled up next to her on the sofa, and he could hear Sam bouncing around the room, soft but exuberant footfalls on the carpeted floor. This was the cadence of so many of their evenings at the beach. Writing and reading. Gordo envied the words already on the printed pages of their book. No matter how fast he wrote, he could never begin to keep up with this onrush. He was working on something different, something devoid of the magic of the novel, but the torrent of words—work already crafted, already done—was both soothing and, by comparison to his own meager output, disheartening. A reminder of all he had left to complete before he met his deadline. Dead line. All that remained for him to do before his pen went still and his trickle of words dried up.

Around eight-thirty, Gordo decided to take a break and let Skoll go outside.

"Why don't you take out the shrimp shells when you go?" said Ana. "They won't improve with age."

He had peeled two pounds of shrimp for their dinner.

"Old shrimp heads make such nice room sachet."

Skoll went to the door, wagging his tail.

"Can I go?" asked Jake.

Man, boy, and dog thumped down the stairs. As Gordo

pried the lid from the trash can, Jake opened Petey's hutch to pet him.

"Petey's getting to like the beach," said Jake.

"Jake. Come here." It was a voice from the driveway.

Gordo turned around and saw a figure half-obscured by the corner piling. The sight of the tall thin man almost knocked the wind out of him.

"Jake," Gordo said, "go upstairs."

He grabbed an oar from *Shark Bite* and stepped toward the voice.

"Go on, Jake."

Jake started slowly up the stairs, walking backwards.

Skoll began to growl.

"Who is it?" said Gordo.

"You know." The man was still in shadow.

"Jake, get up the stairs! Tell your mom to call the police. Go! Now!"

Gordo could hear Jake running up the steps.

The figure stepped forward.

"Don't fuck with me," said the man. Tall, thin, intense eyes.

Gordo moved faster, drawing back the heavy oar as if it were a javelin. When he got to the foot of the stairs, he heaved the oar. It glanced off the man's hip and clattered on the concrete.

Skoll's growl became a roar.

"Skoll!" Gordo shouted. "Get him!"

With his teeth flashing and his great ruff standing on end, the dog charged. Only then did the man seem to notice Skoll.

Skoll seized the intruder's calf, shaking his jaws back and forth.

The man screamed in pain. He tried to shake free.

"Gordo!" Ana cried from the deck above.

"Get the cops!" he shouted. "Don't come down."

Then the man struck Skoll in the face with something hard. A wet, heavy thud. The dog yelped and released his grip.

"Fuckin' dog!" the man shouted. "I'll kill that fuckin' dog!" He reached for his leg.

Gordo bounded halfway up the stairs. Turning, he shouted, "Skoll! Come!"

Once inside, he locked the door and grabbed the Beretta. At the front window, he searched for the man. No one.

Jake rushed to Skoll, who was panting loudly.

"Oh God, are you all right?" asked Ana.

"Jake, you okay?" said Gordo.

Jake had his hand on Skoll's head. "He's bleeding."

"Skoll's got a gash on the side of his nose," said Ana.

Gordo crossed to the window overlooking the deck.

"The guy hit him hard. I could hear it."

"With what?"

"I think it was a pistol."

"Oh God!" Ana was crying. "We've got to get out of here."

"What's going on?" It was Sam from his bed. "I hear a *siwen*."

"Jake could have been shot," she said through her tears. "We've got to get out of here. We've got to get off this goddamn island." Ana was shaking.

"Mom, I'm sorry," said Jake. "I just wanted to go see Petey."

She embraced him.

"Jake, Jake. I wasn't blaming you. Nothing's going to happen to any of us."

The siren grew louder until they could see the lights of the police car turn into the sandy road.

"Skoll bit him," said Jake. "I heard the man scream."

"Thank God for Skoll," said Gordo.

"I don't want that man to come back," Jake said.

Sam, carrying his pillow, began to stroke the dog.

"Thank *Lahs*, too."

"Lars, too."

• • •

"You have a friend by the name of Tom," Lino Gabilondo said. It was not posed as a question. Then the detective looked away, letting the name float in the space between them.

They were near the white stucco band shell in Menard Park, a windblown skeleton of a park across Seawall Boulevard from the beach. Gordo took his boys there from time to time, and it was always an adventure to discover the extravagant vandalism to the playground equipment. Only the palm trees and oleanders seemed to thrive.

"EVA FUCKS!" appeared in black spray paint on the white surface of the band shell. The concave side, a small amphitheater, faced away from the Gulf. Wooden benches had to be hauled in for each band concert during the summer; they were subject to being stolen or destroyed if left in the park for more than a day or two.

He had told Lino of the events of the night before at the beach house.

"Tom?" Gordo was confused. They were talking about the shooter. What did Tom have to do with it?

"Tom's a close friend. What about him?"

"Your friend knows where you were living on the West End?"

"Sure."

"Maybe you shouldn't tell him where you've gone."

"Now I know you guys are crazy. First you suspect me—as if I've shot myself. Now you think Tom's mixed up in this." Gordo could barely restrain himself. He'd thought Lino was different. Different from Grover Hampton and Aldo Martelli and all the rest of the fuck-ups. There was only so much stupidity you could tolerate without going crazy. Gordo was near the edge.

Lino ignored his hostility.

"I can't say more," he said. "Not right now. We're looking at somebody. And it seems like there could be a connection . . . to this Tom. So if I were you, I'd keep my whereabouts to myself."

"I'd trust Tom with my life." Tom, the opera-loving vigilante, was his friend. The Man in Purple. How could he possibly be connected?

Gordo leaned forward and examined Lino's face. He was looking for the lie in his eyes. Some flicker of insincerity. Was this just more cop bullshit? He remembered old Hector Gabilondo. Lino's uncle. A favor to be repaid.

Gordo just said the name.

"Hector."

The young policeman seemed to understand.

"We're not sure. Don't even try to figure it out. I can't tell you enough to start. I'm just telling you what I'd do if I was you. What my uncle would say."

"I want to be someplace where I can see what's going on," said Gordo.

"Then you better get off the island."

"How did that guy find us out there?"

"Maybe from someone close to you?" asked Lino.

"You think one of our friends—maybe Tom, maybe our parents—called up the shooter and told him our address?"

"He could have followed you."

"I don't think so. There's not that much traffic out there in the winter," said Gordo. "I haven't been followed."

"Could have followed Ana."

Gordo realized Lino was right.

"Did Grover and Tiny have something against me?" he asked.

"I don't know. Why?"

"They didn't just seem indifferent; they seemed hostile."

"Some people still resent the Colonel," said Lino, choosing his words with care. "I admire what Pat Hayes did, but not everybody does. And look at it from their standpoint. You and Ana are a couple of yuppies, with your big old house on Batavia and your kids in private schools. Grover and Tiny are a part of old Galveston. Pat Hayes put an end to the good old days. There are lots of reasons why they might not like you."

"They didn't have to like me. I just wanted them to do their jobs."

Gordo stood there, unwilling to believe that his life could be twisted this way. By the memories of Sam and Rosario Maceo and a dozen other dead Italians. The Free State of Galveston. That's what the place had been called in those days. Finally, he didn't believe it. Ana had only been three years old when it all came to an end on the island. There had to be something else.

"What did they find out at the beach?" he asked.

"Jerry Peyton is going to go over this with you, but I would appreciate it if you didn't tell him we'd—"

"I know," said Gordo.

"He's got the case—"

"I know."

"There were some tire tracks. Motorcycle tracks. Just outside the subdivision, near the end of the beach road," said Lino. "We don't know for certain that they were your man. But if it was, looks like he ran across the dunes at the end of your street. The motorcycle tracks pick up on the other side. He goes east on the beach until he hits the paved road. Not too shabby. He's heading east while the cops responding to your call are going west on the main road."

"For somebody who looks deranged, this guy sure thinks things through."

"Crackhead psychos can be smart too," Lino said.

"Why did you call him a crackhead?"

"Like I said, we're looking at somebody."

Gordo hesitated. He didn't know if it was worth going into.

"Last I heard, Ana's brother was using crack. At least it was the flavor of the month."

"Give me his name."

• • •

"He said I shouldn't tell Tom where we are. Tom! Can you believe that?"

"The cop told you that?" asked Ana.

"Gabilondo. Lino Gabilondo. He said they were looking at somebody who had some connection to Tom."

"Well that doesn't mean they're looking at Tom," said Ana.

"Don't you think it's weird that the police are telling us not to trust one of our best friends?"

"At least it's an indication that they've ruled you out as a suspect."

"My mother doesn't have an alibi," he said.

"Look, at least it means they're doing something," she said. "At least it means they're not treating it as an 'inactive' file anymore."

"And something else." Gordo approached the subject with care. "Lino said the guy they're looking at is a crackhead. At least he implied that."

"So?"

"So there's a chance it could be somebody Allen knows. He's the only crackhead we know."

"I don't think Allen's involved. He's not interested in us. He's only interested in getting high."

Ana was seated on a sofa by a wall of glass overlooking the Gulf. She was striking in the light of dusk, her pale hair and bare shoulders set off by a black sleeveless top and black pants. Above her jaw, however, a small knot of muscle pulsed. She was a grinder. So much so that she slept with a plastic retainer to protect her molars.

"Maybe so. But he is a white guy in his thirties who does crack and hangs out on the island. It could be somebody in Allen's circle of friends."

They had moved to the Colonel's. Ana's parents had sold the big house in which they'd raised their children and bought a place on the twelfth floor of a beachfront condominium. The high-rise building, only a few years old, had been built on the site of an old antisubmarine bunker that remained from World War II. Drugs were a sensitive subject in the household because Ana's parents had battled their son's addiction for years. Pat Hayes, who had been able to fix so many things during his life, could never fix Allen. In fact, his countless interventions, his pattern of protecting Allen from the consequences of his actions, his enabling—or coddling as Ana viewed it—had made things worse. Allen was a thirty-nine-year-old man whose parents had never stopped treating him as a fifteen-year-old boy. The fact that Allen wandered in and out of Ana's parents' lives, and their home, was the reason Gordo had stayed clear of the Colonel's house for years. He tried to minimize the contact between Allen and the boys. Jake and Sam didn't need to witness Allen's explosive, drug-induced outbursts any more often than they already had. As much as Gordo loved his father-in-law, he could not accept the way he was dealing with Allen and his problems.

Ana and Gordo feared that someday her parents would fall

victim to Allen's drug buddies. They might be robbed, their house set on fire, or worse. And Allen's enormous presence in their lives was something the Colonel refused to talk about. He considered it his private misfortune, and he intended to keep it private. So Ana and Gordo were rarely informed of Allen's transgressions. They usually heard about them through the grapevine—someone at the courthouse, the jail, or maybe through a bail bondsman sharing an elevator. Never from the Colonel himself.

All this was terribly painful for Pat Hayes. What he had done for so many others—guided people through adversity, challenged powerful opponents, helped the injured or the aggrieved redeem themselves—he could not do for his son. If he had not been so skilled and resourceful, would he feel less inadequate for not salvaging Allen's squalid life?

Gordo had stumbled into the subject recently.

"Are the little men holding up all right?" the Colonel had asked.

"Jake and Sam seem to be fine," Gordo replied. "They are incredibly tough kids. They've been so strong through all this." He was thinking of the episode with the phone repairman, and it still pained him. He had been too embarrassed to tell the Colonel about it.

Shouldn't you put the gun away? Gordo could still hear Sam's innocent voice.

"They are wonderful boys. Our biggest achievement."

Pat Hayes looked wistful. "I'd give my kingdom to be able to say that." But the Colonel could not allow himself the luxury of sadness. "I'd also give my kingdom," he said, his tone a bit brighter, "to stick around long enough to see how Jake and Sam turn out."

Gordo touched his father-in-law's shoulder. "There should be a statute of limitations for parenting," said Gordo. "After some point, a person is who he is. If a person's not responsible for his own life—then who is?"

"Statute of limitations," the Colonel repeated. "Maybe you're right. I just want someone to tell me what the limit is."

• • •

Ana was still seated by the window when Allen walked through the front door.

"Allen," she said casually.

Gordo waved to his brother-in-law. "Hey."

Allen's skin color usually ranged from ashen to a jaundiced yellow. A thin man, whose eyes looked much older than his years, Allen had his father's handsome features but on a smaller scale. The Colonel had an enormous head and a shock of white hair that made him seem bigger than he was. Allen was the dehydrated version, brittle and leathery with dark circles beneath his eyes and hollow cheeks.

"Oh," Allen said flatly, clearly surprised to see them. "Have you seen Daddy?"

"He's not back from work. Mother's in the kitchen with the boys."

Allen drifted out of the room.

"I can't believe he's still got a key," Ana whispered. "My parents are crazy!"

"He doesn't look too good," said Gordo.

"He's using something."

"Seemed a bit out of it."

"He could be up, down, in between," she said. "Who knows?"

"Here we are living in hiding from somebody the police think is a crackhead," he said, "and in comes Allen, probably straight from the crack house, waltzing into your parents' own home." Gordo realized that there was too much bitterness in what he was saying. None of this was Ana's doing. But just seeing Allen made him punchy.

"He'll leave when he gets what he wants," she said.

"Which is?"

"Food or money."

"He didn't look like a man with a hearty appetite." Sometimes Gordo hated Allen. Sometimes he felt sorry for him. Most of the time he was indifferent. But tonight, in his emotionally raw state, he couldn't muster much sympathy. He wondered how much Allen had been told about their problems. He wondered if someone in Allen's circle of friends could be involved. But why? Allen didn't have any reason to harm Ana. But then he hadn't needed a reason in the past to harm everyone around him.

"We need to decide what to do, where to go," said Ana. "We can't stay here very long. I'll go crazy."

"Are we ready to leave?"

"I wouldn't mind taking a break from work. I've been working ever since law school. I could spend more time with the boys. I'll get something for my share of the law firm. We'll have money for a while."

"I could take all my old business, the magazine work and the corporate clients, and find some new ones."

They had talked about the Hill Country around Austin. Gordo and Ana had spent their college years there and vowed to return.

"I want a place with rocks," he said. "Big ones."

"I could plant a garden," she repeated. It was becoming their litany.

"I want cactus and hills and maybe a creek in the back."

"We could use the public schools."

"What a relief. No more tuition."

"No more Esther Quinn and her three-hour board meetings."

No more Corky Elliott, Gordo thought.

"Do you think we can sell Pilot House?" she asked.

"Why not? It's beautiful."

"I mean the shooting. Do you think people will want to live there?"

"I'll call Troy," he said.

Troy, their friend who specialized in selling houses in the historic district.

"Let's go to Austin this weekend," he proposed. "Take the boys. See what we can find."

"This is scary," Ana said.

"Not as scary as staying here."

Gordo leaned back and let this information pour over him. This was how people changed their lives. Imagining the answers to lots of little questions. How? Where? When?

He was ready to be uprooted. He didn't know where they would end up, but it would be someplace very different. Cutting the cord that tethered them to Ana's law firm would be the hard part. But Ana had not been all that fond of her work to begin with, and it had been getting less gratifying with each passing year. She was weary of legal confrontation. More than just legal confrontation, it was the personal confrontation. Litigation, she said, was getting more like mud wrestling than advocacy. People who thrived on conflict were better suited to the grind. Not necessarily better armed with intellect or analytical skills, but better suited to decades of acrimonious conversations and combative forays into court.

Every day Ana was forced to deal with people who thrived on confrontation. "Professional assholes," she called them. People who loved to spar on any subject and in any setting. Conflict with store clerks, waitresses, airlines, their spouses, and, of course, opposing lawyers. She was sick of it, she had said on many occasions.

Tall and self-possessed, Ana was often mistaken for possessing abundant confidence. He knew that wasn't true. She lacked the craving to brawl. What she craved was quiet. A place where she could raise children, garden, and read. She wanted to have time to cook again. At least that's what she told Gordo. But could she really adapt? Would she miss the action? The money?

Ana abandoned the sofa to help her mother with dinner, leaving Gordo staring down at the seawall below. When Jake was a baby, strapped into his car seat, Gordo had started each morning with coffee, a donut, and the newspaper. A quiet ritual together with Jake, usually sleepy and dozing, as the sun rose over the East End. When he finished the paper, Gordo would drop Jake off at the babysitter's house and start his workday.

In 1983, anticipating the landfall of Hurricane Alicia, he had sent Ana and newborn Jake off the island to higher ground. *Time* hired him to report on the storm for the magazine. As the hurricane bore down on the island, almost all of the members of the press camped out in the corridor outside the Weather Service in the Federal Building downtown. Gordo had gone there, taken one look at the media circus, and realized that while trapped inside the windowless, fifth-floor corridor, the reporters would be unable to report on anything other than their own discomfort. He decided to ride out the storm at Pilot House, where at least he would be able to see the weather firsthand, and where he would be much closer to people actually affected by the hurricane.

During the long, black night when the eye of the hurricane and its 130-mile-per-hour winds came ashore, Gordo listened to the Weather Service reports, made notes of what little he could observe, and tried to keep the elements at bay. In the middle of the night, water began gushing into the dining room. Like the sorcerer's apprentice, Gordo mopped furiously to keep pace with the torrent. Two exterior walls that formed a right angle acted like a funnel, forcing wind-driven rain into the vertex where the walls met. Taking the path of least resistance, the water rushed past the dining room window—

through the shutters, under the window sash, over the sill, and onto the floor—as if shot from a fire hose.

Later that night, Gordo heard a crack, followed by a deep thud that shook the entire house. Something big had struck. Branches were thrashing the shutters in places where there were no trees. Eventually he discovered that the four-story pecan tree in the backyard had toppled onto the roof directly over his bed.

During the height of the storm, a cameraman, a sound technician, and a TV reporter from Houston—two men and a woman—drove their van to the seawall to get "up close and personal" with Hurricane Alicia. Gordo heard the story from a colleague who spent the night at the Weather Service.

Chase Morgan, an attractive on-camera reporter in her twenties, was especially keen on reaching the seawall. Gordo had seen her on TV. A thin, pretty face with a sharp nose and hair dyed an unconvincing shade of blond. He'd seen her primping in the corridor of the Federal Building earlier in the day.

The van headed south into a black pool. The local power grid had been knocked down, so there was no electricity. As the trio drove blindly toward the Gulf, inching through the blackness with no visibility, they lost track of where they were. Bouncing off curbs, pummeled by debris, and swallowed up in winds so loud they could barely understand one another while screaming inside the van, the threesome realized they had to stop. Terrified and disoriented, the cameraman got out on his knees and crawled through the rain, trying to find a landmark. An arm's length from the front of the van he discovered that the pavement vanished. They had driven onto the edge of the seawall and were inches from plunging to their deaths. The horrified cameraman climbed back into the truck and the trio slowly found their way back to the safety of the Federal Building. "Just like a drowned water rat," was how one of the newspaper reporters described the young woman. Gordo tried to picture the scene. Pretty Chase Morgan, whose name evoked some grandiose Wall Street merger, as a drowned water rat.

Gordo peered down at the seawall, not far from where the van nearly drove into the sea. Pilot House had come through that storm with minor damage. Three broken boards from the fallen pecan tree and a few errant shingles. It wasn't easy to call Troy about listing the house for sale.

He reached for the phone.

• • •

Sam entered the room.

"How's dinner coming?"

"*Gwandma* says it's almost *weddy*."

"Good, I'm hungry."

"Dad."

"Yes, Sam."

"When is that man going to leave us alone?"

"Are you worried about him?"

"Yes. I don't like him," said the boy. "I'm glad Skoll bit him."

"Me too. I think we'll just leave the man behind."

"*Wheah* will we go?"

"Well, I'm not sure. Someplace in the Hill Country."

"Galveston doesn't have hills," said Sam.

"No, it's flat."

"It's got lots of *watah*."

"The Hill Country's got lakes," Gordo said. "Big lakes. Lakes that are twice as long as the island."

"Lakes that *awa* as big as the ocean?"

"Not that big, Sam. But big enough for us to spend a lot of time exploring them."

"I'd *wather* stay here. When can we go home?"

"Remember, Sam? We're not going back to Pilot House. We're going to find a new home."

"Not me."

Eighteen

"Lino, there's something I've been curious about," said Gordo.

"Yeah?" Lino was seated at Pier 22, a fish house on an old shrimp dock in the harbor, wearing a tan poplin suit, blue shirt, and red foulard tie.

In spite of the dazzling springlike weather, he had insisted they eat indoors.

"Needless to say, you don't dress like a cop. In fact, you're better dressed than most of the lawyers hanging out at the courthouse."

"Really?"

"Don't give me this 'really' bullshit," Gordo said. "You know what I'm talking about."

Lino shot him a knowing look, his heavy eyebrows drawn low, bisected by a wrinkle of skin. His poker face.

"Is there something I don't understand?" Gordo asked.

"You know Amado's Fine Tailors over on Market Street?" asked Lino. "Been there forever."

"Sure."

"Amado's my great-uncle. And my godfather. He made my first communion suit and every suit I've worn since."

"Amado Ruiz?"

"That's him."

"Of course."

Suddenly, Gordo got it. How could he have missed it? Lino didn't act like a cop because he didn't intend to stay one.

"You're in training," Gordo said.

"Huh?"

"You've got your eye on something."

"What are you—"

"I can probably figure this part out," Gordo said. "Let's see, Steve Purdy is thinking about running for the state senate, right?"

"You'd have to ask him. I wouldn't know."

"Yeah, right. What did you say you majored in? Political science? You're going to run for his seat in the legislature."

Lino gave him an incredulous look.

"You need Pat Hayes. You need him because nobody in this county knows or gives a damn about Lino Gabilondo. You need those precincts on the mainland. How could I have been so stupid?"

And for once, Gordo could see that Lino did not know what to do. If he wasn't candid now it would only look worse later.

"All this business about returning some ancient favor was just a way for you to get to the Colonel."

"No . . . my uncle Hector," Lino said haltingly, "he wants to help . . . because of what Pat Hayes did for the family."

"You need votes on the mainland. You need the labor boxes."

Lino looked pained. His careful exterior suddenly collapsed.

"Look, I don't care," Gordo said. "You'd probably do a

good job. I really don't care. In fact, I'll take you over there to Pat's office to talk to him about it. It's not a big deal. I knew you weren't just a cop. I should have figured this out a long time ago."

"So we can meet with your father-in-law?" Lino asked. Gordo was impressed at how quickly he recovered his poise.

"As long as you're not a crook, it's okay. Somebody's got to be in government. Pat never considers ambition something to be ashamed of. He likes to help people. It's what he does. He won't endorse anybody until the filing deadline—when he knows all the horses in the race. But he'll be generous with his advice. And it's better to get to his office early in the game, so it doesn't look like an afterthought."

"What about you?"

Yes, thought Gordo, this man could be a politician. He craves approval.

"Me?" he said. "I'm getting out of here. And you don't want the endorsement of anybody who's dodging bullets."

Through the window, he watched a couple on the sun-drenched deck of the restaurant. In her late thirties, the woman had dark lustrous hair and an olive complexion. Good cheekbones. She was beautiful. There was a kind of youthfulness in the man's face, the kind of face that would have been described as cute in his youth. But the features were now softened by small pads of flesh behind his chin and beneath his eyes. Receding hairline and sad eyes. Gorgeous day. Gorgeous wife. Gordo studied them carefully.

Beautiful women need husbands too.

His friend Paul, who had married many times, had made that observation years ago. Paul knew firsthand, Gordo presumed, although they had met after most of his marriages had run aground.

Beautiful women need husbands too. He had repeated it to himself more than once. He knew the man's problem. The sad-faced man on the deck. Odd how it came to him, how he could understand a thing so completely that it had to be true. This perfectly presentable fellow with the expanding brow possessed the quiet sadness of a man married to a beautiful woman. The constant awareness that his wife was the target of admiration by other men. The secret suspicion that some day he might wake up to find his good fortune swept away. And the man could never share his burden with anyone.

"You put Plexiglas in your front door," Lino said.

"I told Grover and Tiny. So what?"

"Why did you do that?"

"Because Jake put his handlebar through the window," explained Gordo. "The alley behind our house is just oyster shell. You get cut up when you fall on it—you know that. So the boys ride their bikes on the sidewalk in front of the house. The side gate's always padlocked. Easier just to bring their bikes through the front door."

"Did you know that Plexiglas is three times stronger than glass?"

"What are you up to?" asked Gordo.

"That stuff cut the muzzle velocity of the bullet that hit you by at least half."

"You've been doing some homework?"

"My cousin sells industrial plastic."

"So the Plexiglas might have saved my life?"

"That's what I'm saying."

"Jesus," said Gordo.

A quarter inch of plastic. Scrawny Pat Hayes high above the English Channel. Jake and Sam at the Smithsonian exploring *Flak Bait.* Oyster shells in the alley and a handlebar punched through glass. The gun blast ringing in his ears. One moment linked to another by a gossamer thread.

Gordo took a sip of water.

"God bless the inventor of Plexiglas."

"Whatever," said Lino. "Does the name Juventino Campos mean anything to you?"

"No. I think Jerry Peyton asked me the same thing. Who is he?"

"What about Jason Morrow?"

"No. Why?"

"They share a house, at least some of the time. This Juventino is a suspect. Another shooting. Twenty-five caliber. They live about six blocks from you."

"Where?"

"You need to stay clear of these guys."

"Where's the house?"

"Near Tremont and Avenue Q."

"What happened in the other shooting?"

"Guy ended up shot in the head. Looks as if the victim and the suspect dated the same woman."

"Are these the crackheads?"

"You could say that."

"One of these guys is connected to Tom?" asked Gordo.

"Works for him."

"Which one?"

"Right now you need to let us do our job," said Lino. "I don't want you saying anything to your friend or anybody else. We don't have enough information, and you don't want to screw things up for us by spooking somebody."

"Tom's had lots of people work for him over the years," said Gordo.

"I never said he was involved."

Nineteen

Gordo intended to take the family to Austin for the weekend. But on Wednesday, he got a call from the real estate agent informing him that an offer on Pilot House would be forthcoming.

"The buyers have a few questions about the house," said Troy, the agent. "Can you be available this weekend?"

"I was planning on being out of town."

"They're serious prospects. They just haven't owned a hundred-year-old house before and they need a bit of hand-holding. I think we can get a good contract out of this."

"They know what happened? I don't really want to talk to them about the shooting."

"You won't have to."

Gordo sent Ana on to Austin, to check out the real estate market and the schools. It would be good for her to have a weekend off. Off the island. Away from Corky. She would stay with Kate, one of her law school classmates whom she hadn't seen in a while. Kate had children in grade school, and she could tell Ana which neighborhoods had good schools. Ana's mother and the Colonel would help take care of the boys.

"Have fun," Gordo told her as he helped her load her car. "Music, margaritas, Sixth Street. You'll have a great time."

"It's not like we're going bar hopping. Kate's got kids. Remember?"

"Watch out for termites."

"Watch out for homicidal maniacs," she said. But he could sense that she was almost giddy with the prospect of getting away.

"I love you," she said.

They kissed. She hugged him. He kissed the hollow behind her collarbone and drank in her smell.

• • •

Gordo wasn't sure why he was back at Pilot House Saturday morning. The prospective buyers, a couple from Houston, would be there at ten. Surely the realtor could have handled the appointment.

"Are they moving to Galveston?" Gordo asked his agent.

"I think they're toying with the idea," Troy said. "They want to get an old house here for weekends. See if they like it. Apparently the husband could telecommute. He's in computers or something."

Gordo looked the place over with a buyer's critical eye. He wished he'd replaced the flooring on the side balcony that had buckled with age, something he'd planned to do for years. Why didn't they ever change that light fixture in the staircase? He could remember resolving to do that the first week they were here. But there was so much improvement, too. Old carpet removed, pine floors refinished. Plaster ceiling medallions restored. The elaborate balcony railing faithfully rebuilt, right down to the decorative grooves on the edges of the fretwork. He could still remember that the grooves cost $200 extra.

He hoped they would be nice people.

Gordo opened a few windows to air out the closed house. In doing so, he saw that the live oak in the backyard was putting on its pale green spring leaves. The Colonel had carried that tree through the front door on his birthday years earlier. Now twenty feet tall, the oak had come into their lives about the same time Jake was born. It was just starting to assume its role as a real shade tree.

When the doorbell rang, he snapped back into the present. Two shadows through the lace curtain.

"Troy, they're here," he called out.

A pleasant middle-aged couple with grown children, the Andersons almost seemed too mild-mannered for such an old and demanding house. Were they ready to combat dry rot, termites, and peeling paint? Did they want a Victorian house badly enough to put up with the inherent friction of living in the historic district? But Gordo warmed to them when he heard their questions.

"Do you know when the house was built and who built it?" asked the wife.

"Do you have any old photos of the house?" she inquired.

"Are there shutters for all the windows and doors?" the husband wanted to know. "Are they cypress?"

"Do you know if the gingerbread is original?"

"Have you ever sanded the siding down to bare wood?"

Good questions. These weren't people acting on impulse. These were the kind of people who subscribed to *Old House Journal.* But what did he care? He just wanted a fair price for the place. Then he realized that he wanted more. He wanted people who would be good owners—good stewards for his cypress palace of memories. People who would care for Pilot House.

They worked their way through questions about the condition of the furnace and the roof and the chimney. They wanted to know about Hurricane Alicia. Gordo understood why they had asked him to come. They were getting much more information than their realtor could ever provide. And clearly, they were serious prospects. If he had to get rid of Pilot House, he wanted to sell it to people like the Andersons.

• • •

That evening, Gordo met Lars in the lobby of the San Luis, the Colonel's condo. Looking even more weathered than usual, Lars was bearing fresh red snapper from Aransas Pass.

Gordo gave the old Norwegian a hug.

"You smell like fish!"

"You should smell the Jeep. How are you?"

"Still in one piece."

"I'm sorry about that business at the beach. I wish I'd been there."

"Skoll was there. He was enough."

"My Norse wolf," Lars said affectionately. "How is he?"

"He's being pampered over at Tom's. He got a gash in his lip. I'm pretty sure the son of a bitch hit him with the butt of his pistol. The vet says he'll be fine. Seems to be getting along with Siegfried and crew."

Lars laughed. "Those Dobermans give him any trouble and he'll make a snack out of them."

Upstairs at the Colonel's, Gordo opened a good Riesling and prepared the fish. Pat Hayes and Lars, who enjoyed each other's company, talked in the next room. Ana's mother, Sonja, read to the boys. Checking in on them in the living room, Gordo was struck by Sonja's wide cheekbones and full brow. There, beneath the white hair and creased skin, was the shape of Ana's face. The sight of her reading to the boys made him happy. High above the beach in Pat's impregnable tower, they were safe. Things were going to get better.

Spirits ran high at the dinner table. Lars told fishing tales and stories about his eccentric friends living on the water at Aransas. Gordo made a toast.

"To Skoll, the wolf who chases the sun," he said, citing the Norse mythology. "And to his owner. Friend, wanderer, and piscator."

"*Piscatuh*?" Sam said.

"Sounds like something you do in the bathroom," said Jake.

"A fisherman. Lars—who caught our dinner."

"I don't like fish," said Sam.

"To candor," Lars added.

Two bottles of wine later, when the adults were sitting in the family room feeling sated and lethargic, Ana's brother and a friend came in.

The Colonel snapped out of his relaxed state and began to dote on his son in the ineffective way Gordo had observed for years.

"Allen, come on in. Shake ole Lars's hand here. You remember Lars from Minnesota. Introduce me to your friend."

Allen extended a droopy hand in a way that made it clear he neither remembered nor cared who Lars was. Allen's skin was the sallow yellow of dried peaches left too long in the pantry. His friend had stringy hair, sunken cheeks, and glazed eyes.

"Daddy, I need to talk to you."

"Sure. Come on into the study."

Whatever Allen needed it wasn't talk.

Allen's presence, with its potential for ugly conflict, set everyone's teeth on edge. Gordo knew that the Colonel, in an effort to regain the equilibrium of the evening, would give Allen whatever he wanted. Of course, it had to be money.

When Allen left, he seemed to take the group's bonhomie with him. Lars pleaded exhaustion from his long drive and his need to reclaim Skoll. He was insistent that he would stay on at the beach house, which was under lease for the rest of the month.

"You're sure you want to stay there?" Gordo said. "That guy knows the house."

"He's not interested in me," replied Lars. "Besides, I don't think he's too eager to get reacquainted with the wolf."

Before Lars got away, the phone rang.

"Gordon, it's for you," said the Colonel.

Gordo grabbed the kitchen phone.

"Really?" he said. "Really!"

Pat and Lars stepped closer.

"Wow. I guess that forces the issue."

"What is it?" asked the Colonel after Gordo left the phone.

"We've got an offer on the house. Full asking price. Cash."

"That's great," Lars said. "Right?"

"I suppose," Gordo said without enthusiasm. It was beginning to sink in.

"Do you think the buyer is solid?" asked the Colonel, who didn't seem to welcome the news.

"It's a second home. I don't think there's any question about financing."

"What did you mean about 'forcing the issue?'" asked the Colonel.

"The issue of whether or not we really want to leave," said Gordo. "Oh, and one other thing. They want us out in fifteen days."

• • •

Gordo tried to reach Ana, to tell her about the house. But Kate's husband told him it was "girls night out."

"I'm home with the kiddies. I bet the women will be late."

The next morning, Gordo took the boys to St. Stephen's. They stopped by Pilot House on their way to church to pick up the contract on the house.

"What's a *contwact*?" asked Sam.

"A promise to sell our house," said Gordo.

"Can't we take it with us?"

"The house?"

"Houses move," said Sam. "I've seen it on TV."

"Pilot House belongs here, Sam."

"But it's *owah* house."

"Your mother's up in Austin looking for a new house for us."

Gordo picked up a manila envelope on the floor beneath the mail slot. Beneath it was a plain white envelope, which he ignored.

He took out the contract. There it was. The full price. One more sign that it was time to go. Standing there, with the boys in their Sunday outfits, he made peace with the move. Time to go.

Jake picked up the white envelope.

"What's this?" he asked.

The front of the envelope was blank.

"Probably something else from the realtor. Open it up."

Jake tore open the envelope and discovered a get-well card illustrated with a dopey cartoon character whose arm was in a sling. He handed it to Gordo.

Just relax,
Don't get stressed,
Hope that soon,
You'll feel your best.

Beneath the printed message was a child-like scrawl in blue ballpoint:

"See you soon!"

"Why are there two bullets in *heah*?" asked Sam, holding the white envelope.

"Let me see," Gordo said. He was seething, his hands shaking. But he tried to control his anger in front of the boys.

His seven-year-old son dropped a pair of shiny .25 caliber bullets into his hand.

Twenty

Ana called from Austin on Sunday.

"Did you close down the bars last night?" Gordo asked.

"We tried, but we've just become too domesticated," she said. "We made it back out here by one."

"Out here?" he asked.

"By the lake. That's where Kate lives now."

"Which lake?"

"Lake Travis."

"Way out there?"

"It's not way out there any more."

"They moved the lake?"

"They moved the town."

Gordo and Ana had spent time around the area during their college years. They had hiked in the hills and gone swimming in Lake Travis. Back then it had seemed beautiful, pristine, and remote. Impossibly remote for anyone who worked in town.

But, as Ana explained, better roads and urban sprawl had

fixed that. The city had drifted west and now Lake Travis was considered well within commuting distance.

"We've got an offer on Pilot House," he said grimly.

"Good."

"You're taking this well."

"I want to make an offer on another house."

"What? Already? What are you trying to do, buy the bartender's house?"

"We went to Bee Cave Elementary on Friday," said Ana. "Kate showed me the school and introduced me to the principal. They actually have public schools that work here."

"Bee Cave?" said Gordo.

"Near Bee Creek."

"Bee Creek?"

"It's beautiful here. Anyway, I met one of the second-grade teachers and she told me about a house near where she lived. You need to come see it."

"When?"

"Tomorrow," she said.

"I've got—"

"I'll pick you up at the airport. Mom will get the boys to school."

"Do you think you might be rushing into this deal a little too fast?"

"Are we getting lots of money for Pilot House?"

"Speaking of Pilot House," said Gordo, "There's more news." Then he told her about the get-well card they'd found and the bullets inside.

"That son-of-a-bitch!"

He let Ana vent.

"Goddammit!" she shouted. "Tell my mother to keep the boys home from school tomorrow. We've got to get the hell out of there."

• • •

Gordo called Jerry Peyton about what had happened at Batavia Boulevard. He would have preferred to deal with Lino, but he was stuck with this new detective, who had replaced the inept Grover Hampton and Tiny Martelli.

Peyton insisted on coming to collect the evidence that afternoon.

"I thought you were off on Sunday," said Gordo, letting Peyton into the condo.

"Is Colonel Hayes here?"

"He took my sons out for ice cream."

Colonel Hayes. He hadn't heard that before. Peyton must think Pat Hayes really is a colonel. Once again, Gordo was impressed by how little the cops knew about people in the community. He'd heard that much of the police force now lived off the island in more rural parts of the county where housing was cheaper.

"I wanted to pick up the evidence before it was compromised," said Peyton.

"Unfortunately, Jake and Sam and I all handled the card, so I'm afraid it's already pretty compromised. We didn't know what it was."

"We still may be able to lift a print. You and your sons will have to come in and get fingerprinted."

"The boys will get a kick out of that."

"You know Norm Zweiger?" asked Peyton.

Gordo pictured Zweiger in uniform at the police station. The bad cop. He remembered Zweiger's stepdaughter and her testimony before the grand jury.

"I don't know him. I know of him."

"How?"

"Served on the grand jury. The one that indicted him a couple of years ago."

"That's just great," said Peyton.

"Norm Zweiger was indicted for sexual assault," said Gordo. "I don't see what he's got to do with any of this?"

"Maybe nothing. Juventino Campos—do you know him?"

"Juventino? You asked me that before, didn't you? One of the crackheads? What kind of a name—"

"I've never heard of it either," said Peyton. "So anyway, we're pretty sure Zweiger has something to do with this Juventino. Don't you wish your mother'd named you Juventino?"

Gordo could tell that the detective liked to repeat the name, taking pleasure in ridiculing it—no doubt a name originating from some parched Mexican village in the middle of nowhere.

"Are any of these crackheads tall and skinny?" asked Gordo.

"Seems like all crackheads are skinny," said Peyton. "We have the description you gave us. We're looking."

"And you think that Zweiger could be mixed up in this?"

"Let's just say," said the detective, "that Zweiger is not what you'd call the poster boy of law enforcement."

• • •

In the car driving from the airport, Ana explained that the real estate market in Austin was beginning to heat up. After the crash that accompanied the fall of oil prices, the market had endured several years of doldrums when thousands of listed homes went unsold. While property in the desirable neighborhoods within Austin was getting outrageously expensive, houses as far outside the city as Bee Creek were still reasonable.

"The teacher at the school described it as one of the older homes in the neighborhood," said Ana. "Then I found out it was built seven years ago."

"Seven years old and it's ready for a historical marker," he said.

Ana explained that the floor plan wasn't ideal, and the décor included far too much floral wallpaper, but the house had "good bones." Lots of porches like Pilot House. There was a bedroom for each boy with a shared bath. And a room that could be converted to a study.

"And a big stone fireplace," she said.

"Do you have room for a garden?" he asked.

"That'll be a challenge," she said. "It's pretty rocky and most of the backyard is below a big cliff. What there is above the cliff is pretty shaded. But we can haul in topsoil. I could put in beds here and there. It looks dry. We might need to learn about native plants."

"You sound like you've given it a lot of thought," he said.

"It's really nice. It's not perfect, but I don't know if we can do much better within our price range."

Gordo was trying to approach the house with a skeptical eye. The place was a long drive from Austin. Back in the 1970s, this place would have been considered off the edge of the map. And in fact, a glance at the Austin city map he found on the floor of the car revealed that Bee Creek was indeed off the map. The hamlet was too far out and, Ana explained, the subdivision was too new to be on any but the most current county maps. As they traveled west of the city, he was impressed by the long vistas and dramatic topography. Years of living fifteen feet above sea level had conditioned him to flat blue horizons interrupted by nothing more than seabirds and ships.

"It really is beautiful here," he said.

"The boys could roam through the woods," she said. "Ride their bikes in the street and walk to their friends' houses."

All taboo in Galveston.

On first glance, there was something about the neighborhood that put him off. The upstanding pose of the houses and the enforced neatness of the streets, driveways, and front yards. The realtor had proudly informed Ana that it was illegal to put your trash out the night before garbage day.

What a transgression! But he was used to the East End of

the island and its inner city chaos, where people had been known to leave a washing machine on the porch of a shotgun cottage for years at a time.

The sun emerged, and the day grew warm. Climbing out of the car to meet the realtor, Gordo immediately noticed the lack of moisture in the air and the aromatic scent of cedar. A faint memory. The cedar-lined hall closet at his parents' home on the bayou and the smell of winter coats coming out of storage on the first cold day of autumn. How long had it been? Thirty years?

From the street, he could see that the house did have character. The solid white stone façade, the cedar shingle roof, and double-gallery porches gave it an honest face. There was something familiar about it. Then it occurred to him—here was Pilot House in stone. Pilot House without the gingerbread. Pilot House's plain, raw-boned cousin.

Once inside, they found abundant windows that bathed the rooms in natural light. He liked the wide-plank pine floors and stone fireplace. Upstairs, the bath off the master bedroom seemed enormous compared to the minuscule Victorian bathroom they had all shared for years.

But it was the backyard that charmed him completely. A deep ravine cut through the land behind the house, and from the cliff he could hear the creek flowing below.

After the real estate agent left, Ana and Gordo plunged down a rocky trail and savored the stillness of the ravine. Beneath the canopy of trees, they looked up toward the house a hundred feet above them.

"I can't see the house, can you?" he asked.

"Nope. Let's check out the creek," she replied eagerly.

They removed their shoes, cuffed their pants, and waded in the cold creek water.

A herd of deer, ignoring them, raced headlong through the hollow just above the creek. Gordo and Ana stood in the flowing water shivering from the cold and giggling from the beauty and elegance of the passing deer.

"This water!" she shouted. "I'm afraid I'm going to pee in my pants."

"In another minute I'm not going to be able to feel my feet," he said.

"Can you believe this place?" said Ana. "Can you imagine having such a place right outside your back door?"

"It beats the alley behind Pilot House."

They sat on boulders and let their feet air-dry. Like a shoe salesman, Gordo pulled on Ana's socks and then her shoes. Climbing the ledge above the creek bed, he found an enormous feather.

"We'd have wild turkeys for neighbors," he said.

"They're probably pretty good neighbors."

"Wouldn't the boys love this?"

"These woods go on for miles," she said.

Gordo approached her from behind and put his arms around her. He could feel the knobs of her hipbone on either side of the gentle roundness of her stomach. She had lost weight, growing even thinner under the stress of these past weeks. Better not to mention it.

"I guess you found us a new home," he said, nuzzling her neck.

Ana kissed him. The purity of the air and the silence of the woods seemed to consecrate their embrace. He pulled her close.

"The next chapter," he whispered.

"I feel so incredibly free."

He didn't have to say it. She didn't need to hear it. They both experienced the stark contrast between these innocent, sun-dappled woods—all rock and water and trees—and the dark, complex path their lives had taken on the island. *Malhado.*

Crossing the hollow, they passed a large rock, cleanly split down the center like an enormous cloven hoof. He showed Ana, and leaned her against its soft, feminine curves. He kissed her again. The woods were still and private.

"It's sexy down here," he said.

Ana smiled and turned away from him. She bent toward the rock, bracing her palms on either side of the fissure, and gave her ass a provocative shake.

Gordo reached around her, unfastened her jeans, and pulled them and her panties down to midthigh. His hand wandered across her bare skin. Then he entered her, probing gently as she grew wet. Within moments, as he had done countless times before, he felt the inaudible *thunk* of slipping inside to the hilt, his scrotum pressed against her cleft.

"I love to be inside you," he whispered.

At least that's how it registered in his mind. *Thunk.* The feeling of going as far as he could go, sheathed in her interior folds. Sometimes he thought that nothing more complicated than that sublime *thunk* could keep two people together. Could keep *them* together.

All gentleness gone, they hammered against each other like rutting deer, snorting and rattling hardscrabble beneath their feet. He looked down at the flexing muscles of her ass—pale flesh lightly dusted with goosebumps. As Gordo drove into her, a low-pitched noise, almost a growl, escaped from his throat. Ana's flanks rose. She was up on her toes now.

Bowed before the cleft in the great rock and Ana's own, Gordo felt like a celebrant at a Mesozoic altar of rear entry.

Her gasp set him off, as it often did. They broke their grip slightly, but he was still inside.

"Jesus," he said. "I like this place."

Ana, wordless, inhaled.

Dry air poured over their exposed wetness. Ana reached for the waistband of her jeans, and with a shimmy, her nakedness was gone.

He was still zipping up when she took his hand and bolted toward the cliff. "Come on. Let's go find that realtor!"

• • •

By the next morning, back on the island, his euphoria was gone.

"Tell me about Norman Zweiger," said Gordo. "Jerry Peyton mentioned him. Wanted to know if we knew each other. If Zweiger's mixed up somehow, that changes everything."

Gordo was getting testy. He knew none of this was Lino's fault, but Lino represented the cops, and Lino was the only person he trusted enough to bitch at.

"If he's got some link to the shooter," said Gordo, "then every time I talk to the police I'm putting my family at risk. It also seems like there are three investigations. Jerry Peyton's investigation of the investigation that Grover Hampton and Tiny Martelli blew off, and your investigation of the job Peyton's doing"

"No," Lino said calmly. "One investigation. Peyton's continuing what Hampton and Tiny started. And now I've been asked to help him."

"How did that happen?"

"I talked to my boss," said Lino. "Pointed out a few things."

"Do you realize that if I get shot again, you're not going to get elected dog-catcher?"

"You're not getting shot again because you're not going to be here. You need to get off the island."

"You mean I need to get out of your jurisdiction. You don't want me shot on your watch."

"Just get out."

They had met at Adoue Park in the East End. Children were playing on the swings. Large oak trees shaded the perimeter of the park, which otherwise had a worn, ill-kept look.

There were bald patches in the grass and rust splotches on the slide. Gordo looked at the generations of thick, encrusted paint on the playground equipment and thought of lead poisoning.

"I'm just wrapping up loose ends. We're moving as fast as we can. Can't the police protect and serve for just a little while longer?"

"Fuck the loose ends. You can let somebody else do it."

"Why are you suddenly interested in getting us out of here? You know something you're not telling me."

Lino polished off the dregs in the paper coffee cup he was carrying. He wadded it in his fist and tossed it in a barrel overflowing with trash.

"I don't trust Zweiger. Nobody does," Lino said.

"Why don't you make this easy and just tell me what you know?" Gordo was growing more concerned.

"It's complicated."

"So is my life."

"These crackheads," Lino explained. "We're looking at one of them for popping a guy at the Dunes Motel on the beach. I told you a little about them. Twenty-five-caliber pistol. Girlfriend of the victim's hanging around with the crackhead now. Maybe there's a connection. One of the crackhead's roommates is Campos. Campos may know Zweiger. There're several other fuck-ups who float in and out of the place. One of our guys is watching the house and here comes Zweiger bopping down the front stairs like he owns the place. You follow?"

"I'm trying." Gordo picked at the flaking paint on the leg of the swing set like it was a scab.

"That's why you need to get out of here. Usually, I see two connections, I get real suspicious. Three, and I'm starting to rule out coincidence. Twenty-five-caliber gun—sound familiar?"

"I got that part."

"Twenty-five-caliber gun. Dope. Cop. Oh, and one other thing. Your friend, Tom? Your neighbor?"

"Yeah?"

"He's got that employee who lives at that same house—at least part of the time."

"Tom?"

Lino paused.

"Look, the East End is so small, some of these connections may really be coincidence. Most people here are only twice removed from a major asshole. But I'll be honest. I don't like this loop. The crackhead. Zweiger. Your friend. Your friend's employee. And a goddamn .25-caliber pistol that keeps turning up," said Lino. "Too many people too close for comfort. I don't think we can control the information. That's nothing new around here. But the stakes are higher for you. Think about that phone call at the beach."

"Can't you compare the bullets?" asked Gordo. "See if the same gun is involved? The gun from the motel shooting?"

"We're working on it. The DPS lab is in Austin. It's going to take some time. Some big backlog."

Gordo imagined a lab full of bullets, each one having torn through some person whose life had changed forever—or ended—as a result. So many stories. Most worse than his. It was hard for him, knowing that he was being hunted, not to feel at the center of a drama unfolding around him. A drama that people should care about. But he was just one more shooting victim among many. Nothing special at all. Gordo didn't want to contribute any more evidence to the crime lab. He didn't want to feel the heavy punch ever again.

Lino was right. Fuck the loose ends.

• • •

"Ana, it's really time to go," said Gordo. "Time to get the kids away from here."

"What happened?" She had just driven in from Austin.

"Lino thinks we need to leave. They have some suspects, a

house full of crackheads. Zweiger has some connection to them."

"The cop?"

"Right. And one of the guys in the house works for Tom."

"That might explain how the guy keeps finding us."

"It makes it a lot easier if there's a cop giving out information."

"But why?"

"Lino hasn't figured that out yet. He just doesn't like the way the pieces are falling into place."

"I hate this town," she said. "Those fucking cops. And why is there a goddamn crack house six blocks from our home? This wouldn't happen in most neighborhoods. Sometimes I think there's something evil about this place."

Malhado.

He was startled by the harshness of her words. She was talking about home. The place where she had grown up, where Jake and Sam were born.

Gordo was swept up in their need to get off the island. He didn't have to linger over their memories. Nevertheless, he had thought he would feel worse about reaching this decision.

"Maybe self-preservation is preventing me from getting sentimental about leaving," he said.

"I'm not sentimental," Ana said. "I just feel relief. I wish it was as easy to get out of the law firm as it was to sell the house. When can we leave?"

"Lars can help us clear out the beach house," he replied. "That won't take long. We'll have to withdraw the kids from school. I just don't know where we'll go. Do you think we can move up the closing on the Bee Creek house?"

"The sellers are eager to wrap it up," she said. "It's just a matter of the mortgage company pulling things together. Why don't we call the owners and find out if they'd rent the house to us until the closing?"

"I married a smart woman," he said. "We could camp out there until the furniture arrives. We should take sleeping bags. The big job is going to be moving our stuff from Pilot House."

"How will we do that?"

"I'll schedule a moving company as soon as possible. I could drive back for moving day. We won't have time to sift through our things."

"I'll hand off my active files tomorrow," she said.

All her resistance was gone. She was ready to go.

"I can't begin to finish everything at the office," she said. "But I can drive down later and stay here with my parents."

Ana gazed out at the beach.

"We're doing the right thing, Ana."

"We should have done this right after the shooting."

Galveston was her home. Her town. He had come to love it. More so than most natives, who had experienced a lifetime of its failings. Like a convert more devoted to the church than a person born into it.

"Sam's not going to like this," he said.

Ana winced at the thought.

We can go. But we have to take the Pilot House.

"We'll just have to make it an adventure for him," he added.

"What do you make of this business about Tom?"

"Tom would never do anything that would endanger us," he said. "But he could be passing information about us inadvertently. His employee might ask how we're doing. Tom might tell him. Why wouldn't he?"

"Do you think you should talk to Tom?" she asked.

"Lino thought that might backfire. That Tom might start asking the guy questions and spook him. I think I won't tell Tom any more than I need to right now. He'd be upset if he thought he'd put us at risk. Besides, it's time to leave the police work to Lino and concentrate on getting out."

Twenty-One

Gordo met a guy from the moving company the next afternoon. His name was Oscar Nuñez. Already, Pilot House seemed abandoned and forlorn.

"Where are we taking this stuff?" the man asked.

"Near Austin."

"Get transferred?"

"In a way."

The moving agent didn't pursue it. He just set about estimating the size of the load.

"You packing or you want us to do it?"

"You'll have to do it."

Oscar Nuñez was short, but he looked powerful. He nodded. "I can schedule the move for the eighteenth. The packers will have to come the day before."

"If I can't get back, I'll arrange to have someone here."

"I see from the sign the house sold already. Great old place. Kind of a tough neighborhood though."

"I know what you mean," Gordo replied.

"A lot cheaper if you pack yourself," said the man, opening the kitchen cabinets. "Makes no difference to me, of course."

Gordo imagined how difficult it would be to unpack, not knowing where any single item was inside the mountain of boxes.

"No time," he said. "We've got to hit the road."

"I came here twenty-two years ago to be with a woman," said Oscar. "Expected to stay a couple months. Woman's long gone. I'm still here."

"The mainland is only about a mile away," Gordo said. "But sometimes it seems like it's on the other side of the ocean."

"Amen."

Oscar, carrying a clipboard, surveyed each room. In his mind, the man counted the boxes it would take to move them, thirteen years of their lives now catalogued in terms of packing crates.

Cabeza de Vaca hadn't intended to stay long either. The explorer, whose surname was Alvar Núñez Cabeza de Vaca, arrived suddenly. Gordo knew de Vaca's account.

> *Near land a great wave took us and cast the boat out of the water as far as a horseshoe can be tossed. The boat ran aground with such force that it revived the men on it who were almost dead. When they saw they were near land they pushed themselves overboard and crawled on their hands and knees. When we got to the beach, we lit a fire by some rocks and toasted some of the corn we had and found rainwater. With the warmth of the fire, the men began to regain some of their strength. Little did we know that it would take six years to accomplish our escape from this place, which we would come to know as Malhado, the isle of misfortune.*

Gordo, who couldn't do much more than watch Oscar Nuñez, mused about their new life, their life away from *Malhado.* The house in Bee Creek was so much like what he and Ana had envisioned that it was spooky. A few years earlier, before the boys' school day regimen so dominated their mornings, he and Ana used to get out of bed early and go downstairs to meditate, do yoga, or to listen to some self-improvement tape that she'd ordered, no doubt from *Yoga Journal*, *New Age* magazine, or perhaps *Vegetarian Times.*

Gordo extracted a zafu—the firm, round meditation pillow designed to keep one's butt the optimal distance from the ground—from its place hidden between the sofa and the bookcase. Ana kept two squirreled away there, "his" and "her" zafus for the family on the go. He didn't always approach the predawn exercises with enthusiasm, but he knew there was value in this quiet time they shared together. It was useful to step away from the chaos of life from time to time. To reconcile where they were trying to go and what they were trying to achieve with their daily struggles. To see if the struggle made sense. Even if there were times when he felt like an arthritic contortionist trying to duplicate some tortuous yoga posture.

One series of these morning sessions was devoted to "creative visualizations." It was his least favorite and, seemingly, one of the least productive. But during those sessions, the mellifluous voice on the recording had instructed them to envision a place where they wanted to be. Any place, although it seemed to presume that you wanted to be someplace else. He had envisioned a stone house on a cliff above a ravine.

That was the eerie part.

A faint memory of a quote.

Lord, spare us from what we most desire.

• • •

The day they left, Gordo expected it to hurt more.

Pilot House. His friends. Their life of thirteen years. But the moment the car hit the causeway, with the ground falling away so rapidly that it made him feel airborne, he was too distracted to be sentimental. Distracted by keeping an eye on *Shark Bite*, the boat he was towing. On Ana's car ahead. On Lars's Jeep behind him. Ana had Sam and Henry the gerbil in her car. Gordo had Jake, who was asking an incessant stream of questions about life at the end of the day's drive. And Lars was towing a U-Haul trailer containing, among other things, Peter, the rabbit, inside his hutch. The whole shaky caravan was shooting over the causeway at fifty-five miles an hour, and Gordo just couldn't muster any feelings beyond relief and his immediate concern for a safe trip.

A squall from the Gulf was moving ashore. The rain started pelting the windshield on the downward slope of the causeway. He hoped none of them had to stop suddenly. He had stuffed the trailer tightly, including his heavy table saw and some power tools for work he would do at the new house.

"What's this place like?" asked Jake.

"It's nice. The house is on a cliff overlooking a ravine. There are woods below the cliff and there's a creek. You're going to like it. You just have to watch out for the deer."

"Why?"

"There are so many they might step on your toes as they go by."

"Nooo!" Jake insisted. "Not really."

"You'll see."

"What's the school like?"

"Beautiful. It's on a hill all by itself. You can see for miles. And right next door is a ranch."

"A ranch? What for?"

"Raising cattle."

"Why do they need cattle at school?"

"The ranch was there first, Jake."

"Really? Are there cowboys?"

"Well, I suppose there's a rancher who takes care of the cows."

"Cool!"

Gordo kept checking the rearview mirror. As they swooped down the far side of the causeway, the wind was intense. If it was going to happen at all, this was a likely place for the mast or some of the boat gear to come loose.

"And your bedroom looks out over the cliff."

"Sam really doesn't want to leave," said Jake. "He told me that if we didn't like the new place we could come back and get Pilot House back. Is that true?"

"We can always come back, Jake. But we sold the house. You know that. Your little brother is going to be fine. It's okay for him to be upset. He's leaving his home. Sam's always been strong-willed. He needs to see Bee Creek for himself. To make up his own mind."

"Tell me about the bees."

• • •

It took Cabeza de Vaca six years to get off the island. Gordo and Ana had been here thirteen. They moved to Galveston with an aging beagle and hardly enough belongings to furnish the second floor of Pilot House. For the first couple of years the only furniture on the first floor was a table and chairs in the kitchen. The rest of the rooms were bare. For entertaining, they took guests upstairs.

Today, they had two boys, a rabbit, a gerbil, two cars, a U-Haul trailer, a boat trailer, and Lars's Jeep packed tight. The Carrots of Wrath. And Pilot House was still full of their furniture, clothing, toys, bicycles, cookware, and the rest of their household. He couldn't believe how much they'd accumulated during those years. And, as he checked the rearview mirror, he noticed that his few gray hairs seemed to be increasing on a daily basis. Getting shot—that would do it as well as anything.

At the town of Derringer, they all stopped at a small bakery.

The tiny hamlet owed its existence to the fact that Highway 71 cut through the handful of buildings that comprised Main Street. *Shark Bite*'s sail had unfurled from the mast a bit and was beginning to billow. Ana took the boys inside. They remembered the bakery from previous trips and were eager to get kolaches. Lars took a cup of coffee to Gordo, who was adjusting the rigging on the boat. The sky was clearing, and the terrain was changing as they headed west. Derringer was on the edge of blackland farm country. In another forty miles, the soil would turn red as they passed through a pine belt, before they encountered outcroppings of limestone.

Sipping the coffee, Gordo said, "Glad to leave the squalls behind."

"We're starting to see bluebonnets," replied Lars. He felt a special affinity for bluebonnets, a botanical cousin to the lupine that grew along Minnesota's north shore of Lake Superior.

"I feel better already. I feel like I'm leaving a whole lot of things behind."

"This is as good a time as any, I guess," said Lars, "to tell you that I found something at the beach house this morning."

Gordo finished tightening the nylon strap securing *Shark Bite*'s stern. He picked up his coffee cup and gazed west, where the highway disappeared beyond a gentle rise.

"Tell me."

Lars pulled an envelope from his pocket. Using a napkin from the bakery, he removed a folded sheet of paper by its corner. The page fell open and he placed it on the seat of the boat. It seemed to be a handbill.

Gordo leaned over the varnished-fir gunwale to read:

A decree made known this day from a servant of the Lord
God will do his work
And the whirlwind will vanquish the chaff.
Warnings have been issued

Precious time is left to repent.
But the hearts harden beyond mending
What is God to do, but to strike to break the hardness.
It will come and only those who know the safety of His bosom
Will know rest and peace.
The remainder will fear for their lives.
They will fear for their loved ones.
They will live in fear and trepidation.
They will know only horror in these last days
Before He arrives.

"What is this?" asked Gordo.

"Found it wedged in the door of the rabbit hutch this morning," said Lars. "Did you read the postscript?"

Gordo deciphered the jaggy scrawl at the bottom of the page.

The whirlwind is coming!

And the whirlwind will vanquish the chaff.

"What's this shit?" he said. But as he said it, he remembered where he'd seen the angular scrawl before. Or could he be sure?

"I should have told you sooner," said Lars. "But I knew you had a lot on your mind this morning. I figured it was more important to get you people off the island than it was to take this note to the police."

"You think it's him?"

"Don't you?"

"I'm glad you didn't show it to me earlier," said Gordo. "Because it would have bothered me a lot more three hours ago. Now we're a hundred miles away from that asshole and getting farther all the time. I can't tell you how good it feels to be out of there. Even the air feels better."

An hour out of Houston, they had left the boggy, moisture-laden air behind.

"This changes things," said Gordo. "It doesn't sound like a whacked-out crackhead, does it? Well, fuck that son-of-a-bitch. He's going to have to find somebody else to obsess about. Fuck him and his fear and trepidation!" He was smiling at his friend.

"I guess that tells us the shooter's some kind of religious nut," Lars said. "That sounds like something out of the Old Testament."

"Sounds like a cheesy imitation of some prophecy," said Gordo. "I'm glad he didn't bother you. Or Petey."

"I didn't hear anything all night."

"I never thought you staying on at the beach house was a good idea."

"The guy's not interested in me."

"I appreciate all you've done, Lars. We couldn't have pulled things together this fast without you."

"Hey, I've been fishing in the Gulf, walking on the beach, getting lots of sun—all in the middle of winter. This has been a vacation. It's still cold in Minnesota."

Ana approached, bringing kolaches for them both.

"Time to refuel," she said.

Gordo carefully replaced the handbill inside the envelope and tucked it in his pocket. No reason to worry Ana with it now. He would send it to the police. He smelled the yeasty kolache—a soft and buttery cross between bread and pastry—and then tore into it, his teeth sinking into the spicy sausage within and clicking slightly as they severed the casing. The waxy but comforting sensation of pork fat and butter on his tongue. As a fallen vegetarian, he felt an illicit pleasure in such fare.

"Kolaches like these are worth the drive to Derringer," he said.

The boys walked toward them slowly, concentrating on their food. Gordo drained his coffee cup and used it to scoop rainwater out of the boat hull.

"We're about to hit bluebonnet country, boys."

"Flowers?" said Jake. "Who cares about flowers?"

"We *cayuh* about kolaches," said Sam.

Standing there, bailing the boat, Gordo watched his sons licking their sticky fingers in the cool dry air. He smiled at this family on the move. Some problems were best solved by time, others by distance. Motion.

He gave *Shark Bite*'s transom a spirited slap, as if the vessel were a pack animal.

"Let's go, folks," he said.

With each passing mile, things were getting better.

• • •

Two hours later, they surmounted the final hill, a crest near Lake Travis, and then swooped down to the rim of a deep ravine. Gordo caught sight of the limestone chimney—their chimney—above the tree line. A stone beacon that signaled they were nearing their new nest. One last gentle corner, and there it was. The sturdy white stone house they had decided to buy on that impulsive afternoon. The image of Ana, standing in the creek with her legs crossed and laughing, returned to him.

"That's it," he said to Jake as they approached.

"It's made of rock," said the boy.

"We won't have to paint it."

"Where's the cliff?"

"You'll see."

• • •

Slowly, the three vehicles pulled into the driveway. Lars eased stiffly out of the Jeep after the long drive. Gordo inhaled the fresh, cedar-laced air. He went to the Volvo and took Ana's hand.

"Hey, trail boss, we're here." He kissed her.

She was grinning.

"What do you think, boys?" she said.

"Can we see the inside?" asked Jake.

"I like the Pilot House *bettah*," said Sam.

"Come on," Ana said, leading them to the front door.

Gordo unlocked the trailer to check on Petey in his hutch. The rabbit cowered in the corner.

"Sorry, Petey. We're going to find a nice place under the trees for you. No more road trips."

"Need a hand?" offered Lars.

They lifted the hutch out of the U-Haul and carried it to a relatively flat area beneath a stand of cedar. Gordo picked out rocks for the downhill legs of the hutch to make it level.

He picked up a slab of limestone the size of a melon.

"Rocks, Lars. Rocks!"

"You act like you've never seen one."

"It feels good to own rocks. Our own cliff. I've spent most of my life about fifteen feet above sea level. According to the U.S. Geological Survey, the property falls one hundred feet between here and the creek. Wait till you see what's down below. It's like having our own Stonehenge down there."

• • •

A little later, the boys began to wander around the yard. Gordo, sensing that they were ready to explore, stopped unloading the caravan and took each boy by the hand. He led them to the cliff.

They carefully approached a limestone promontory, where Gordo warned, "If you fall off, you'll crack your head open on a boulder and probably land on a cactus to boot. So stay away from the ledge! No pushing or shoving near the cliff."

The boys were impressed. They could see limestone slabs the size of Volkswagons littered throughout the ravine. In

Galveston, they'd never excavated anything bigger than a seashell. Yet here great sheets of rock were sprouting up from the earth. A real rock garden. Gordo took them down the steep trail below the cliff.

Halfway down, they encountered a difficult stretch of hardscrabble. Not only were there no handholds, but there was a small stand of prickly pear on the edge of the trail.

"Look," said Sam, "a *flowah.*" He reached with his free hand for the beautiful yellow bloom.

Gordo grabbed his arm. "Sam! See the spines?"

"Spines?"

"It's a cactus," chided Jake.

"They're like needles. If you brush against them, they'll end up in your skin. We'll have to pull them out with tweezers. Lots of them."

"Ouch," said Sam.

"Bad ouch."

They examined the papery blossom, its brilliant yellow unfolding on the tip of a green cactus pad, protected by new clusters of spines. This early in the year, the new spines were not yet rigid. But some of last year's spines stood guard until the new arsenal matured.

"The flower will close up at nightfall," said Gordo.

"Why?" asked Sam.

"I don't know. Why do we go to bed at night?"

"To sleep."

"Flowers don't sleep," said Jake.

"I guess not," replied Sam. "Maybe they just nap."

Deeper into the ravine they came upon a large live oak. A boulder the size of a small outbuilding was resting against the trunk of the tree, on the uphill side. Gordo hadn't seen it when he and Ana had come down the week before.

"Why doesn't the *wock* push over the *twee*?" asked Sam.

"Roots," Jake replied.

"See how big the *wock* is?"

"Deep roots," said Gordo. He helped the boys up onto the flat top of the rock. It was like a small terrace.

"I think someday the *twee* is going *ovah*," said Sam.

"We'll keep an eye on it," replied Gordo.

"This is big land."

"What do you mean, Sam?"

"Things *awe* big."

Sam was right. Galveston was made up of insubstantial grains of sand. Here, the texture of the land was big. Big views, big cliffs, big trees. The boulders looked like giant gravestones. For Gordo, the place evoked some prehistoric era. Deep in the ravine, he could imagine a time when dinosaurs crashed through these woods.

"I wonder what did that," Jake said, examining a rock almost as tall as his shoulder, split down the center.

It was the cloven rock Gordo and Ana had discovered, the altar at which he had taken her from behind on that first day. Gordo was stirred by the memory of her leaning over the fissure in the boulder.

"Water, I guess," Gordo said. The rock attracted the curious, he thought.

"How can water do that?" asked Jake.

"Moisture's trapped inside the rock," said Gordo. "Then the temperature drops below freezing and the water expands."

"This place is *stwange*," said Sam.

Jake picked up a rock and threw it toward the creek. Sam reached for his own to throw. Gordo spotted something curious. A rock with rounded curves flowing into a tight spiral. He picked it up and turned it over. The shape of the pale gray rock was soft and effeminate.

"Look at this, boys," he said. "It's a nautilus shell. A fossil."

Jake and Sam closed in around him.

"A seashell?" asked Jake.

"This part of Texas was a shallow sea a hundred and twenty million years ago. Back then this was probably a beach."

"Seashells? Here?" Jake said incredulously.

"I told you this place was *stwange*," said Sam.

"So we're back on the beach," said Jake.

Gordo looked over these boys he and Ana had made. He still didn't know how they could be so wise and unflappable during the chaos since the awful night that changed their lives.

"Right, Jake," he said. "A very old beach."

• • •

The house had wood floors throughout, even in the bathrooms. They were pine, soft wood that scarred easily, making them look older than they were. That evening, Gordo and the boys made pallets on the floor with thin camping mattresses and sleeping bags. Sam wanted everyone to sleep together, so they put four bags side-by-side on the floor of the big bedroom. Lars, who traveled with a mattress from the berth of his sailboat in the back of his truck, made himself at home in Jake's bedroom.

"It's like camping inside," Sam said.

Devoid of furniture, their new home seemed cavernous, even though it wasn't quite as big as Pilot House.

Ana had packed one box with a few basic dishes and kitchen utensils. She put together a simple meal of scrambled eggs and toast.

"I'm sorry we don't have more," she said, "but I was just too exhausted to go to the store."

"Scrambled eggs is one of my favorite suppers," said Lars.

"When will my toys come to the cliff house?" Sam asked.

"About a week," replied Ana.

"Cliff House," said Gordo. "That has a nice ring to it."

"Mom, you should see what's down the cliff," Sam said. "We found an old beach!"

Before bedtime, they all carried mugs of hot chocolate out to the second-story deck off the bedroom. This far out in the country, with almost no ambient light, the stars were bright and infinite.

"Wow," Sam said. "So many *stahs.*"

Lars pointed out constellations he had used for navigation during his sailing voyages. Then they fell silent, the only noise the sound of the creek flowing in the ravine. Batavia Boulevard felt very far away.

• • •

The next day, he got Lino on the phone and told him about the handbill Lars had found at the beach house. The prophecy.

"Send it to me," said Lino. "Guy sounds a little whacked out. Guess we knew that."

"I've been thinking about Norman Zweiger," said Gordo. "What exactly is his connection to this Juventino guy? I mean, why is a cop hanging out with crackheads and murder suspects?"

"As you know, Zweiger's not exactly a Boy Scout. He seems to have a stubborn marijuana habit he picked up in Vietnam. At least that's what I've heard. Lights up every night to wind down from his stressful day in law enforcement. We think his dealer is Juventino Campos."

"Get our new address out of the file," said Gordo. "Right now. The Bee Creek address. I gave it to Jerry Payton before I left town. Go get the file."

"Okay. It's right here. The file hasn't left my desk. I'll make sure I take it out. But we're gonna need some kind of address."

"Use the Colonel's office address. Zweiger would explain a lot." Gordo could see it now. The whole blurry landscape coming into focus.

"If he's been talking," said Lino. "If he knows stuff."

"That's how the information could be moving around."

"Zweiger's not close to the case," said Lino.

"Where we've been staying. Our unlisted phone number at the beach. It's all in the file."

"It's possible. But he's got no beef with you."

"How can that guy still be a cop?"

"Zweiger's crazy. That's part of it. Nobody's itching to cross him. Not even the chief. You have to spend too much time watching your back. The guy's a nut."

"Galveston's finest, I guess," Gordo said. "So why don't you bust him for possession and get rid of him? Last I heard cops weren't supposed to be smoking marijuana."

"We're working on it. We've got to do this by the numbers. Else we'll get him right back like last time. When he got acquitted. Besides, the homicide guys don't want us to spook their suspect."

"Hey, we wouldn't want to spook anybody."

Lino didn't respond.

"What about the ballistics report on that .25-caliber slug?" Gordo asked. "The one you pulled out of that guy's head at the Dunes Motel?"

"DPS lab in Austin says they think it's a match."

"A match?"

"Same gun that hit you."

"Damn." Gordo didn't think there could be anything good about this piece of news. "What do you make of that?"

"Time to find the gun."

Twenty-Two

After three nights of sleeping on the floor in the new house, Gordo bought a bed.

"We can use another bed anyway," he said. "Sam will get the bunk beds, and Jake can have our old one."

The new queen-size bed was delivered the next day. It was the only real furniture they had. Gordo had packed a plastic outdoor table and chairs in the U-Haul, along with two file cabinets topped by an old door he was using as a desk for his computer. But the boys, after having been cooped up in the Colonel's high-rise condo for two weeks, were overjoyed by the woods and all the wildlife in their new backyard. They were already getting familiar with individual members of the roaming herd of deer. Blackie. The name Sam bestowed on the graceful black doe. Humpy. The one with the hump in its nose. There was also a limping doe whose foreleg was turned ninety degrees, so that the bottom of her hoof was pointed sideways. Presumably, she had been struck by a car. They called her Break Like the Wind.

On Tuesday, the sun rose on a clear sky and the temperature climbed into the eighties. Ana baked that afternoon, and they took a brown paper bag of still-warm oatmeal raisin cookies down to the creek. Spring rains had filled the creek with clear rushing water.

Gordo couldn't believe he could be at work in his office one moment and wading in the creek moments later. He was working more in the evenings because of all the interruptions during the day, but breaks like this one were worth it.

They returned to the stretch of creek where Gordo and Ana had first waded. On a rock ledge, they munched cookies laced with lots of raisins and pecans.

"Let's swim," Jake said.

"Me, too," said Sam.

Both boys hurled their clothes onto the bank and carefully eased their tender feet into a limestone basin. Sam kicked water gleefully. Then he squatted in the pool, his bare bottom inches away from the flowing water, as he sifted through stones in the shallow water. Jake headed upstream, a naked explorer.

Under the canopy of cedar elms and oaks, the only noises were Sam singing softly to himself and the sound of water pouring from one rock shelf to another.

"The boys like it here," said Ana. "I like it here."

"The closing is only nine days off," Gordo said, reaching for another cookie. Pointing the cookie to the center of the stream, where a surveyor had driven a metal spike with an orange plastic ribbon, he added, "Then half of this creek will be ours."

"As long as I can listen to it," she said, "I don't care who owns it."

• • •

Gordo was sitting on the deck outside the back door with a beer in one hand as he stroked Skoll's ruff with the other.

Looking out over the ravine, he felt more relaxed than he could ever have imagined in Galveston. The neighbors on their new street, a sprinkling of families with young children and a good number of retirees, were easy to get along with. Some of the retirees, who had moved out to the lake area a few years earlier when it was more isolated, were growing frustrated by the growth and the higher school taxes. But for the most part, they were an educated and tolerant lot. Gordo reveled in the freedom of the place. Freedom from the threat of violence and crime and the petty vexations of urban living. People in Bee Creek left their doors unlocked.

He decided not to install a security system. He didn't like the pressure it subjected them to every time they came home. The race to subdue the beeping keypad to avoid setting off the alarm. The blaring siren when someone punched in the wrong code. This was not a place for jangled nerves.

"We're more than two hundred miles away from the island," he said. "The biggest security threat here in Bee Creek is getting between a horny buck and a doe in heat!"

A few days into their new life Lars announced he was going to New Orleans to visit friends.

Gordo figured it was Lars's sixth sense of when people needed privacy. Or maybe he'd just decided that they were safely out of danger and his job was done. Ana and the boys were saddened by the news. Lars had been there for them. A stabilizing force. Quiet, watchful, quick with a smile or a word of comfort. They would miss him.

"We'll have furniture later in the week," said Gordo, "so you don't have to leave in order to have a bed."

"It's time."

He offered to leave Skoll behind for a week or two.

"Skoll likes it here," Lars said, adding that he could swing back to Bee Creek before heading north toward home.

"You know we love him," said Gordo. "Especially the

boys. But look, you're going to come back and take Skoll away sooner or later. Take him to New Orleans. It'll save you a few hundred miles on the way back."

"You're sure?"

"I want things to be normal. That guy is some delusional crackhead who probably never gets off the island. We're safe here. And I don't want to export all that tension and fear from Galveston. I'm unloading the Beretta and locking it up."

"If that's what you want," said Lars. "You're probably right."

As usual, he was way ahead of them. He'd already packed most of his things into the Jeep. Somewhere in his travels, Lars learned that quick departures were the easiest.

Sam had his arms around Skoll's neck that morning. Gordo could see a dog in their future. He could also see that Sam was crying. For Lars? For Skoll? For something that was already gone, left behind in Galveston? No point in asking. Hard enough as it was. Crushing hugs. Now Ana was crying. Lars growled in disapproval at her tears. But he didn't come up with any words either.

"Let's go, boy," he said to Skoll, who jumped into the back of the Jeep. Then the old Norwegian was gone.

• • •

Ana didn't care for the front door at the new house, with its ornately curved oak panels and leaded-pane glass. She thought it belonged in a suburban neo-château. She was right, of course, but Gordo, who had worked on a few doors at Pilot House, knew what a hassle it was to hang a door properly. So that it closed smoothly and didn't bind or sag. And this was the front door. He'd let someone else do it this time.

Out toward Dripping Springs, Gordo found a woodworker who made furniture out of recycled longleaf pine in a barn-like workshop. He started the project by milling old timbers into thick, resinous slabs, exposing heavily grained amber wood. Planed anew and still bearing rust stains from nails driven a hundred years earlier, the wood had a warm appearance that invited one's touch. The carpenter made a simple door with two glass panels over two wood panels. They ordered fluted glass panes from Dallas. After the door was constructed, the exterior side received a coat of spar varnish and the interior side was rubbed with beeswax.

Two weeks later, the carpenter showed up to hang the door.

"I love it!" Ana cried.

Outfitted with pewter-finished hardware, it was perfect for the rustic stone exterior of the house. That day Ana went out and bought a large Tuscan pot of creamy terracotta and planted it with flowers and grasses in a variety of shades of silver and purple.

"To go with my new door," she announced.

"A work of art," Gordo said.

Two days later the glass company called.

"They said the glass in the door wasn't tempered," Ana said. "Some kind of mix-up."

"What does that mean?"

"Door glass is supposed to be tempered so it's safer if it gets broken. They said it's in the building code."

"What are we supposed to do?"

"They'll replace the glass for free," she said. "But we're going to have to figure out how to get the new stuff into the door."

Gordo groaned. He didn't like the idea of taking the door apart to install new glass. He'd have to bring the carpenter back from Dripping Springs.

• • •

Halfway between the house and the cliff, Gordo hung a hammock. On this lovely spring afternoon in the hill country, he shared it with Ana, their heads at opposite ends. The air was dry and at least twenty degrees warmer than the day before. Pale green clouds of new leaves floated over the ravine.

"I'm amazed that after being so attached to Galveston," he said, "I could feel so much a part of this place."

Ana flopped a leg across his, causing the hammock to rock slightly.

"So quiet," he said. "I can't believe we used to live thirty feet from a street where sirens wailed every night."

"It shows how conditioned we were."

"And now?"

"We're de-conditioning," she said.

"What about the work? No law practice? Are you bored yet?"

"You don't realize the toll practicing law is taking," she said, "until you stop doing it. All those tense, aggressive people. The constant fear that you're going to miss some deadline for motions or interrogatories. That you're going to screw up. Even though you're doing everything you can to stay on top of things. Even though you've got a reliable secretary and a well-organized office. Sometimes stuff slips past. It never happened to me, but I saw it happen to other people and I knew how easily it could happen to anybody. So even when the day is over, and you've done your best work and the client is happy, there's that nagging suspicion that at the stroke of midnight—while you're sleeping—some deadline will pass and you've screwed up.

"I always felt pretty good about the work in front of me. It was the stuff I might not even be aware of that bothered me. Now when I go to sleep, I know there may be legal malpractice taking place, but it's not my malpractice."

"Have you talked to anybody at the law firm lately?"

"I spoke to Dave this morning," she said. "He had one

interesting piece of gossip."

"Let's hear it."

"Corky knocked up Joe Clayton's daughter."

"Not the one who used to babysit for us? She'd be too young."

"That was when Jake was a tiny infant?"

"Still, she couldn't be but—"

"Twenty-four."

Gordo shook his head. He spied a fox nonchalantly moving down the edge of the cliff. On patrol for dinner, perhaps.

"What are they going to do?" he asked.

"Big wedding at St. Stephen's."

"Corky's what? Forty-eight or forty-nine?"

Ana didn't answer. Her expression grew serious.

"About Corky," she said. "I'm sorry about all that."

Gordo placed a finger over her lips and nodded toward the approaching fox, who kept right on coming as if he owned the place. As casually as he might examine a passing squirrel, the fox stopped and looked directly into their gaze. Gordo admired the animal's thick gray coat and rust-colored chest.

Gordo didn't need to know more about Ana and Corky. It still bothered him. Sometimes, just before sleep, he could see them together in his mind. *Let it go.* Ana didn't need to know everything about Lisa Pierce. Neither of them had been at their best during those turbulent weeks. Let it go.

The hammock swung silently as they watched.

After a moment, the fox lost interest in them and resumed his stroll along the cliff.

• • •

Later, before he turned off his computer for the night, Gordo checked his e-mail, where there was a message from Lino Gabilondo.

Gordo,

Just learned that Allen Hayes was convicted of unlawfully carrying a weapon two years ago. A pistol—.25 caliber. Did you know? Pat Hayes represented him and got a year's probation.

Lino

"Did you know?" Gordo asked Ana.

"It's news to me."

"Don't you think your father should have said something?"

"He should have," she said. "But he's so used to covering up stuff for Allen, it's second nature to him."

"But if it involves your safety, the safety of his grandchildren—"

"You don't understand the way he is about Allen. He gives Allen the benefit of the doubt every time. He's been doing this for years."

"I think I need to talk to your father," said Gordo.

"I'll talk to him," she said. "He's probably going to say he never saw any connection. Any reason to mention it. That he never would have thought to mention it."

"Your father the FBI agent," said Gordo incredulously. "At this point, anything that might shed light on our situation is serious—is worth mentioning."

"I know. I'm just saying that my parents have been in complete denial about Allen for years. It's no surprise that they might be reluctant to admit that he could be mixed up in something. And we don't know that he is. It's not just my parents. Most parents don't immediately link their children to crimes."

"Allen's not your normal little brother," said Gordo.

Ana sighed. "I'll talk to Daddy."

• • •

On Saturday, what would be the final crisp morning of spring, Jake went out to feed Petey and Henry. There was frost on the cars in the driveway.

Henry, the gerbil, who always slept on Petey's back in cold weather, lay motionless on the wire mesh.

Jake reported this news with concern. "Henry's asleep, and I can't wake him up."

"Maybe he's *tiyud*," Sam said.

Gordo looked at Ana with concern. Henry was an old friend.

The whole family filed out the back door. The hutch was located under a canopy of cedars near the cliff. Petey was keeping his distance from the gerbil.

"Why don't you give him a pat?" Ana told Gordo. "See if he has a fever."

Gordo gingerly touched the gerbil's back.

"No fever," he said.

"Any particular temperature?" Ana inquired gingerly.

"Well, he's not ice cold, either."

"He's just sleepy," Sam pronounced. "Let him sleep."

"Maybe we should take him inside," said Jake. "I'll get a shoebox."

All that morning, the boys kept a vigil for the resting Henry. Then, during lunch, Jake screamed.

"Henry!"

And to everyone's astonishment, there was Henry, holding his head above the shoebox.

"Lazarus," said Gordo.

"Henry Van Winkle," said Ana.

"I told you he was sleeping!" said Sam.

"Henry!" Jake repeated, now holding the gerbil to his cheek.

"I'd have sworn that gerbil was a goner," Gordo whispered.

"I was getting worried," she said.

For the next half-hour, Henry was his old self again. Running around the house, hiding behind the sofa, crapping on the floor. But then, he seemed to tire, and the boys put him back in the box for a nap.

By evening, Henry was still prostrate. Jake called his father to take a look. Gordo picked up the animal, and realized that now he was indeed cold. He also seemed to be stiffening up. Gordo didn't know what to say. Returning Henry to the box, he said, "I don't know about Henry, boys. I'm afraid he's not going to get better."

"He hasn't moved in a long time," said Jake.

Jake understood but was trying to protect his little brother's feelings.

"Let's leave Henry alone for now," Gordo said, trying to ease into the subject. "But he may not recover this time."

Sam studied Henry in his box. "He's dead," he said casually.

"Do you think so, Sam?"

"Not *bweathing*. Can't live without *bweathing*."

"Well, you've got a point."

Jake, looking sad, grew quiet. Petey was a family pet. But Henry had been his.

"I'm sorry, Jake. I really am." And Gordo felt his own eyes water. Henry was the first loss from their old existence at Pilot House. He'd survived the weeks on the beach and the trip to Austin. He'd been a part of their past that had made the transition, and now he was gone.

"Let's have a memorial service for Henry," Ana suggested.

"A funeral?" asked Jake.

"A chance to say goodbye to him," she said. "Tomorrow. In the woods."

• • •

The next day, the whole family set out for the woods. They crossed the creek and climbed the other side of the ravine, a heavily wooded slope which Sam had christened Secret Hill, because he had discovered it, and he was sure that its existence was a secret. Jake carried the shoebox, and Gordo carried a shovel. After digging the grave, Gordo turned to Jake.

Silently, Jake nestled the box into the hole.

"There."

His father covered the box with rich black earth from a hundred years of composted leaves. Then they built a pyramid of stones, each about the size of a cantaloupe.

"Let's all say a few words about our old friend Henry," said Ana. "He brought joy to our family," she said.

"He was my friend," said Jake, looking painfully sad.

"He was awfully good at hide and seek," said Gordo. "And he was a good roommate for Petey."

"He's dead," said Sam.

"We know that, stupid!" said Jake.

As Gordo was collecting his shovel, the boys noticed some thick vines hanging from the tall trees. Jake swung out over the sloping hillside.

"Wow!" said Sam. "Help me do that."

Gordo lifted the boy up to get a firm grip on a vine that was at least an inch in diameter.

"Can you hold on?" he asked.

"Let me go!"

Sam screamed in delight as he floated out over the sloping floor of the woods, with its thick carpet of last autumn's fallen leaves.

Ana put her arms around Gordo's shoulder.

"Henry will like it here on Secret Hill," she said.

• • •

On Monday, after Gordo finished his work for the day, he went downstairs to join Ana. She was working on dinner, trying out a new recipe from Martha Rose Schulman's latest cookbook.

"Hi, honey, I'm home," he called.

"How was your day?"

Gordo gave her a kiss on the cheek.

It had started as a joke and had slipped into a part of their new routine.

This domestic scene, Ana leisurely working her way through an ambitious recipe at 5:30 on a weekday evening, stood out in high relief from their prior life. In those days, if there was food on the table at something approaching the dinner hour, he had put it there. But so often, soccer practice, Cub Scouts, or karate class consumed those hours, and everyone returned to an empty kitchen. Having Ana at home was a luxury. It was as if they were on some kind of extended vacation.

"Sam's been invited over to Daniel's house this week," Ana said.

He put his arms around her and whispered, "That's great."

They both were anxious about the boys making new friends. Sam was more of an extrovert, but this would be his first visit to a friend's home in Bee Creek.

Jake had always been shy. He wasn't quick to reach out and make friends, but with time, he slowly wove himself into the social fabric of his class or baseball team. At St. Stephen's, he'd always been well liked. But he'd known those kids since kindergarten.

Jake and Sam had been giving favorable but not ecstatic reports from their new schools. Ana and Gordo were concerned that they might be having a hard time with the adjustment and were just putting up a brave front. They had discussed telling the boys' new teachers about the trauma of the shooting but decided against it.

"Jake and Sam might do better in the long run if they aren't known for having bullet-dodging parents on the lam," Gordo said.

Ana knew he was only half joking. "We can always tell the teacher later if one of the boys seems to be having a problem."

"They're tough," he said. "Tougher than we are."

"They seem to handle it better. People say kids are resilient. That they adapt better than adults. Maybe it's true."

"What do we know about Daniel's family?"

"Not much," she said. "His mother sounds nice. But the best part is that they live just two streets over."

"Really?"

"Sam and I have been going down that street on our walks together. I think I even know which house, from what Daniel's mom told me."

"A friend in the neighborhood," he said.

"Within walking distance."

Ana was making baked chicken with forty cloves of garlic.

Gordo poured them each a glass of white wine before she put him to work making crostini.

"That's the good news," she said.

"Hmm."

"I talked to Sam's teacher today after school. She said he's having trouble keeping up in his reading class."

"Did she have any ideas about what's wrong?"

"She said he needs a lot of practice and repetition. More than she can give him in the classroom."

"It's hard to imagine that Sam, with his big vocabulary and—"

"I know, I know. She said she knew he was very smart and that he had a bigger vocabulary than lots of adults. But he just can't read. He doesn't have the skills to sound out the words fast enough to keep up."

"Do you think Cooper School—"

"She said it probably wasn't the school's fault. Some kids pick this up later than others do. She said, 'If it's any comfort, I've never taught a smart kid who didn't learn how to read. It's not a matter of whether he can learn, it's just a matter of when.'"

"What can we do?"

"There's a special reading group he can go to. But they'll have to pull him out of his reading class."

"Special ed?"

"That's not what they call it. She also recommended a book so we can work with him at home. I'll go into town tomorrow and get it. But she warned me, it's got a hundred lessons. Can you imagine how much work it would be to get Sam to do anything a hundred times?"

"A test of will," Gordo said with resignation.

The second-born, Sam acted like it was his mission in life to test limits. He could listen to his mother read to him for hours as he paced the room, engaged in imaginary sword fights and striking foes with karate kicks as waves of prose washed over him. His was the most stubborn and unyielding personality in the house.

"Fifty lessons for me," she said, "fifty for you."

"Oh boy."

"Could you go get some herbs? Basil and thyme."

Gordo went out the back door. The house had decks overlooking the ravine off the first and second stories, with connecting outdoor stairs. He liked the arrangement, with the top deck protecting the lower one from the harsh light of the afternoon. In the rocky soil between the deck and the cliff, he put in beds with stone borders for Ana's herbs and native plants. The biggest threat to the project was the deer, who seemed to relish anything green, even the plants that were sold as "deerproof."

He reached over the black plastic netting they were using to discourage the deer, and snipped off a few sprigs. Crushing one of the deep green basil leaves, he breathed in its summery aroma.

The garden was a tangible expression of Ana's optimism. That the future would bring sunshine, rainfall, and a good harvest. They were just native plants and herbs. Nothing fancy.

The stone work had been hard. Gordo had piddled with masonry, repairing the eroded mortar in the brick piers of Pilot House back in Galveston. One day, on his belly, he was amazed to find that he could see daylight between the bricks that supported the old house.

"The house is floating on air," he reported to Ana, horrified that the brick piers might collapse if Jake jumped off his bunk bed onto just the right spot. Gordo had tried to fix it, but it was excruciatingly slow work and he ultimately hired a mason. But for Ana, and her dream of a green cliffside, he had mixed mortar in a big new wheelbarrow from the building supply store on the highway and hauled rocks up from the cliff. Eventually, he had ordered limestone from a rock yard.

"I can't believe I'm paying for limestone when we are surrounded by the stuff." But the work was a balm for his sedentary weekdays, when he seemed bound to the phone and computer. A satisfying soreness set in after a weekend of hauling rock, mixing mortar, and setting the stones. The only physical complaint that lasted more than a couple days came when, after he'd worn holes in the fingertips of his leather gloves, he'd scoured the skin off the pads of his fingers.

"I don't mind the sweat and toil, but I don't really want to contribute my skin to your stone borders."

Ana had massaged his weary back, but it had taken almost a week for his fingertips to recover. She bought him a replacement pair of heavy gloves and the work proceeded. Earlier in the week, he had more rock delivered to start a stone path from the front porch to the driveway. The rocks lay in a pile near the front door. First thing Saturday morning he would be mixing mortar again.

Herbs in hand, Gordo could see that the plants had already put on some growth during the moist spring. And the curving stone path he had built had weathered a bit and was beginning to look like it had been there for years. Ana's tiny kingdom was beginning to emerge beneath the cedars and the oaks on their sun-washed cliff.

But was it real? This life that felt like an extended summer vacation. Would Ana ultimately need more movement in her life? And would they have enough money? The check she'd received from her partners for her share of the firm's assets would see them through the rest of the year. And fortunately, Gordo's work was plentiful for now. But what about the future?

A turkey vulture sailed serenely over the ravine on an updraft. On the ground, it was an awkward bird with a droopy neck that hopped around its meal of carrion like an arthritic scavenger. The bird's blood-red wattle, which flopped back and forth as it circled a dead raccoon in the middle of the road, made it even more menacing. But in the air, it was a graceful black presence. Gordo, having experienced the stench of dead deer rising up from the ravine earlier in the spring, considered the vultures' work a public service.

He was growing to love this house on the cliff. The hundred-foot plunge into the ravine, the prickly pear clinging to the rocky slope, the oaks and the cedar elms, and the massive slabs of limestone. It was uplifting to look out on this little piece of the Hill Country and know it was theirs. Last night's rainfall had caused the creek to swell. The music of rushing water filtered through the trees. Two months ago, he didn't think it would be possible to replace the sense of home they had felt at Pilot House. Now he wasn't so sure. Cliff House. He liked the sound of it.

This was where Jake and Sam would careen into their teenage years. Gordo knew the bucolic life on this cliff would not last forever. He assumed that within a few years they would be wrestling with imperfect report cards, teenage drinking, reckless driving, and the other detritus of parenting during the home stretch. Maybe they'd get lucky and be spared some of it.

He took one more deep breath of the fragrant air and went inside to help Ana.

Twenty-Three

The next morning he got a phone call from Lino Gabilondo.

"I'd like you to look at some photos. Could we meet in Austin?" asked Lino.

"What's going on? Have you found the gun?"

"We're looking at the guys who live in the house I told you about."

"The crackheads?"

"One of them fits the description you gave us. If you can ID the guy, then we'll get a warrant and search the house. If we could find the gun, it could help us with the Dunes Motel homicide."

"And my case?"

"You ID him, that's a big step."

"So you want to drive all the way to Austin?"

"I could use the break."

"So who's your suspect?" asked Gordo.

"His name is Rory DuBose. Does that name mean anything to you?"

"Never heard of him. Why would he be shooting at me?"

"We're working on that part. Not clear. Some kind of fixation maybe. Maybe something about Ana."

"Ana?"

"We're thinking he may have seen her at the law firm."

"Why?"

"Just a theory."

"But what could he have against Ana?"

"Look, it's no secret that she's a good-looking woman. Sometimes that's all it takes."

"What would this guy have been doing at the law firm?"

"We're not sure," said Lino. "It's not worth fretting over. We might be wrong. You can ask Ana if she recognizes the name. But there's not much to be done until you see this photo."

They arranged to meet at a restaurant in Austin on Thursday.

"Ana talked to her father about Allen," Gordo said. "He said it never occurred to him to mention Allen's conviction and the .25-caliber pistol. I suppose that could be true."

"Don't you think it's strange?" asked Lino.

"I can't explain it. But Lino, I appreciate the work you're doing."

"Just doing my job."

"So were Tiny and Hampton."

"I think I've got a better idea about your friends in the police department," said Lino, his voice lower. "We can talk about it when I get to Austin."

Gordo hung up. Rory DuBose. He would remember a name like that. It sounded like Lino was closing in on some answers. Gordo felt relief in the prospect of learning who and why. But he also was uneasy. Lars, erstwhile lawyer and public defender, hadn't seen much good in prosecution—even if they could find the shooter.

You're better off if they don't find the guy.

So where to put your faith? Criminal justice or geography. The courts or the highway. Putting distance between his family and Batavia Boulevard. Lino's photo could start the process that would force them to place their bet on the courts. Rory DuBose.

He went to find Ana.

"Does the name Rory DuBose mean anything to you?"

"No," she said. "Should it?"

"Lino thinks it may be the name of the shooter."

"What's his problem?"

"He said the guy may have some connection to the law firm."

"I've never had a client named Rory DuBose, or Rory anything."

"Lino's going to bring me a picture of the guy."

"He's going to drive all the way up here?"

"As far as Austin," said Gordo. "I got the impression he wanted an excuse to get off the island. He said he had some information about 'my friends' in the police department."

"That should be interesting."

"I'm ready to get past all that," said Gordo. "What if the only case they have against the guy is me as an eyewitness? Some defense lawyer would grill me about how good a look I got at the shooter. About the lighting. It could get ugly."

"It's not worth worrying about now," she said. "It might not even be the right guy in the photo."

"This place is so nice," he said, sweeping an open palm around him. "I just hate to dive back into that mess we left behind."

"The DA's not going to move on a weak case," said Ana.

"No, he might just piss the guy off really good, drop the whole thing, and then leave us hanging in the breeze."

"Let's see what happens."

"Two days," said Gordo. "It's hard to imagine that face in a mug shot. In my mind, he's this simmering, twitching mass of energy. Too much emotion to fit into a little picture."

He worked late that night, trying to get as much work done as possible. He had a Friday deadline for a magazine piece, and he would lose much of Thursday to his meeting with Lino in Austin. Finally, at about one in the morning, he switched off the light in the office and got ready for bed. As he eased into bed, not wanting to disturb Ana, he heard a car engine start somewhere on the street.

Odd, he thought. His neighbors weren't much for keeping late hours, especially on weeknights. He heard the car's engine labor as it climbed the hill and then disappear, leaving Gordo on the soft threshold of sleep. Only the music of the crickets, whose nocturnal chorus had just begun for the season, remained. Within moments, he was gone.

• • •

Gordo spent most of Wednesday afternoon on the phone. His deadline was approaching for the article on managed health care, and he was dialing sources on one phone line and trying to leave the other open for people returning his calls. Several times, when he was in the middle of an interview, he was forced to ignore incoming calls. Late in the day, he called contacts in the Pacific time zone to stretch the work day. Close to six, he checked his voice mail. Three callbacks and one message from Lino Gabilondo.

"Got something I want you to know. Call me. Still on for tomorrow's meeting in Austin. But call me back."

He played the message twice.

Short, clear, precise.

Ana had driven out to the highway to pick up Chinese food. Gordo, parched from the day's chatter, went to grab a beer before calling Lino, who was probably gone for the day. Then he heard Sam's voice.

He smiled. Sam had been at his friend Kyle's house down the street. The boy, now seven and suddenly craving independence, had permission to roam the street and the ravine behind their house. Gordo was always relieved when Sam returned home. He liked the feel of everyone being at home. His constellation.

"Hey, how did it go at Kyle's?" he called.

"Dad, *you'wa fwend* is *heah.*"

"What friend?" He wondered if it was one of the tree trimmers who had worked there in the morning.

He turned the corner and saw the man standing just inside the door.

"Did you forget one of your tools?"

And then the man looked directly at him.

"What did you say *you'wa* name was?" asked Sam.

The man didn't answer.

"*Wohwee.*"

"Sam, go upstairs with your brother."

A wave of fear swept through Gordo. He tried to stay calm. His fingers were shaking, and he struggled for air.

"Go on, Sam!" he said.

The boy slowly climbed the stairs.

Gordo locked his eyes on the man.

Him!

There was a bulge in the pocket of his camouflage pants. The left pocket.

"What can I do for you?" said Gordo, fighting the quaver in his voice.

"I came to talk," said the man softly.

The exchange was surreal. He had wanted to talk to this man for so long. The angry eyes were calm now. The same hollow cheeks and the blondish stubble of beard that Gordo had seen countless times in his memory. He didn't appear to be in a violent mood. But Gordo needed to get him out of the house!

"I didn't expect to see you again," Gordo said, gently rocking his weight forward off his heels, ready to spring.

"Why not?"

"I just thought you had other things to do."

"This is what I have to do," the man said.

"My son said your name is Rory?"

"Your son was right."

"Rory, why are you here?"

"I'll get to that. I want you to know I was confused last time. I'm not mad at you."

"Oh."

Gordo was trying to figure out a way to get the man away from the boys. He didn't want to do anything sudden, anything that might make the man reach for his pocket.

"Have we ever met? Have we ever talked before . . . well, before the time you came to my house?"

"No."

Gordo decided not to press him. Maybe it would be better to listen. At least until he could ease the man out the door.

"You wanted to tell me something?"

"Just that I wasn't mad at you. I thought I was. But it's not your fault."

"Not my fault?"

"That you are with her."

"Her?"

"Ana."

"Do you know Ana?"

"I know her very well."

"How do you two know each other?"

"I've always known her."

"Always?"

"We were meant to be together. Sometimes that just happens."

"How?"

"Fate. God. Take your pick."

"I don't think she's ever mentioned you, Rory."

"She wouldn't."

"Oh."

Rory's gaze drifted up, as if he were looking at something upstairs.

He saw Jake looking through the banister.

"Jake, you guys go into our bedroom and lock the door, please," Gordo said calmly. "Take care of your brother. You know what to do." The bedroom had a back door and a phone. They had been over this when they first moved here. If there was trouble, lock the door and call for help. Gordo hoped Jake would remember.

"So you know Ana?" Gordo wanted to divert the attention from the boys.

"Yes. I've been around her a lot." Rory seemed to focus on Ana. "Seen her a lot. But we're much closer in spirit."

"Tell me about it."

"She has an important role to play. In the future. When it comes. Ana will help me."

"What's coming?"

"You don't even suspect, do you?"

Gordo had to do something.

"I suppose it's important for you to talk to Ana about this," he said.

"We have a lot to go over."

"She's coming soon," said Gordo. "Why don't we go out front to wait for her?"

"I have work to do here," Rory said, avoiding eye contact. "Like I said. I've never had anything against you. But there are things I've got to do. To prepare." Rory's hand suddenly disappeared into his pocket.

Gordo had run out of time. He rushed at the man, shoving

him against the front door. The intruder's elbow smashed through the glass pane.

Rory screamed, as shards of glass struck the floor. Non-tempered glass.

He pulled his elbow free of the windowpane.

Gordo charged again, driving him back into the heavy door. Rory grunted. Then he spun away.

Grabbing the knob, Gordo threw open the door.

"Get out!"

A blue steel pistol cleared Rory's pants pocket. He inspected his elbow, which was bleeding.

"I was wrong about you, brother."

The door was wide open, but Gordo couldn't risk it. What if Rory didn't follow him? The boys were still upstairs!

"You are one of them," Rory said, raising the pistol.

Gordo ran outside, stopping just past the threshold. The door remained open. He was just outside Rory's line of sight. Gordo would never let the front door close behind him.

Come on! Come on!

Then Rory followed. As he emerged from the house, Gordo hit him in the shoulder with Ana's big terracotta pot. Missing the step below the threshold, Rory stumbled off the porch. Gordo leaped inside and locked the door behind him.

"Jake!" he screamed. "Dial 911! Call the police!"

There was no reply.

Gordo, panting, stood back from the door, with its broken pane.

"You cut me. I'm bleeding," Rory growled as he reached through the window for the deadbolt.

Gordo froze. Rory was on the other side of the door with a gun. He had the bolt in his grasp.

"Dad!"

It was Jake. He held out the fireplace poker. The heavy

iron sword that the blacksmith Eli had made for the Cub Scouts.

"Take it," urged the boy.

Gordo rushed forward and cracked the poker across Rory's hand. As the hand withdrew, a curl of skin peeled off Rory's knuckles as if being drawn across a paring knife.

Gordo, flattening himself against the wall next to the door, heard grunting and swearing above the sound of his own heart pounding. Jake stood on the staircase.

"Did you call?"

"Yes!" said Jake.

"The police?"

"Yes!"

"Go upstairs with Sam, and lock yourself in our bedroom. Now! And don't come out until I get you."

That was when Rory fired the first shot. It sounded like a cannon as it echoed through the house.

Jake was running up the stairs now.

Then Gordo heard heavy footfalls on the porch. Rory was moving away from the door. A car was pulling into the driveway.

Ana!

Gordo peered out the broken window. Rory was in front of the porch, looking toward the driveway, transfixed.

Ana wouldn't know who Rory was!

Gordo couldn't wait.

He flew out the door with a two-fisted grip on Eli's iron sword. He swung it like a club with the heavy handle arcing toward his assailant.

Stepping back, Rory easily eluded the crude weapon. He gazed into Gordo's eyes and repeated the question he had asked during their last encounter. "Who are you?" Then he raised the pistol.

Ana screamed.

Rory looked toward her.

"Ana," Rory said, taking a step in her direction.

Gordo pointed the sword and lunged. Rory backed up, tripping on the pile of paving stones. The gun fired. With his flailing arms and legs, Rory looked like a spider as he fell, grunting loudly as he landed upon the rocks.

Where was the gun?

Rory, frantically trying to get purchase amongst the rubble, rolled over on his side.

Where was the gun?

Gordo stepped forward. He raised the sword overhead and drove it down with all his force. Gordo could feel the sword glancing off bone. He heard a crunching sound and a metallic chink. Metal on bone. Iron on rock. The sword pierced Rory's neck.

A plume of blood swept across Gordo's leg.

Pulsating, keeping time to the man's wildly beating heart. More blood than Gordo had ever seen. As he stood there, watching, Ana's screams began to register. He looked toward her.

"Gordo!" she shouted.

Rory reached up to pull the poker from his neck. He tugged once. Gordo realized that the gun was still there, somewhere in the rubble. Rory's fingers tightened around the iron shaft with greater force, his legs scraped over the rocks, desperate to get a foothold. Gordo picked up a heavy stone block with one hand and, with a great heave, struck the prone figure of Rory DuBose. The rock hit him on the forehead and toppled to the side. Standing over him, gasping for breath, Gordo watched Rory grow still. A river of blood spilled over the white stones. A bright red pool on the ground.

Gordo was breathing in deep, noisy gulps. He looked savage, his clothes covered in blood, a big rock in his grasp. He didn't even remember picking up the second rock.

"Gordo!" Ana cried again.

He turned to Ana.

"It's okay."

He dropped the rock.

"The boys!" he shouted.

Gordo raced inside and up the stairs with Ana on his heels.

"Jake! Sam! Unlock the door!" The door flew open, and he embraced them both.

"Are you all right?"

The boys were crying.

Ana joined them. The four of them locked together, hearts pounding.

"Did he shoot you, Dad?" asked Sam.

"No, son."

Sam said, "*You'wa* bloody."

Gordo stepped back from the boys. Blood from his arms and shirt, Rory's blood, was visible on Jake and Sam's t-shirts.

"It's not my blood." Then Gordo remembered the last time. "At least I don't think any of it's mine."

"We heard shots," said Jake.

"I know."

Gordo tried to listen to his body. He looked down at himself. Mindful of the Galveston shooting, he pulled up his shirt. "Look me over. I don't think I got hit."

Ana was crying, her hands moving over his chest.

"I don't see anything," she said. She turned him around. "I don't see anything."

"We're okay," said Gordo. "We're all okay."

"*Wheah* is that guy?" asked Sam.

"Out front. He can't hurt you."

"Why not?"

"Because he's hurt."

Sam shuddered. "Did you shoot him?"

"No. I hurt him. But I didn't shoot him."

"We were *scahed*, Daddy."

"So was I."

"We didn't know who was coming up the *staihs.*"

"Oh, boys. I'm sorry. I'm so sorry."

"I called 911," said Jake.

"Good boy."

Gordo looked over at the phone, which was hanging by its cord.

"Are they still on the phone?"

"I guess," Jake replied.

A siren broke the stillness.

• • •

Gordo held them.

"Before we go down, I want you to know something," he said. "I'm proud of both of you. You did what needed to be done. I know that wasn't easy."

"We were *scahed.*" Like so much of what Sam said, it was a pure, unfiltered statement of fact.

"Sam, we're not going to have to be scared anymore. Not by that man."

"Is he dead?"

"He's not going to hurt us."

"Can he come back?"

"He's never coming back."

"Good."

"We're going to go downstairs. There will be policemen."

"Like last time," Jake said.

"When we go downstairs, I want you to stay inside. There's a lot of blood. You don't need to see all that."

"You've got a lot of blood on *you'wa* pants," said Sam.

"You just remember, I'm proud of you. You've been strong."

"Dad," Sam asked, "*awe* we leaving?"

"No. Last time we left. This time we stay."

Twenty-Four

People don't kill each other in Bee Creek. The town, which had only been incorporated a few years, had never had a homicide. There were bloody traffic and boating accidents, but the police never had to deal with a person intentionally taking another life. Both police cruisers, the entire force on duty, appeared in the O'Connor driveway.

"I'd better get outside," Gordo told Ana.

He walked across the porch toward the driveway, trying to make eye contact with the officer getting out of the first car, but the man's eyes were locked on Rory's bloody heap. When the policeman did spot Gordo, he reacted with alarm. Bloody clothes and raw emotions—he looked homicidal.

"Come on," Gordo said, waving to the officer. "My son called. You better have a look at this guy."

"What the hell happened?" asked the cop, a beefy man with one hand on his holstered pistol butt, clearly alarmed by the scene. He hurried to Rory's side, pulling on a pair of latex gloves. The second officer, so thin he barely had the hips to hold up his belt and holster, followed him.

"He tried to kill me," said Gordo. "He had a gun. He's from Galveston. I stabbed him with the fireplace poker."

"You did this with a poker?" Squatting in such a way as to keep his uniform out of the mess, the officer checked for a pulse while his partner carefully picked up the pistol. "You better tell the EMS unit to hurry," the big one said. "He's lost a lot of blood."

Looking up at Gordo, he asked, "You know this man?"

"I don't know him, but I've seen him before. He shot me back in Galveston."

"Well I damn sure wish he'd stayed in Galveston."

"He's crazy."

"Newcomers."

Gordo assumed the remark was for his partner's benefit.

The cop was trying to stop the bleeding from the hole in Rory's neck. "What a mess. That the poker?" he asked, tilting his head toward the iron sword in the grass.

Somehow, Rory had pulled it free.

"That's it," replied Gordo.

"You get in a fight with a poker," said the officer, "that's the one you wanna have."

"Cub Scouts." It was all Gordo said.

He could see some of his new neighbors in the street, approaching the spectacle with caution. Welcome to the neighborhood.

"EMS is two minutes away," said the thin officer. Pen in hand, he reached for his clipboard nestled in the grass. "You better tell me what happened."

Lightheaded and gulping air, Gordo stepped over to the porch and sat down on the step. Where to begin? How could he make these men understand what had happened when he hadn't figured it out yet himself?

Ana peered out the door.

"Keep the boys inside," he said.

Gordo looked up at the officer.

"It started in Galveston."

• • •

Lino Gabilondo never made it to Austin. The Bee Creek police called Galveston to get information. To find out who Rory DuBose was and why he was in Bee Creek. To find out who Gordo O'Connor was and why he was in Bee Creek. The task fell to Lino to find some answers. He was also given the task of contacting Rory's next of kin. In the ambulance racing from Bee Creek to Austin, Rory's heart stopped.

• • •

"A person is harder to stop than you would think," said Gordo, talking to Ana that night in bed. "I put two hundred miles between us. I put an iron shaft through his neck. I bounced a rock off his head."

"He did die," she said.

"It's not like the movies."

"You got shot in the chest and walked away," she reminded him.

"I guess people are tougher in real life," he said. "No such thing as a clean shot."

"Life is messier than movies."

And that was true. They had pieced together something beautiful at Cliff House. Something too good to be true? Their idyllic ravine. He remembered his predawn visualization back in Galveston. His vision of a house on a cliff.

And now they had a pool of blood congealing outside their door.

Lord, spare us from what we most desire.

• • •

Within a day of the attack, Gordo learned these things from the reedy police officer who took his statement and his fireplace poker and from his phone conversation with Lino. He understood the facts, but it was hard to absorb them. For months he and Ana had lived with the menacing presence of Rory, which was more real to them than the person whose life drained away on a pile of rocks in their front yard. But he was a real person, and Gordo could not resist his urge, his need, to learn the story of Rory DuBose. To know how their lives became entangled. Random crime, like random events, does take place. But Gordo did not live in a random world. His was a world of specifics, and he needed to know more. Which is why he left Ana, Jake, and Sam and drove to Galveston.

• • •

This time, Gordo didn't need to meet Lino at a coffee shop or a park. At the police station, he almost bumped into Grover Hampton turning the corner outside the detectives' bullpen. There were times in the past months when he had loathed Grover and Tiny Martelli. But today, Gordo just ignored him, the way he might treat a stranger in an elevator. Grover Hampton would know the details by now, as well as the fact that Gordo had killed his assailant with a poker.

Gordo remembered that first visit to the bullpen. The morning after. He was a different person then. Lino shook his hand, looked him over, and led him back into the hallway.

"Where are we going?"

"For a drive," said Lino.

"I've just driven two hundred miles."

"A short drive."

"Where?"

"You'll see."

Lino pointed the white Ford Crown Victoria south on

Batavia Boulevard. At first, Gordo thought he was taking him to their old home. Soon they were sweeping past Pilot House, which looked tall and regal, with no visible clue that they had ever left. But they didn't slow down. Lino continued south to Avenue Q, then turned east. The towering Victorians and matronly turn-of-the-century houses gave way to cottages. The trees diminished, this part of the island having been scraped clean in vicious hurricanes early in the century. Stubby oaks, weather-beaten palms, and overgrown oleanders lined the street. Half a block past Tremont they stopped alongside the curb. Then Gordo understood. They were parked in front of a one-story red brick house with aluminum shutters that seemed to squat behind a chain-link fence heavy with dead honeysuckle vine. The louvers of the shutters were all closed. Pale green blades of grass reached up from hard-packed earth and piles of dog droppings. Even before he spotted the strands of yellow police tape stretched across the front door, he knew this was the house of Rory DuBose.

"This is really why you're here, isn't it?" said Lino.

Gordo followed the detective to the entrance, where a retrofitted interior door, its veneer curling upward from the bottom in strips, blocked their way. A temporary door, he reasoned, for a house whose front door had been kicked in months ago. A house whose front door probably had been kicked in more than once. The crack house that had existed in Gordo's imagination, populated by the hazy figures he'd invented from small bits of information. Men with curious, unfamiliar names.

No small talk now. Lino just peeled off the yellow tape and unlocked the door. He walked through a dim living room with a shabby stuffed sofa and an orange beanbag chair. The room smelled like sour milk. Down a dark hall with scuffed walls to the last doorway on the back side of the house. A broken hasp hung from the door frame.

"We had to pry the door open. He had a thing about security," said Lino.

The world inside that room was very different from the rest of the house. The heavily textured walls were covered with flyers and typed quotations, all of which seemed to be related to some form of Armageddon or apocalypse. The documents were painstakingly mounted with four black pushpins in each corner, each paper parallel to the adjacent one. The bed was neatly made with a white chenille bedspread. Above the bed, a silver crucifix. Inside the open closet Gordo could see a few shirts and pants, all hung an equal distance apart. Several pairs of worn shoes were aligned in a neat row.

Lino pointed to empty rectangles formed by pushpins in the wall.

"I took these down when I searched the room," he said, opening a manila folder he'd brought from the car. He placed a faded snapshot and a yellowed newspaper clipping on a desk near the bed.

The first was a smiling girl with pale blond, shoulder length hair. Ana. Second, maybe third grade.

"Where did he get that?"

Lino pushed the clipping toward him. It contained a photo with a caption.

Ana in a business suit, with a colleague and another person Gordo didn't recognize. He remembered the photo from sometime last year. She was presenting a check from the county bar association to the Children's Law Center, a child advocacy agency. The picture had run in the local newspaper.

"And then there's this." Lino pulled a small picture frame from the envelope.

Gordo recognized the black-and-white photo immediately—he had shot the picture himself. All Ana wore was a white terry cloth robe, which had fallen off her shoulders, and pearl earrings. Sprigs of hair as fine as corn silk escaped from a knot behind her head, reflecting soft window light. Ana gazed directly into the camera.

"He stole that from our house," said Gordo. "I thought it had been lost in the move."

"So he didn't crawl through your kitchen window empty-handed after all."

"Who was this guy?"

"Rory DuBose was born in Galveston in 1953," said Lino. "We think his father worked on the wharves. Father died when Rory's a kid. His mother worked at East End Academy. Not sure what she did there. So Rory went to the school there for a couple of years."

"Ana."

"That's my question. Do you know if Ana went to East End?"

"Primary school, I think," said Gordo.

"So you see—"

"It's a school picture."

"Ana probably gave it to him," said Lino. "The way kids exchange pictures in grade school."

Gordo turned the photo over. The reverse side was blank.

"What's this got to do—"

"Rory's mother remarried, and the family left the island. Apparently they knocked around Texas. Not sure where all they went. Something happened, and Rory ended up on his own. Couldn't get along with the stepfather, maybe. But then he was having trouble getting along with everybody. As a juvenile, he gets mad at some girl in Corpus Christi and cuts her and ends up getting sent to the Medical Branch for a psychiatric work-up. Ten, fifteen years later he gets nostalgic for Galveston, I guess, because he's back here working as a painter, laborer, odd jobs. That kind of stuff. He and Juventino Campos worked on a house-painting crew together, before Juventino decides to become an entrepreneur."

"The dealer."

"Right. Over the years, Rory has his ups and downs. Ends up back in the psych ward at the medical school once or twice. Couldn't get him to leave the library one night at closing. Voices were telling him to go to the periodical department and remove all references to Charles Manson. Nothing too violent. Just crazy."

"Ana didn't know the name."

"It was the third grade," said Lino. "How many names you remember from third grade?"

Gordo went over to a small bookshelf made from three planks resting on cinder blocks. Four videotapes: *Taxi Driver, Raging Bull, Day of the Jackal, Three Days of the Condor.* A row of books. He read the titles: *2000: A Date With Chaos, In My Own Words: Pope John XXIII, The Armageddon Manifesto, Millennium Apocalypse, My Daily Missal.* He reached for the missal. Latin on the left, English on the right. Gordo owned this very edition until Vatican II. His copy had the same bookmarks made of red and gold ribbon glued into the binding. As a boy, he had resented the fact that the ends of the ribbons frayed after a year or two of use.

Then he picked up a copy of *Lives of the Saints.* Inside the front cover was the impression of a rubber stamp. "Property of St. Patrick's Catholic School."

"I think I know where Rory went to school before East End Academy," said Gordo. The book fell open to the pages devoted to Joan of Arc. Now he remembered this image of Joan from his own childhood. An image forgotten so many years ago. A young, freckled Gordo had often visited the page and admired the picture of her. Tall, lithe, blond, fair. It could be Ana. Ana with her hands bound behind her, standing defiantly atop a thicket of sticks. Ana about to be burned at the stake. Rory, too, had been fascinated by this painting of the martyr-to-be.

"Find something?" asked Lino.

"A picture I haven't seen in a long time."

"Another picture of Ana?"

"No." Gordo held out the cover of the book for Lino to read.

"*Lives of the Saints?*" Lino shrugged.

"What happened to Rory? His body. Did he have family?"

"We reached a half-sister in Shreveport. She had the body given to the medical school. You ever go into the anatomy lab when you were a kid?"

Gordo didn't answer. Lino had forgotten that he did not grow up in Galveston. He was more relaxed with him in this strange house and under these strange conditions than in any of their previous encounters.

"We used to sneak in there," said Lino. "Scared the shit out of us. Bodies the color of liverwurst. In a way, you could say that Rory went back home. 'Course, they would have liked it better if you hadn't made such a mess of him."

"The autopsy showed that when Rory's arm went through the glass in our door, he cut tendons in his arm," said Gordo. "His left arm. He couldn't really fight."

"He did have a gun."

Gordo replaced *Lives of the Saints.*

He surveyed the room. "It's like a monk's cell."

"Rory was a hell of a lot neater than his roommates," said Lino. "I'll give him that."

"Who are the roommates? Where are they?"

"Juventino Campos we picked up for drugs. He's out on bond, awaiting trial. Jason Morrow, who we liked for the Dunes Motel shooting, cleared out. We haven't been able to link him to the gun. Without that, we don't have squat on him. There was one other guy, Theo Smith. This part of the story will get your attention."

• • •

They met on the Flagship Hotel pier. Gordo brought two cups of coffee. The pier was T-shaped, and below the seaward railing a staircase descended to a fishing platform nearer the water. They stood at the rail, sipping coffee, overlooking the anglers. Fish scales on the pier, reflecting light, blinked at them like stars in daylight.

Lisa Pierce. Very pregnant, her due date some four weeks away. She seemed to talk as deliberately as she moved. Her face a bit more oval and her hair dark and glossy.

"Eric's been offered a job at Washington University in St. Louis," she said. "Tenure track and a chance to work with a famous tropical disease specialist. The baby comes in early May. We leave June first."

"No time for postpartum depression."

"No time for anything. I'll be nursing the baby and packing boxes at the same time."

"Sounds like a good opportunity for him."

"As Eric puts it, 'We'll be on hard money.'"

"Hard money?"

"As opposed to soft money—grants. With soft money, if a grant doesn't get renewed, you're out of a job."

"Are you happy about it?"

"Eric will be teaching more. Less time for traipsing through jungles. And we can use the money."

Gordo watched a fisherman land a silvery sand shark with a loud, watery slap. He looked irritated about having the writhing, toothy creature at his feet. The fisherman took a club, what looked to be a broken baseball bat, and pounded the shark's head to no obvious effect. Gordo diverted Lisa's attention back toward the beach.

"Will you miss the water?"

"I loved running on the seawall," she said. "But the town's felt claustrophobic to me for the last year or two. I just wouldn't admit it to myself. We're not from here. And if you're not born here, it's hard to ever really fit in."

Gordo had brought Jake and Sam here to fish or sometimes just for donuts at dawn. They'd come one night before a tropical storm and seen surfers throw their boards from the high pier and then jump in after them. The boys marveled at the surfers as their baggy trunks inflated during the long, slow fall to the water. Swimming to their surfboards, they rode steep, powerful waves through yellow pools of light. Gordo might never again experience the excitement of a coming storm hours before landfall.

"Sometimes I think about you," she said.

And he knew what she meant.

"Sometimes the strongest memories," he said, "are memories of things we don't do."

She touched his face.

"I have to go. I want to be back before bedtime," he said. "So they're not alone."

Gordo opened the door of her car.

"Have a good delivery. Always a high-octane experience."

"For the dad!"

"Make a pretty baby."

"I'll work on it."

"Adios."

"What does that mean?"

"Adios?"

"I've heard it a million times, of course. But what does the word mean?"

"Literally, it means 'Go with God,'" he said. "Godspeed. Happy Trails."

"Well then," she said, satisfied with his answer, *"adios."*

Then he kissed her on the cheek and again above her forehead at the hairline, inhaling the smell of her. He stood back at arm's length and looked her over. The brown eyes, thick mane, and magnificent bulk of her.

"Glorious."

After she drove away, he returned to the railing. The shark lay dead and bleeding on the pier. The fisherman was casting anew. Gordo watched a wave break over the sandbar. Then he slowly drove the length of the pier and down the narrow apron to the seawall, where he turned west toward home.

Twenty-Five

As Gordo unlocked the front door, he touched the square of plywood tacked over the broken glass. Ana's new door. He would have to fill the nail holes when the glass was replaced. Once inside, he could smell the dinner he had missed. Marinara sauce, perhaps.

Jake and Sam ran out on the upstairs landing to greet him.

"*You'wa* back," said Sam.

Gordo felt the boy's words in his gut. As if there had been some question about whether he'd make it back. He hoped he hadn't scared them by leaving.

"Back to stay," Gordo said.

No one asked him about the trip. He'd told the boys he had to return to the island to talk to the police.

When he got upstairs later, Ana was reading to the boys in their bed. Gordo pulled off his shoes and crawled in with them. There was a time when the four of them neatly shared the bed. The boys were bigger now, like two large dogs splayed across the foot of the bed. Gordo felt a deep weariness. But he was back in his nest and grateful to be there.

The Once and Future King.

Ana's clear and animated reading voice.

The World had been expected to end in the year one thousand, and, in the reaction which followed its reprieve, there had been a burst of lawlessness and brutality which had sickened Europe for centuries...

Jake and Sam were in the grip of the story, and Gordo was reluctant to break the spell.

Only after the boys were put to bed did Gordo tell her about his day.

"It seems that Rory was at East End Academy while you were there. A classmate, I assume."

"I don't remember him," said Ana. "But it was so long ago. I could only name two or three people from there. And they went to school with me for years after."

He told her about the photo and the clipping and the red brick house on Avenue Q.

"But between primary school and now, what got him interested?" she asked.

"There was a guy named Theo Smith. He lived at the house from time to time, with Rory and the others. Smith and his sister were clients of your firm in some kind of wrongful death case. Lino found the correspondence when he searched the house. Dave handled the case. He told Lino you had nothing to do with it. Smith's mother was killed; Dave sued and got a nice settlement for the clients. Very straightforward. This Theo Smith says he once asked Rory to give him a ride to your office to talk to Dave. Rory goes inside with him and sees you somewhere in the office. Rory later tells Smith he knows you."

"So what? He starts obsessing about me because he sees me after thirty years? What's this got to do with you? Why shoot you?"

"We can only speculate. But it seems obvious."

"That's insane," she said.

"I was in the way," he said.

"And the car Rory drove here? It was registered to Theo Smith," he added. "Lino told me that another guy in the house, a guy named Juventino Campos, was dealing drugs. Norman Zweiger, our friend the bad cop, was buying pot from Campos. Lino figures Zweiger was giving Rory information about us."

"But why?"

"As Lino put it, 'Gratuitous mind-fucking.' He remembered the grand jury. He probably just did it for the hell of it. Because he could. Lino figures Zweiger got our Bee Creek address from snooping through the file in his office."

Gordo explained that Zweiger had been arrested on drug charges and that he was expected to plead out. He probably wouldn't get hard time, but his days as a policeman were over.

"What about the other cops? Tiny and Grover?"

"More than anything, they were incompetent. Lino said they called us 'Yuppie scum.' They didn't like me, and they didn't like your father."

"The rackets?"

"Remember," Gordo said, "Tiny's name is Aldo Martelli. He would have grown up with gambling all around him."

"I'm so grateful to be away from that awful place," she said. "I want to be somewhere normal."

"Lino's filed for county commissioner."

"I thought you said he was interested in the legislature."

"Not enough money in it for him to support his family," he said. "The commissioner's job has a decent salary, and while he's at it, he can go to law school."

"Does he have much of an opponent?"

"Jacobson from the city council. He strikes me as old and tired."

"And Daddy?" she asked.

"Sounds like Pat's going to support Lino."

She nodded, showing no more interest than if they were talking about a political race in Honduras.

"And what about Allen?" said Ana.

"Your brother might have crossed paths with some of these guys, but Lino doesn't think he was involved."

Ana seemed relieved. "I didn't think so."

"I saw Pilot House," he said.

"How did it look?"

"Like we never left. Your roses are in bloom."

Ana couldn't remember Rory DuBose. After all, it had been more than thirty years since they shared a classroom. And Rory, no doubt, had been a shy, reticent boy. Beautiful women go through life making deep impressions on people they meet. It's not something that takes any effort. The beautiful are few, and the plain are many. That was just the way things were.

Ana could not remember Rory, but Rory could never forget Ana. She was always there, like a religious fervor. Like his vision of the apocalypse. Beauty, art, religion—they had an intoxicating appeal to the higher self. A whiff of death in all three. Searching, striving, grasping. Reaching for a beacon of perfection in an imperfect world.

Growing up among the sweet Italian girls of St. Patrick's, doe-eyed with olive skin and dark brows, Rory was moved by Ana's lofty ethereal beauty. Her Protestant, Nordic otherness. This Gordo completely understood.

He had Ana. Her beauty was his gift and burden. He would be there for her and Jake and Sam. As long as she would have him. Rory, in the throes of his convoluted desire, reached for her and missed.

• • •

Ana's period was late. Gordo walked around exhilarated by giddiness and apprehension.

"I'll be sixty by the time the child graduates from high school," he said. "Sixty-four before she finishes college."

"Why 'she'?" Ana asked.

"We've already got two 'he's'."

"Which makes it more statistically probable that we'd have three."

"Well, I'm calling her 'she.' I can call her what I want."

"You seem ready to start painting the nursery."

"I'm psyching myself up for this. In training, so to speak."

"You want a daughter?"

"A beautiful, blonde little Ana? Who wouldn't? Of course, I already know what she'll be like. A red-haired, freckle-faced hellion, who will devote her life to making us miserable in our old age."

"In that case, maybe I should retire from motherhood while I'm ahead."

"Are you excited?" Gordo was clearly excited.

"I hadn't even been thinking about it until you brought it up. Not much, at least. Too many false alarms over the years to take all this very seriously. You know that."

"Did you ever stop to think that this false alarm could be the last one?" he said.

"Maybe you get your grins from wondering whether every little queasy twitch is the beginning of three months of morning sickness, but I don't."

"We'll name her Hannah."

"You're not handling this middle-age business very well," she said, "are you?"

• • •

Gordo had considered throwing the blood-stained rocks off the cliff. But instead he used them to finish the walkway. Mortar sealed Rory's blood within the pores of the rock. He did not tell the others. And so, in a small, private way, he built a stone memorial to the man who had loved Ana from afar. To the man who said he was his brother. A marker to remind him that this chapter of his life was over and to heed Jake's advice on that distant day at the beach. Relax.

Ana's period came after all. False alarm. The last false alarm?

• • •

The next summer, sixteen months after the shooting, they were back in Galveston. Gordo's mother rented a beach house for a week in June and invited her brood. The whole family. Returning, knowing that there was not someone there who wanted him dead, was different. He relaxed in a way he hadn't since that awful February night.

Back on the island, he was flooded with familiar sights and sensations. The dunes were low and patchy, rearranged and diminished by some recent tropical storm. Wildflowers in two shades of gaudy yellow grew in clumps in the dune grass.

The clear evening sky was turning orchid. Mottled blues, reds, and purples wheeled above them as the children played in the powerful, choppy surf. Squalls had blown in several times each day. Drenching rain that lasted five or ten minutes, often with the sun shining through the downpour. Gordo frequently studied the sky to keep from getting caught in the surf or in the sailboat during one of the small blows. But despite his vigilance, he couldn't predict what would happen from one minute to the next.

The beach house reminded him of their time in hiding. The O'Connors on the lam. The safe house that turned out to be unsafe. Black nights when the murmur of the wind would startle him into consciousness.

Sam's treasure hunt birthday party. The Norwegian *au pair* man. The Carrots of Wrath.

Gordo cooked spicy red beans and rice and filled a galvanized tub with beer on ice. The Colonel and Ana's mother came. So did Judge Greta Radkey and Tom and his wife, Samantha. Tom wearing a violet Hawaiian shirt, a throwback to his days as the Man in Purple. Lino Gabilondo, the newly elected county commissioner, dropped by briefly. Lots of stories and laughter, even more gossip. No one mentioned the shooting, the shared experience that drew them together.

Later, Gordo found himself alone on the deck overlooking the Gulf. He remembered those days of living in real time. Living on the edge. The edge of land, the edge of emotion, the edge of violence. He began to cry.

He hoped he wasn't going to become a sentimental old man who wept at weddings, funerals, and sappy movies. But he was afraid that his father hadn't passed on his stoic New England countenance. Maybe it was the latitude. Maybe he cried for the part of Jake and Sam's lives that were spent and beyond recovery. And of course, Rory DuBose had nothing to do with that. The boys were just growing up.

Gordo listened to the wash of the surf and inhaled the astringent air. He loved this place. He always would. But he could not live here anymore. The island was a vault of memories. Rocking babies on the porch swing at Pilot House. Building *Shark Bite* with Jake and Sam. Stepping off the third sandbar.

The place where they had become a family.

• • •

There is a riptide in Galveston that on occasion flows seaward alongside the rock jetties. The wind, the currents, and the tides all come together in some inscrutable alignment to create a powerful torrent that hauls everything in its path out into the Gulf. Half a dozen times a summer, more than that during a particularly stormy season, people are swept to their death. Children floating in inner tubes, lovers holding hands, strong swimmers, grown men—all kinds. If you are in its path, you will have to fight for your life.

When Rory came into their lives, Gordo found himself in the grip of the riptide. Suddenly he was forced to fight.

The way to ride out the riptide is to let the current take you, using your energy not to overcome it but to stay near the surface so you can steal an occasional breath as the water drags you away. Eventually, the current spits you into calm water. If you have enough strength left, you survive. Swimmers who thrash and tear at the riptide drown in the process. Their swollen bodies wash up within a day or two, sometimes more.

That terrible spring, the tide swept him out to sea. But Gordo made it ashore.

Twenty-Six

Today was the summer solstice. The longest day. He was sitting on the deck, overlooking the cliff and the ravine. A few hours earlier the sun had fallen in a fiery red splash. But it was dark now and a breeze was pouring up the canyon, toward the lake. The boys were both sleeping over with friends.

When they moved to this cliff, he saw their life here as a second chance. A chance to remake what they had built on the island. But of course, that was not possible. The boys had moved to another point in their young lives. Jake had turned ten. The four of them around a birthday cake. The throes of adolescence—with puberty on the way. Life was sweet, but different. They had all lost a certain innocence. They couldn't recapture that giddy happiness of babies in their midst, discovering a fresh new world every day.

So they moved on. And in the process, was he growing complacent about the gift of survival? He immersed himself in daily life, increasingly less aware of the fact that each day was a day he would have missed had Rory's bullet pierced his heart.

Do people in remission experience this? Falling back into the ordinariness of life?

Rory took something from him, and he took Rory's life. Gordo would gladly return one for the other.

He went inside and drew a bath for Ana. He lit candles along the sill of the large window next to the tub. He opened the window and studied the gently rocking treetops below the cliff. Ana slipped out of her robe and eased her pale hips into the hot water. Gordo washed the valley between her shoulder blades. He used his razor, sharper than her own dull, waxy one that she always left in the shower, to shave her legs. Then her underarms. He had done this when she was pregnant with Jake and it had become a part of their ritual. He sponged hot water across her narrow shoulders and left her deep in a nest of bubbles and candlelight.

Naked, he went downstairs to the kitchen. At the spice cabinet, he took out a heavy brown bottle of Mexican vanilla. Holding the bottle to his nose, he let the rich potent aroma fill his nostrils. The scent of flan in a distant kitchen. He poured a drop on his finger and painted a stripe down the length of his cock.

The windows were open, and the insects were singing as if to herald this final exhalation of spring. The summer heat would soon be upon them in earnest.

Another season vanished, and Gordo was still searching. Whatever he had learned was not enough. He would be forty-five in a month. A life half gone. Maybe more. He couldn't slow the torrent of time sweeping past.

He wished his father were still alive. To see Jake and Sam. To talk. To be with his aging mother. At night, his father wore flannel pajamas, a Pendleton wool robe, and leather slippers. Gordo smiled at the memory.

Climbing the stairs, he could feel the alcohol in the vanilla evaporate from his cock, his balls swinging with each step, cool varnished wood beneath his feet. When was the last time he'd climbed stairs naked? Simple pleasures. The color of Ana's skin, still pink from her bath. Gordo quickened his pace, taking the stairs two at a time. Eager.

Ana loved the taste of vanilla.

• • •

Gordo expected to sleep a different sleep with him gone. The sleep of a person who is no longer a target. But Rory had sensitized him to the potential for harm, and that potential remained like the after-image of the sun after you've closed your eyes to it. He and Rory shared a time and space, however briefly. They occupied the intersection of cause and effect, of violence and fear. Be there, be conscious, be focused. Gordo's life had depended on it.

What is the equal of such a primal experience? The first breathless taste of love? Childbirth? Watching someone you love die? Sex, birth, death. It seemed like an awfully short menu for creatures whose appetites last a lifetime.

Gordo was reaching for a lesson. What had he learned? People occasionally asked that. The lesson. And it was the question behind lots of other questions.

I wish I knew.

There was something. It was small, but it was all he had to offer. He was planting trees. Planting them and taking care of them for no apparent reason other than a powerful urge to do so.

A shovel was good for about six inches in the rocky soil. So he bought an eight-foot iron bar with a chisel blade on one end. By driving the sixteen-pound bar into the hole he could chip away a cavity large enough for a sapling's root ball. It was slow, backbreaking work. Breaking through layers of limestone, a calcified beach 120 million years old. Even on a cool day, sweat flowed off his brow so steadily that he needed to keep a towel handy to wipe off his glasses. It took brute force, but he always excavated deep enough to plant.

"Dad, are you *cwazy?*" Sam asked one recent Saturday, with a faint hint of his imperfect speech. Ana had sent him out with a glass of lemonade. Gordo had been pounding away with the iron bar, making room for a Mexican plum.

"We have trees! Lots of them," said Sam. "Too many to count. Go look off the cliff, and all you can see are trees, trees, trees!"

"I know," Gordo explained. "But I'm planting different trees. Monterey oaks. Cypress trees that will grow a hundred feet tall. Maples that will turn flame red in fall. Trees that will be beautiful someday."

"Dad, you'll be dead by then."

"I know, son. But I will enjoy the part of their life that I do get to see."

At that moment, he realized that what he was doing was akin to parenting. If you're lucky, you never get to see your children's final outcome. You do the planting, you do the nurturing, and then you die before you get to see how things turn out.

Sam's words echoed in his mind: "Dad, you'll be dead by then."

Well, I could be dead by now. But I'm not.

Gordo told his son, "You're right, Sam. But I'm not dead yet. So we will have trees."